PRAISE FOR JANICE CANTORE

"This is the start of a smart new series for retired police officer–turned–author Cantore. Interesting procedural details, multi-layered characters, lots of action, and intertwined mysteries offer plenty of appeal."

BOOKLIST on *Drawing Fire*

"Cantore's well-drawn characters employ Christian values and spirituality to navigate them through tragedy, challenges, and loss. However, layered upon the underlying basis of faith is a riveting police-crime drama infused with ratcheting suspense and surprising plot twists."

SHELF AWARENESS on *Drawing Fire*

"*Drawing Fire* rips into the heart of every reader. One dedicated homicide detective. One poignant cold case. One struggle for truth. . . . Or is the pursuit revenge?"

DIANN MILLS, bestselling author of the FBI: Houston series

"This hard-edged and chilling narrative rings with authenticity. . . . Fans of police suspense fiction will be drawn in by her accurate and dramatic portrayal."

LIBRARY JOURNAL on *Visible Threat*

"Janice Cantore provides an accurate behind-the-scenes view of law enforcement and the challenges associated with solving cases. Through well-written dialogue and effective plot twists, the reader is quickly drawn into a story that sensitively yet realistically deals with a difficult topic."

CHRISTIAN LIBRARY JOURNAL on *Visible Threat*

"[Cantore's] characters resonate with an authenticity not routinely found in police dramas. Her knack with words captures Jack's despair and bitterness and skillfully documents his spiritual journey."

ROMANTIC TIMES on *Critical Pursuit*

"Cantore is a former cop, and her experience shows in this wonderful series debut. The characters are well drawn and believable, and the suspenseful plot is thick with tension. Fans of Lynette Eason, Dee Henderson, or DiAnn Mills and readers who like crime fiction without gratuitous violence and sex will appreciate discovering a new writer."

LIBRARY JOURNAL on *Accused*

"Cantore provides a detailed and intimate account of a homicide investigation in an enjoyable read that's more crime than Christian."

PUBLISHERS WEEKLY on *Accused*

"Janice Cantore's twenty-two years as a police veteran for the Long Beach Police Department [lend] authenticity in each suspense novel she pens. If your readers like Dee Henderson, they will love Janice Cantore."

CHRISTIAN RETAILING on *Abducted*

"[*Avenged*] offers plenty of procedural authenticity and suspense that will attract fans of Dee Henderson."

LIBRARY JOURNAL

"Cantore . . . delivers another round of crime, intrigue, and romance in her latest title."

JOYCE LAMB, *USA Today* on *Avenged*

"Set in a busy West Coast city, the story's twists will keep readers eagerly reading and guessing. . . . I enjoyed every chapter. *Accused* is a brisk and action-filled book with enjoyable characters and a good dose of mystery. . . . I look forward to more books in this series."

"*Accused* was a wonderfully paced, action-packed mystery. . . . [Carly] is clearly a competent detective, an intelligent woman, and a compassionate partner. This is definitely a series I will be revisiting."

"*Abducted* is a riveting suspense . . . [and] the many twists and turns keep the reader puzzled. The book is a realistic look into the lives of law enforcement officers. *Abducted* is one book I couldn't put down. Can't wait to see what Carly and Nick might be up to next."

BURNING PROOF

BURNING PROOF

COLD CASE JUSTICE

JANICE CANTORE

TYNDALE HOUSE PUBLISHERS, INC.
CAROL STREAM, ILLINOIS

Visit Tyndale online at www.tyndale.com.

Visit Janice Cantore's website at www.janicecantore.com.

TYNDALE and Tyndale's quill logo are registered trademarks of Tyndale House Publishers, Inc.

Burning Proof

Designed by Jennifer Ghionzoli

Edited by Erin E. Smith

Published in association with the literary agency of D.C. Jacobson & Associates LLC, an Author Management Company. www.dcjacobson.com

Library of Congress Cataloging-in-Publication Data

Cantore, Janice, author.
  Burning proof / Janice Cantore.
    pages cm. -- (Cold case justice)
  Summary: After months of investigating the brutal homicide of a young girl, Detective Abby Hart finally has the evidence she needs. But when the arrest goes terribly wrong, Abby begins to doubt her future as a police officer. As she wrestles with conflicting emotions, old questions about the fire that took her parents' lives come back to haunt her. "There is proof." PI Luke Murphy can't stop thinking about what Abby's former partner, Asa Foster, mumbled just before he died. When he uncovers a clue to the murder of Abby's parents and his uncle, he's reluctant to tell Abby, despite his growing feelings for the beautiful detective. A decade-old abduction case brings Luke and Abby together, but will his secret tear them apart?
  ISBN 978-1-4143-9669-9 (sc)
  PS3603.A588B87 2016
  813'.6—dc23
                                    2015032517

Printed in the United States of America

22	21	20	19	18	17	16
7	6	5	4	3	2	1

ACKNOWLEDGMENTS

I'D LIKE TO ACKNOWLEDGE the help of Pastor Bill Gallagher, Detective Stephen Jones (ret.), and Commander Lisa Lopez; the encouragement of Don Jacobson, my agent; and the overall support of Kitty Bucholtz, Marcy Weydemuller, Cathleen Armstrong, Kathleen Wright, Wendy Lawton, and Lauraine Snelling, my writing friends, for always being there to listen to the ideas as they bounce around—some good, some not so good—and to always tell the truth about what is what.

And thanks to Erin Smith, my awesome editor, and all the great people at Tyndale that I am blessed to be able to work with.

Therefore the Lord waits to be gracious to you, and therefore he exalts himself to show mercy to you. For the Lord is a God of justice; blessed are all those who wait for him.

ISAIAH 30:18

PROLOGUE

"IF GEORGE SANDERS weren't already dead, I'd kill him."

Kelsey Cox said nothing, knowing better than to interrupt when her boss was this angry. As if validating her silence, the tirade continued.

"He made this mess, opening his mouth when he should have stayed quiet. Feeding Detective Hart gossip that could ruin everything. He didn't even know what he was talking about, for pete's sake!" The last two words were punctuated by pounding the conference table.

Sanders had been a small-time criminal with a big-time mouth. He'd tried to implicate Governor Lowell Rollins in a twenty-seven-year-old triple murder. Any other cop would have seen the allegations as laughable. But since Abby Hart's parents were among the victims, she'd taken every word seriously.

Sensing an opening to calm the situation, Kelsey spoke up. "But he is dead. There's no way to verify anything he said. Don't you think she'll stop?" Kelsey sat across the conference table from her employer.

"Looking into her parents' deaths? I doubt it. Not if she's anything like her father."

"But the Triple Seven case is closed. What could she possibly accomplish? There's no proof connecting the governor to anything. Gavin—"

"Gavin, like Sanders, should have kept his mouth shut. If he was going to blow his brains out, he should have done it before he said anything."

Cox flinched. The image of Gavin Kent's suicide outside Governor Rollins's Long Beach residence was all too fresh in her mind's eye. And the fact that anyone could be so callous about his death abraded her heart; she still loved him.

"Oh, don't get your back up." Her boss smacked the table. "If you can't move on, I can't use you."

Embarrassed and angry that she let her guard down and was so transparent, Cox gritted her teeth. "I have moved on."

Standing, she turned her back to the boss and looked out the window. The beautiful blue, early fall sky did nothing to assuage her anxiety. "What do you want me to do about Hart?"

"Keep tabs on her for now. The governor will officially declare he's in the senate race soon. She'll have one more chance to accept his job offer."

Kelsey couldn't hide the shock, jerking back around. "You want her working *here* with Lowell?"

"Of course. Keep your enemies close. But if she doesn't take the offer . . ." A cavalier shrug. "I'll come up with another, more permanent solution."

Cox put a hand behind her on the windowsill to keep from sliding sideways. In another time and place the thinly veiled threat her boss made to stop Hart would not have shaken her so. In spite of her long law enforcement career, stepping up and doing the unpleasant—even the illegal—for a greater good was a no-brainer. But the mention of it now rocketed her back to the day she'd watched the governor's right-hand man, her lover, put a gun to his head and pull the trigger. She'd lost her balance that day, feeling as though the bullet had struck her as well, knocking her off a cliff, where she now hung by one hand, like a stuntman in the movies.

Unlike the movies, there was no rescuer rushing to the precipice to grab her hand and pull her up.

And every so often something would happen that made Kelsey feel like her fingers were being pulled back. Any minute now she could lose her grip completely. She hated Hart as much as her boss did—even more—but the woman was not a threat. There was nothing she could prove. Another murder was a risk, a finger being peeled back.

"Hart can poke around until frogs grow beards. All she'll get is frustrated." As soon as the words were out of her mouth, Kelsey wished she could take them back. Her boss did not take kindly to being questioned.

"Nothing, I mean nothing—not Hart, not that irritating PI Murphy, and not you dragging your feet—is going to get in the way of Lowell being a senator. Is that clear?"

Cox nodded, having to look away from the vicious, murderous glint in her boss's eyes.

"Can you do the job or do I need to find someone else?"

"You can count on me," she said as she was dismissed for the afternoon.

CHAPTER

MONDAY MORNING Detective Abby Hart filled her coffee cup as soon as the pot finished, then settled in at her desk and turned on the computer. She yawned, covering her mouth with the back of her hand, still a little foggy without caffeine. She'd participated in a beach volleyball tournament over the weekend. It'd been hard and tested her conditioning, but she and her beach partner had triumphed and taken home the trophy.

As she stretched and grimaced at the sore muscles that screamed, she was glad the office was quiet; she was first in and anticipating a court appearance later in the week. A reminder about her scheduled meeting with DA Drew in an hour popped up on her calendar. Homicide cases could take years to get to trial. When they did, she needed her head to be right back in the midst of the investigation as if it were fresh. She had several cases pending in various stages of the court process. The one Drew wanted to discuss was a gang shooting that occurred nearly a year ago. It was due to go to jury selection soon, so she planned to review all the pertinent details. A sharp pang of sadness sliced through her as she scanned the summary. She'd consulted on the gang shooting with her first partner in homicide, her mentor, Asa Foster. He was retired at the time, but still a great resource. His death a few months ago still stung.

Shoving the sadness aside, she looked at the rest of her to-do list. She also wanted to review her most pressing open homicide case, spending her day after the meeting with the DA going over the Adonna Joiner homicide details. She heard footsteps but didn't look up because it was bound to be just another office mate or her partner, Bill.

"Abby."

The sharp, clear voice demanded her attention. Lieutenant Jacoby strode toward her desk. Something was in the works. The LT wasn't usually in until later. He dropped a manila envelope in front of her. "Glad you're here early. Just got this regarding the Joiner case."

Abby reached for the envelope. "I planned on pulling that file and calling the lab for an update."

The brutal rape and murder of a ten-year-old girl was a study in firsts: the first case she and her new partner, Bill Roper, had caught on their first on-call shift. Together they'd hit it hard for forty-eight hours and gotten nowhere. Then frustration set in. For the months since, it was their priority case. Evidence had been collected from the victim's body, but there was no hit in CODIS, the national offender database. Abby and Bill had knocked on doors and collected voluntary DNA swabs from several persons of interest, only to be stymied by a backlog at the lab. She often called Clayton and Althea Joiner, the victim's parents, to touch base. In fact, she planned to pay them a visit tomorrow.

She looked at the envelope and realized that it was from

the forensics lab. Her head snapped back and she stared at the lieutenant. "They got a match?" She undid the clasp and pulled the contents out, tense now and wide-awake.

"They did." He pointed. "Halfway down. They got a match from one of the samples we took to exclude."

Abby read the finding and was up out of her chair. "Unbelievable. It's Curtis. I had a feeling."

Javon Curtis, a single man, a loner living two doors away from the victim in a house he'd inherited from his mother, had been Abby's number one suspect. He had no prior record and cooperated completely, even willingly providing the buccal swab that just implicated him, but her gut had told her something was off about the man.

"As soon as Bill gets in, go pick him up and bring him in for an interview. Hopefully he'll open up."

The adrenaline evaporated like smoke. "I have a meeting scheduled—"

"DA Drew is in the loop on this. Knowing you, you'll have a confession before noon." Jacoby gave her a half salute and left the office.

Abby looked at the clock. Bill should be in any minute. She couldn't sit back down. She did a happy dance all the way to the file cabinet to pull the Joiner file.

"Hallelujah!" she said to the empty office. "I knew it was him. I just wish we could have proved it two months ago."

She wanted to call the young victim's father. He'd been waiting to hear that his daughter's killer had been identified, and Abby knew better than anyone what that kind of wait was like. But she decided it would make more sense to have the suspect in custody first and, as the LT had hopefully implied, have a confession. The killing of Adonna Joiner had been horrific, and the close-knit neighborhood she'd lived in was volatile.

Abby sat at her desk with the file and remembered that the suspect, Javon Curtis, had stood next to the grieving parents at many of the numerous press conferences while they pleaded for any witnesses to come forward. What a Judas. She and Bill were the only ones who suspected him, but there was no evidence. When Curtis claimed to have been out of town at the time the murder occurred and provided his buccal swab for testing in order to exclude, she'd wondered then if her instincts had betrayed her.

He snowed everyone with his easy compliance—tried to throw us off. Abby's annoyance was tempered by the knowledge that he couldn't fool the science of an exact match. But match notwithstanding, she wanted a confession. Abby hated relying solely on DNA in court. As strong as a DNA match like this was, she wanted an admission and, if possible, a little contrition. She rarely got the contrition; usually criminals only felt bad about getting caught. But a case where someone actually expressed remorse always made her feel a little better.

Abby had kept tabs on Curtis and a finger on the pulse of the neighborhood in the months since the murder. There had been understandable anger over the lab situation. But the Joiners were patient, churchgoing people. They had faith they'd get their answers, and Abby was overjoyed that it appeared their faith would be rewarded today.

Bill walked in, and Abby hit him with the news before he could fill up his coffee mug.

It was just before 9 a.m. when they arrived in the quiet neighborhood and knocked on the front door of the suspect's residence. The only precaution they'd taken was having a black-and-white cruise the alley to be certain the man didn't flee. But neither Abby nor Bill expected the suspect would give them any trouble.

He didn't. Javon Curtis invited them inside his house and then quietly accepted being handcuffed after they informed him that DNA identified him as at least a rapist and at most a killer.

Then everything went sideways.

Abby stepped out of the house onto the porch, Bill and Javon behind her. Bill pulled the door closed, and Abby turned to take the first step down. She snatched her weapon from its holster as training kicked in.

There was a man on the lawn pointing a gun at them.

From the corner of her eye she saw Javon try to bolt left. Bill grabbed at him while conflicting emotions swirled through Abby's insides like a debris-filled tornado. The man with the gun was her victim's father, Clayton Joiner.

"Put the gun down now!" she ordered, reflexively shifting left to shield Bill and Javon.

Joiner ignored her, also stepping to the left. "He murdered my baby!"

"Please, Clayton." Abby's gun was up and on target. A thousand questions begging—most of all: *How did Clayton know?*

"He'll be charged; he'll pay. Put the gun down."

Something like a sob and a groan escaped his lips. He raised his gun and fired.

So did Abby.

CHAPTER

"I USED TO LIKE *Hee Haw.*"

Luke cast a sideways glance toward Woody in the passenger seat. "What? Was that a show or a catcall?" His truck bounced down the rough dirt road, on the way to check on an address in rural Riverside County. Robert "Woody" Woods had come along for the ride, and they'd been chatting about a lot of things, eventually getting to TV shows.

"Ha. It was a music show, and funny, a comedy. Wholesome, too. Nowadays you turn on the TV and all you see are people playing musical beds."

"Yeah, I can't argue with you there. I'm very careful about what my daughter watches. Seems like I have to say no more than I can say yes. . . . Looks like we're here."

Luke Murphy pulled his truck to the side of the dusty dirt road and turned off the ignition. He looked around at the bleak, dry landscape and wondered if they were on a wild-goose chase. Rural Riverside County was a world away from his normal stomping grounds in Long Beach. They'd stopped at the local sheriff's substation for directions since his GPS didn't seem to recognize the address he was looking for. The deputies had told him it was in a dead zone, and even with their guidance, he wondered if perhaps he'd taken a wrong turn. But this was a neighborhood of sorts. The lots were large and the structures far apart, but the presence of mailboxes told him the area was not too remote for mail delivery.

"It's a perfect hiding place, if this is your guy," Woody said.

Luke agreed but said nothing. He really didn't think they'd find the fugitive he was looking for here. Together they climbed out of the truck and met at the tailgate.

Deciding to work this like a training exercise, Luke turned to Woody. "If you were still in uniform, how would you handle this?"

"Well . . ." Woody rubbed his chin and did a slow 360, taking in the whole area. "Once you're certain this is the place, I'll follow the fence toward the rear of the house, keep an eye on things there. Fugitives have been known to make backdoor getaways. If he does split, I'll try to get a plate for you. If not, just pick me up after you talk to the guy."

"I don't want to put you in jeopardy."

Woody frowned and gave a dismissive wave. "I'm old and retired but not feeble, and I am armed." He tapped the fanny pack that Luke knew held a small .380 automatic. Woody had applied for and received a concealed carry weapon permit.

Luke chuckled and walked to one of the bent, dented, and aged mailboxes and double-checked the number he'd written down. "Yep, this is the right spot. You want me to give you a few minutes?"

The lot looked to be fenced all the way around. Woody started to walk to the corner of the enclosure. "Just a couple. It looks like when I reach the third fence post, I'll be out of sight of the front door. If he hasn't seen us already, I'll be fine."

"10-4."

As a private investigator, Luke specialized in finding missing people. This particular case was not his. He'd said yes as a favor to a PI from Arizona who'd called and asked if he could check out this address. Luke didn't normally do work for other PIs; he had enough of his own. But the Arizona PI's story was compelling, so he agreed to help. She'd admitted it was a long shot, one in a million, but she wanted him to look for a convicted murderer who'd absconded from parole. The provocative thing about her case was that the guy had been on the lam for thirty years.

Luke was intrigued when the Arizona PI told him the story of Oscar Cardoza, how he'd been hitchhiking in Montana in 1975. He shot and killed the man who picked him up, then stole the victim's car. Eventually apprehended, tried, convicted, Oscar spent several years in prison before becoming eligible for parole in 1984. He was paroled to California because he had family here, and that was when he disappeared.

Since the state of Montana didn't seem to be in a hurry to find the man, the grandson of the murdered man, who now lived in Arizona, had hired her, hoping she'd pick up a thirty-year cold trail. The first thing she'd found out was that the family member Oscar had been paroled to, his brother, was long dead, but he had lived in Riverside. She then uncovered a couple of aliases Oscar had used over the years. One, Dan Parker, was the name that led the PI to this address, the name of the owner on record. And that was why Luke was with Woody in the middle of nowhere, standing at a battered mailbox looking for any signs of life in a run-down double-wide trailer.

Oscar would be in his sixties now. Luke had a copy of the wanted bulletin with a picture of the man at twenty-five upon conviction, and an age-enhanced photo of what he could look like now. The age-enhanced photo didn't impress him. It could never account for what a person might go through over the years that could age them. But Oscar did have a couple of distinguishing marks. He had prison tattoos on his knuckles and a large tattoo of a woman on his left arm. Unless the man had spent money to have the tats professionally and cleanly removed, Luke was certain he'd know right away if he'd found the fugitive or not.

This search, with all its uncertainty, was a welcome break for Luke. He and Woody were in the process of interviewing and testing for a task force job with the federal government, investigating cold cases. But things had stalled in the process. Since Woody had retired after thirty-four years as a police officer, he'd taken to working with Luke, even considered getting his own PI license. In the last three months, together they'd found two girls who were just eighteen and who didn't want to go home, but at least now their folks knew they were okay. Their most satisfying find was a war veteran suffering from PTSD who went off his meds and disappeared. Luke and Woody found the poor kid living under a bridge in Pasadena. It did Luke's heart good to reunite the young man with his mother and mental health professionals who could help him.

Woody seemed to like the work, and while Luke's old partner was still going through therapy to rehab a badly broken ankle and was not even certain she wanted to come back to the PI business, Luke was happy for the company and the help. They'd be partners if and when the cold case squad ever got up and running. In the meantime it was nice to know they worked well together.

Woody was well along the side fence line as Luke approached the gravel driveway leading to the manufactured home. There was a padlocked gate across the drive, and No Trespassing and No Soliciting signs were posted. Luke walked to the lock and studied the structure, trying to ascertain whether anyone was home. All the blinds in front were drawn, so it was a good bet they had not been seen yet if someone was there. There was a bit of landscaping in front of the tired, bleak structure—pots and containers with plants and flowers that were green and colorful, indicating that someone was watering and caring for them. There was also an old car off to the side, a minivan Luke guessed was from the eighties, but it didn't look broken-down. In fact, the driveway and area in front of the house were free of weeds. Someone moved the van and drove it in and out with some regularity.

Taking a chance, Luke cupped his hands in front of his mouth. "Hello! Is anyone home?"

Woody was out of sight behind the house now, but Luke was sure he'd heard.

He repeated the question a couple of times and waited. Just as he was about to give up, the door to the home opened and an old man stepped out. A jolt of fear spiked in Luke. He thought the man had a gun, but as the man moved forward, he could see that it was a cane.

"What do you want?" the man hollered in a strong voice that belied his appearance.

"I'm looking for someone. I wonder if you can help me."

The man cursed, and Luke feared he'd disappear back into the house and that would be the end of the inquiry.

But he seemed to reconsider and made his way down the stairs. He walked okay, just slowly, and it appeared that he needed the cane only for balance. Luke sized him up. While he knew you couldn't judge a book by its cover—or a fugitive by his wrinkles—he didn't get any dangerous vibes from the guy.

"Who do you want?" the man asked when he reached the gate.

"I'm a private investigator and—"

"A private investigator?" He frowned and Luke studied him. He could be the face in the age-enhanced photo, but this guy looked to be in his eighties, not his sixties. Was that the result of a hard life on the run? He was about four inches shorter than Luke and thin. His skin was tan, creased, and leathery, like someone who spent a lot of time in the sun. From his sharp jawline to his thin frame, there was nothing soft about him; he was all hard angles. His bald head sported a couple of scars and a clean Band-Aid on the right side.

"Yes, here's my identification." Luke pulled out his ID and handed it to the man, reaching over the gate, hoping he'd take it. That would give Luke the opportunity to look at his hands.

The old man did what Luke hoped: reached out and took the ID. Luke saw faded ink splotches on the man's knuckles. He'd read that the tattoos originally spelled *HATE* on the right and *COPS* on the left. A blurry *H* was all Luke could make out for certain. Further up on the left arm was another tat. It could have been a woman, but on the old, wrinkled arm, it was just a blotchy mess.

Luke had his man. His pulse jumped, not with fear, but with satisfaction that this trip had been a success, in spite of his doubts. He and Woody had discussed the possibility and planned to return to the sheriff's office, tell them what they'd found, and let law enforcement proceed with the arrest. Montana would extradite, so Luke knew the sheriff would make an arrest.

All I have to do is ask a couple of inane questions, say good-bye, pick Woody up, and head back to the sheriff.

"And what do you want with me, Mr. Murphy?" The old guy looked up at him and handed back the ID.

"I'm looking for Dan Parker. Does he live here?"

"Dan Parker?" The man chuckled. "That's a name I haven't heard in a long time."

"Do you know him?"

Something in the man's demeanor changed—it was subtle, but Luke caught it and it made his guard go up. He wished he'd parked his truck closer. There was no cover out here if this leathery fugitive got contentious. It was not Luke's job to get into a confrontation, especially out here in the middle of nowhere. If the man had a weapon, elderly or not, he was dangerous.

The deputy's voice saying, "Dead zone" rang in Luke's ears. *Yeah,* he thought, *and a great place to hide bodies.* His and Woody's.

"I used to know him. What's he done? What do you want him for?"

"I don't want him at all. Someone in Arizona is looking for him. I'm just doing an Arizona PI a favor." He gave a generic explanation about the woman's call and professional courtesy.

The man took a step back and rubbed his chin. "Do you want to come in the yard and look around?"

"No," Luke said, "I'll take your word on it. You have an honest face. Is Parker here?"

The man seemed to think about it, leaning on his cane and

studying Luke. For his part Luke watched as conflicting emotions crossed the man's face. An angry frown gave way to resignation, he thought.

"What took you so long?" he asked after a long minute.

"You're Oscar, aren't you?" Luke asked by reflex, hands at his sides, balanced stance, bracing himself for whatever might come next.

Nodding, the man leaned his left hand on the cane and reached into his pocket with his right. Out came a small handgun—a .22, Luke guessed as he stared down the barrel.

CHAPTER

-3-

"**HEY!** Earth to Molly. You with me here?"

Molly shook her head to clear the confusion from her mind and turned to face her partner.

"Yeah, yeah, I'm with you." *Am I?* she wondered as she bent to help him with the ambulance stretcher after tossing the emergency equipment bags on top. They pulled the gurney from the back of the ambulance and jerked it toward the crash, to the scene that had captured her attention and sent her insides twisting into a fist of paralyzing fear.

They were on a lonely stretch of two-lane highway out in the desert, crowded now with emergency vehicles, lights flashing, and stinking with the acrid smell of flares. It was a single-car crash; the driver probably fell asleep and wrapped the car around a tree.

Firefighters had ripped the crushed car open with the Jaws of Life to free the passenger, a young girl about the same age Molly had been when she was trapped in the trunk of a car ten years ago.

But Molly's ordeal had not been the result of an accident.

And now the horror of that black day clutched at her from the past, seizing her by the throat. And she didn't know why. She'd worked through that day long before this, put it behind her, come to terms with it. All the normal platitudes had been applied to her situation and she'd moved on. The fact that she did this job—well, according to the commendations on her wall—bolstered her confidence.

So why was the past, that dark incident, stalking her, striking with sharp teeth at her heart when she could least afford it?

Concentrate, she told herself as she gritted her teeth, knowing her partner and—most of all—this young girl depended on her to keep it together.

But it was only the grip she had on the rail of the stretcher that kept her hands from shaking. She wondered if she'd lose it altogether right here and suddenly need rescue herself.

CHAPTER

-4-

LUKE SAW HIS LIFE pass before him. He thought of his daughter, his mother, and he thought of Abby Hart.

He stepped back and looked for cover or an escape route. The gate still separated them. There was no way he could take the gun away from the fugitive.

"Kinda sorry you did that favor now, aren't you?" Oscar said, viciousness in his eyes.

Luke peered over Oscar's shoulder and held his breath. Woody, gun in hand, was slowly creeping up behind him.

Cardoza noticed Luke's gaze and sneered. "You think I'm gonna fall for that trick, you're crazy. I haven't stayed free all these years by being stupid. Step over to the padlock. I'll show you what I do with nosy PIs." He dropped his free hand to the ring of keys on his belt.

"Think." Luke raised his hands, stalling, giving Woody time to get closer. "I don't have to tell anyone you're here. I can keep a secret."

The old man cursed. "The only reason I won't shoot you

where you stand is because I can't drag your body where I want it. You shouldn't be poking your face into other people's business."

"And you shouldn't be hiding out on a property with holes in the fence." Woody placed the barrel of his gun in the old man's back.

Luke watched the shock spread, saw Oscar blanch. The gun dropped from his hand.

Hands raised, he stammered, "Aw, I was just trying to scare you. I wasn't serious."

"Yeah, right," Woody said. "And I'm a big gray-headed Easter bunny." He unclipped the ring of keys from Oscar's belt and tossed them to Luke. "Open the gate, partner. Let's secure this clown."

Luke caught the keys and fumbled with them for a moment before he found one that looked as if it fit the lock. He slid the key into the padlock and let the chain fall, then pulled the gate open. He always carried plastic restraints with him but had never had to use them before this. Once he had Oscar's hands secure, Woody put his gun away and picked up the dropped .22.

The fugitive's tone changed. "Why, you guys just might be doing me a favor. I'm dog-tired. Not going to fight you. Tired of running and hiding and looking over my shoulder. Don't figure now that prison will be any worse."

Woody just glared at him, and Luke had to stifle a chuckle. All cop, even out of uniform, Woody's expression and posture would brook no nonsense.

"Do you have a working phone in your house?" Luke asked Oscar.

"Nope. I'm as off the grid as I can be."

Luke had not planned on transporting the man but saw no other course of action.

Woody seemed to read his mind. "You live with anyone? Anyone else home?"

Oscar shook his head.

"I've got him," Woody said. "Why don't you go check out the house, then lock it up?"

"Great idea." He looked at Oscar. "Do you need anything from inside?"

"Nah, what's the point?"

Luke turned for the house. As he walked away, he heard Oscar try to get on Woody's good side.

"Look, sorry about the gun bit, really. For thirty years I've been looking over my shoulder, wondering if the feds would kick down my door. I'm done with it. Get me to jail."

Woody's harsh response told Luke he didn't believe the guy and would not be letting his guard down. Luke smiled, glad he and Woody were a team. With a quick glance back when he reached the steps, Luke saw that Woody had Oscar's arm and was moving him toward the truck.

Luke hurried into the manufactured home. The place was a mess. Oscar was a hoarder. Newspapers were stacked everywhere, leaving a narrow walkway resembling a maze. There was also trash and boxes, containing who knows what. The smell nearly knocked Luke back. Mold, body odor, decay, rot. It surprised him that the outside of the property was so neat.

He called out to see if anyone else was home and heard nothing. After a quick look through, he gratefully backed out of the place and locked the door. A thorough search would have to be left to the deputies. Taking a deep breath of fresh air, he jogged to the truck. Woody had already put Oscar in the backseat. He was studying the handgun Oscar had dropped.

"He had a round in the chamber. Could've been ugly."

"I thank you, my friend. How'd you know to move up so quick?"

"I think there are bodies buried in the yard."

"What?" Luke felt his hands go numb.

Woody nodded, expression grim. "I could be wrong—it might be pets or something else—but there are mounds there. He's buried something. The hair stood up on the back of my neck, and I knew I had to get out here and watch your bacon."

It took a moment for Luke to find his voice. "Thank God you were with me today."

"I second that. Someone was watching over the both of us today."

Luke tried not to kick himself for not taking this more seriously. He'd really believed it was going to be a wild-goose chase and had not been on guard nearly enough.

On the road returning to civilization, Luke kept his questions to himself, but Oscar got talkative. His demeanor was on a switch: evil and murderous one minute and harmless old codger the next. He told them about his life on the run. Claimed he hated the deserted area he lived in but it was the only place he felt safe. He'd been supporting himself with an old friend's Social Security checks.

"I didn't kill him. He died of natural causes, so I just became him. I'm amazed that the PI in Arizona connected Parker to me. I thought I was so careful."

Luke wondered if the friend was buried in the backyard.

Oscar rambled on about hiding from the cops, how it had

worn him down. Luke listened and thought about how sin would do exactly that to a person. He thought about Abby Hart and the cold case that connected them. He wanted to believe that if there was another guilty party in her parents' and his uncle's murders, they were as tortured by guilt and fear as this shriveled-up old man behind him.

Curious about how it all started, Luke asked, "Why'd you kill that man in the first place?"

"I wanted the car, plain and simple. It was a beautiful '54 Chevy, completely restored with shiny new leather seats and a powerful motor. I still think about that car and how the want of it made me pull the trigger. Dumbest thing I ever did. Don't think I had it twenty-four hours before cops were all over me. Back then I thought I was invincible."

From the look on Woody's face in the rearview mirror, Luke knew he thought everything the old man was saying was hooey.

Luke reached into his glove box and pulled out a pocket New Testament. He carried them to give to runaways. "Don't know how long you'll be able to keep this, but why not read it while you can. Woody can put it in your shirt pocket."

Woody took the little book and showed it to Oscar.

"God stuff? I'm too evil. God would never pay someone like me any account." He made a face.

Woody looked in the mirror, eyebrows raised.

Luke waved his hand. "Put it in his pocket," he said to Woody, then addressed Oscar. "You were wrong decades ago when you pulled the trigger, and you're wrong now. God's forgiveness is for everyone. Just read the book. What could it hurt?"

Oscar shrugged and Woody shoved the New Testament into his shirt pocket. Luke prayed he'd read it.

When they reached the main road, they hit cell service and his phone came alive. So did Woody's. Luke paused at a stop sign to check it and his heart stopped. Looking in the rearview mirror, he knew Woody had seen the same thing. A police shooting in Long Beach. Luke also had a message from his friend Bill. He could put two and two together.

"I see it," Woody said. "Abby called me, left a message. I'm going to call her back."

Luke nodded and hurried to get Oscar to the proper authorities, all the while praying for Abby and her partner, Bill—praying they were safe and it was the bad guy who was hurt by the shooting. From Woody's side of the conversation it sounded as if Abby was okay, and Luke relaxed. He got the feeling Woody didn't want to say much in front of the prisoner, so he didn't ask any questions.

Now he found it difficult to concentrate on Cardoza and was grateful that Woody was with him. Once back at the sheriff's substation, Luke and Woody gave the officers all the information they had about Oscar and left the fugitive in their hands. They were very interested in Woody's take on the backyard. Luke knew they'd have to officially confirm Cardoza's identity, probably get a search warrant for the property, and then contact the authorities in Montana about extradition if no charges were filed against him here.

Luke was finished with his part, and he called to let the Arizona PI know. She was excited and grateful, but Luke didn't want to waste any time being congratulated. He couldn't get back to his truck fast enough.

"What did Abby say?"

"Not much. She wants me to go by her house and let the

dog out. She'll be tied up for a bit. I can call my neighbor to look after mine."

"I'll head right there. NFD?" Luke was learning cop lingo from Woody, like the shorthand for "no further details."

"She promised Bill would call with more. It's the Joiner case."

Luke said nothing after hearing that. It probably meant Abby was the shooter, and that made his stomach cramp with anxiety. He was familiar with the case and guessed that the partners must have confronted a suspect. Luke made a point of following cases involving kids, and this one was about a ten-year-old's rape and murder. He knew that Abby and Bill had evidence but were sweating out a lab backlog. If they had a suspect, the lab must have come through after all. There must have been a hit right away, and since there'd been a shooting, Luke thought that maybe the suspect didn't want to go quietly.

He wished he could fly back to the city. As it was, they were way south in Perris, at least an hour and a half away from Long Beach on a good traffic day. He clicked on the radio station that gave news updates every few minutes and hit the freeway hoping for clear sailing and light traffic.

They were halfway home when Bill called. Luke put it on speaker, asking if they had tangled with an uncooperative suspect.

"Not him. We found him on the couch," Bill said. "He looked at us and held his hands out for the cuffs, saying he'd rather be in prison than hurt anyone else. No, man, it was worse. We stepped out the front door and the victim's father was waiting for us. He tried to kill the suspect, got off a couple of shots before Abby dropped him."

"Abby shot . . ." Luke's voice faded as a horrible picture flashed in his mind. *Abby shot a victim's father?*

"Yeah, it's worse still. He's dead. Abby's pretty tore up about it. But she saved us all as far as I'm concerned. Thank God the father shot wild. He could have killed me; he could have killed Abby."

Luke couldn't imagine being in Abby's shoes. He felt he knew her well enough that being "pretty tore up" was an understatement. All he could think about were her beautiful green eyes, filled with pain and guilt over taking a life.

CHAPTER

-5-

GOD, why did you let me kill him?

Abby threw water on her face from the sink in the locker room after she'd finished with the last interview. It was close to 9:30 p.m. She and Bill had been going over the shooting with everyone in the city for a lifetime, it seemed. She was beyond exhausted, moving around in a walking zombie state.

A day that had begun dreamlike and upbeat turned nightmarish and dark as if a coin were flipped.

She kept seeing Clayton fall and then the life leave his eyes as the paramedics worked on his bloody form to no avail. He wasn't officially pronounced dead until he got to the hospital, but Abby knew there on the lawn that he was gone.

Abby couldn't help but flash back in her mind to another shooting—the day she'd confronted Gavin Kent about her parents' murders. Like Clayton, she'd waited a long time for a suspect, a reason for the deaths that ripped her world apart. And like Clayton, she'd had a gun in her hand when she confronted the monster.

She'd wanted to pull the trigger.

She'd wanted to be judge, jury, and executioner just like Clayton wanted to be.

She and Kent had faced each other, guns drawn. But Kent pulled the trigger and killed himself, wrenching the opportunity away from Abby. And today it was excruciatingly obvious to Abby that she could have been Clayton—a millisecond of difference and she would have been Clayton.

But why is the bad guy safe and the good guy in the morgue? Why, God, why?

"You made the hard choice, and you did your job." Bill said those words to her over and over as if sensing how disturbed she was about what she'd had to do.

Abby listened and tried to take his words to heart, but she wanted to talk to her friend and mentor, Woody. So far she'd managed only a brief conversation with him between interviews. She'd called him as soon as she was able. A retired cop, he understood that she'd be consumed by interviews and investigation for hours, and she wanted him to go to her house and let her dog out.

When they finally were able to talk for a few minutes, he'd tried to quiet her doubts, her self-flagellation.

"Guy points a gun at you, you have to shoot. He could have killed you or your partner. Would you want that?"

Abby leaned against a row of lockers, and the sound of clanging metal reverberated through the empty locker room.

Clayton's wife was inconsolable.

"How could you take his life protecting that monster?" she'd screamed as uniformed officers held her back from scratching Abby's eyes out. In between sobs the woman explained that when Clayton saw Bill and Abby pull up, he just knew. She'd tried to stop him, but he was determined to avenge his daughter.

"I told him to leave it to God, but he wouldn't listen," Althea cried. *"Why didn't he listen?"*

Abby listened. She heard the woman's pain and felt guilt to the core. She knew exactly what drove Clayton Joiner and realized some of the same emotions drove her as well.

How could I kill him protecting a monster?

Her phone chimed and she saw it was Ethan, her fiancé, and felt guiltier. He'd called earlier and she'd never called him back. The interviews she had to give regarding the shooting had left her voice dry and weak. It wasn't Ethan's fault she just didn't want to talk anymore.

Sighing, she answered the call, knowing he only wanted to help and be supportive.

"Hey," he said, "I'm worried about you. Are you still at work?"

"On my way out."

"You sound tired. I can't imagine how you must be feeling."

"I'm numb right now."

"Do you want any company? I can stop by."

"Ethan, I'm just tired. All I want right now is bed. Thanks for the offer."

"I understand. I'll call you in the morning. Can I pray for you?"

"I'd love that."

"Lord, I lift Abby to you tonight. You know what's going on in her head and her heart. Heal what needs to be healed. In Jesus' name, amen."

Abby thought about Ethan's prayer as she drove home through quiet, dark streets. *"Heal what needs to be healed."*

She didn't think healing was possible because there was no way to replay the moment and put the bullets back in her gun.

CHAPTER

-6-

LUKE DROPPED WOODY off at Abby's house.

"Call me when you need a ride home," he said as Woody stepped out of the truck.

"I will," Woody said. "I don't mind hanging out here for a while. Abby will need someone to talk to. Call before you come."

Luke said he would, then headed home to his family, wondering how things had gone so right for him and Woody and so wrong for Abby and Bill. He got home in time for dinner and to catch a news report on the shooting. There were the usual inane comments by people and reporters asking why Abby didn't just shoot the gun out of the man's hand. The criticisms and second-guessing by people who'd never been in a life-and-death situation made Luke angry, and the outrage he heard in the voices of the anchor regarding a victim's father being shot stoked the flames. There were even pictures of crowds forming in front of the police station to protest Abby. He had to retire to his office and throw a couple punches at the heavy bag to calm down.

In the end, it wasn't the heavy bag that calmed him; it was the knowledge that Abby was a believer and that the foundation of her life shouldn't rest on what reporters and onlookers had to say.

He called Woody after dinner, but Abby still hadn't made it home.

"Don't read anything into that," Woody said. "The process after a shooting like this is long and involved. When I spoke to Bill a little while ago, he said Abby was talking to the department psychologist, which is a good thing."

"I agree. I can't imagine being in her shoes. I'll head over after Maddie goes to bed."

"Sounds good, and if you can stop and pick me up a burger or something, I'd appreciate it."

"Will do."

"Is your friend Abby in trouble?" Maddie asked as Luke sat down with his daughter for bedtime prayer. The question took him by surprise because he didn't think she was paying attention to the news broadcast.

"No, she's not in trouble, Mads, but she had to shoot someone today."

"Did the person die?"

"Afraid so."

"But Abby and Bill are okay."

"Yes, they are."

"I'm glad. But sometimes I wish there were no bad people in the world. Then people wouldn't have to get shot."

"I wish that too," Luke said. He kissed her good night and then went to package up the dinner his mother had set aside for him to take to Woody. Luke had mentioned that Woody asked for food, and Grace, who hated fast food, insisted that Luke take some of her casserole to him.

Luke and Woody were set to fly to Idaho tomorrow to fulfill the last wishes of Woody's old patrol partner, Asa Foster. Coincidentally, Asa had also worked with Abby in the twilight years of his career. It was time to nail down the fine points of their itinerary. But Luke wondered if Woody would want to cancel the trip because of the shooting. When he considered how hard this must be for Abby, he knew he'd be fine with it if that was what Woody wanted to do. Luke called to let Woody know that he was on his way.

"She's not home yet. I spoke to her on the phone a couple of hours ago. Maybe you should hang out with me as well. She didn't sound too great."

"It probably wouldn't be a good thing for her to come home to an empty house on a day like this." Luke worked to sound nonchalant, but he was happy Woody had asked him to hang out.

"You're right. I never discharged my weapon on duty, but I know guys who have. It's not easy, and in this case . . . well, it's not so black-and-white."

"Um, is—is Ethan there?"

"No. I spoke to him as well. He said she told him not to come by, that she was tired. Just between you and me and the fence post, I don't think everything is going too well with those two."

"I'm sorry to hear that," Luke said, wanting to pry but not wanting to pry. It was really none of his business. But his concern for Abby made him ask the next question. "Do you think she'd mind if I were there?"

"I'd kind of like your company. You and her speak the same God talk; you might be able to help her more than me. She's taking this hard."

That surprised Luke. He'd spent quite a bit of time with Woody recently. He knew Woody was not a Christian. Other than mentioning the man upstairs from time to time, and letting Luke pray now and then, Woody had never made a statement either positive or negative about Abby's faith or faith in general.

"I'd love to try to help. You should be able to tell if I can help or if we should leave her alone. I'll be over in a few minutes."

Abby knew Woody's car would not be in her driveway. He'd told her that Luke had dropped him off. But when she recognized the truck parked at the curb in front of her house, it gave her pause.

Luke Murphy's truck.

She wanted to see Woody, and she wanted to hug her dog, Bandit, but she wasn't sure about Murphy. The man always seemed to be able to see right through her. Right now she wasn't certain she wanted to be transparent. Sighing, she parked in front of her garage and climbed out of the car.

Woody opened the front door and Abby could have kissed him. He let little Bandit run out and greet her. Picking up the wiggling fur ball and holding his squirming, licking body was a comforting normality on a totally abnormal day.

"Oh, sweetie," Abby cooed to the dog. "It's wonderful to see you." She continued up to the front door. "You too, Woody. Thanks for taking care of Bandit."

"My pleasure."

He held the door open for her, and a wonderful aroma hit her as she stepped inside.

Luke smiled at her from the kitchen. "My mom sent me over with food for Woody. I figured you'd be hungry as well, so I brought extra. It's her potato and ham casserole. I'm heating some up for you."

Words fled. Abby was hungry; her stomach growled even as she inhaled the wonderful smell. She'd totally forgotten that she hadn't eaten since breakfast, and the fact that Luke and his mother so perfectly anticipated what she'd need touched her.

Swallowing, she set Bandit down. "I'm starved; thank you," she said when she stood back up.

"It's great stuff," Woody said, rubbing his stomach.

Abby smiled, thankful for her friends and realizing that having them both here was helpful. "I'll just go wash my hands."

"Dinner will be served as soon as you're back," Luke said.

Feeling better as she sat down in front of a plate of steaming, creamy, wonderful-smelling food, Abby bowed her head for a blessing. When she finished and took a bite, she had to admit the meal was heavenly.

"Mmm, this is great. Please thank your mom for me."

"Will do." Luke sat across from Abby, next to Woody.

Abby ate while Luke and Woody discussed their trip to Idaho the next day. They planned to be gone for three days and hoped to wrap everything up quickly. Asa had left his house in trust, so the estate was not complicated. He'd also left detailed instructions about the dispersal of his personal belongings.

They both shared the story of their arrest in Riverside, Luke acting like a careless bungler, which she knew that he wasn't, and Woody puffed with pride about still being able to be sneaky. That she knew was true. He had taught her the art of being sneaky when you needed to get the drop on a bad guy.

"I wish all tips panned out that way," Luke said after he finished.

"Amen to that," Abby said, feeling full, tired, and somewhat better. "I hope you continue to get that lucky when you're working with the feds."

Woody preened. "It's not all luck, you know. Haven't I taught you that hard work and perseverance makes luck?"

"Of course." Abby smiled and felt it. She didn't miss Luke smothering a chuckle.

"What are you going to do with your time off this week?" Woody asked, referring to the mandatory three days off given to any officer involved in a shooting.

She could tell he was concerned. Woody had the best cop face when dealing with suspects, but Abby often saw through him.

She drained her glass of water before answering. "I have another appointment with the psychologist tomorrow. Coincidentally Ethan and I have a counseling appointment on Thursday." She played with her glass. "Who knows? I may do a little goldbricking and try to take Friday off as well—a six-day vacation." A weak smile was all she could muster for the lame joke.

"You did your job," Luke said, repeating what Bill had already told her. "Joiner made the wrong choice, not you."

He'd read her again and knew she was struggling over her actions. *Clayton made the wrong choice, and I made the hard choice.* Abby just nodded, not trusting herself to speak.

His gaze was so warm and filled with understanding, Abby almost wished it were just the two of them and she could rest her head on his broad, strong shoulder. Almost. Guilt niggled at her as she remembered Ethan's sincere prayer; it was his shoulder she should be wanting.

Later, with Luke and Woody gone, she pulled down a package of Oreos and her Bible. The cookies went down easy, but the Bible didn't hold her attention. So much swirled inside. Luke's comfort, his concern, was somewhat bracing, even more so than Woody's knowledge and his sage advice, and that surprised her. But it was something she didn't want to add to her list of concerns at the moment.

She finished half a glass of milk and four cookies, then took a shower and went to bed. Sleep came, after a struggle with the image of Clayton Joiner lying on the lawn, bleeding, seemingly etched on her eyelids.

CHAPTER

-7-

"I ONLY VISITED HIM up here once, after he retired."

Woody and Luke stopped at the curb, just in front of Asa Foster's Idaho home. Luke waited for Woody, knowing that this was hard for him. Asa had been Woody's patrol partner and his friend for many years. Even after Asa transferred to detectives, he and Woody had stayed close. Luke could feel the depressing finality in this visit, and he'd barely known the man. It must be doubly hard for Woody.

Woody had wanted to make the trip right after he officially retired, months ago. But between helping Luke close up his open cases and jumping through hoops for the federal hiring process, the trip had been delayed over and over. As soon as they finished the last bit of federal paperwork and both of their schedules jibed, they'd made arrangements to fly up together, hoping to beat the winter snowfall.

After Abby's shooting, Luke thought Woody would want to reschedule. When he realized Woody didn't want to do that, he'd almost considered bringing up the idea, asking Woody to reschedule, because he was worried about her. But reality sank in hard, like a twenty-five-pound barbell dropped on his foot; Abby was engaged to another man. Luke chastised himself for even considering it was his place to worry about her.

He worked hard to put Abby out of his mind and concentrate on the task at hand. As he and Woody stood in front of Asa's house, Luke knew Woody still struggled with the loss, even with the passage of time.

"We went fishing on a lake about half an hour away. Caught a lot of fish. He said then that it felt like heaven here." Woody's wistful tone made Luke sad, and he couldn't help but remember the horrible way Asa had died.

The retired detective had wanted to force the California governor to come clean with what he believed was the truth about a twenty-seven-year-old cold case, the Triple Seven murders. Asa had heard the allegations made about the murders by George Sanders and had it in his mind that the governor and his chief of staff, Gavin Kent, were guilty of a triple homicide—Abby's parents and Luke's uncle. Asa was right in one respect: Kent did partially confess, only to immediately kill himself and prevent further inquiry. But not before Asa himself died, cut down by the governor's security man because Asa was a perceived threat to the governor.

Luke was there when Asa took his last breath, vainly tried to stop the bleeding. But the retired detective had been hit in an artery, and there was nothing Luke could do. Asa died while he watched helplessly. His last words were one of the reasons Luke and Woody were here now, at Asa's home.

"There is proof."

Later, after Luke told Woody, they decided that Asa meant proof pertaining to the cold case, to the murders of Buck and

Patricia Morgan and Luke Goddard, Luke's uncle. Kent confessed to killing Patricia Morgan and to setting a fire to destroy evidence in the Triple Seven restaurant. But the entire story about what happened the day Patricia was slain, presumably with her husband and Goddard, had never been uncovered.

Did Asa have proof, here in his home, connecting the triple murder to the governor, a man who was rumored to soon be running for the US Senate as a shoo-in?

As soon as Woody was ready, Luke wanted to go inside and find out.

Finally Woody sighed. "Let's get this over with."

Luke followed him into the house.

It wasn't a big house and it was obviously a bachelor pad—neat, but sparsely furnished. A fifty-inch television dominated the small living room.

"Asa loved NASCAR, said the big screen made it feel as if he were there," Woody commented. He had in his hand a letter Asa had left for him on the last day of his life. He'd guessed that violently confronting the governor would cost him his life. In the letter, Asa gave Woody directions to and a combination for his safe.

"Looks like the bedroom is back here." Luke pointed to the left.

Woody nodded and headed that way. According to the note, the safe was in Asa's bedroom, in the closet under a bunch of boxes. Woody found it straightaway. It was a square metal box, two feet by two feet, and Woody needed Luke's help to pick it up and put it on Asa's unmade bed.

"Asa wanted to be certain no one ever ran out of the house with this," Woody said as he bent to work the combination.

Luke said nothing, but he held his breath. If there really was proof in here about who killed Abby Hart's parents and his uncle, it would be the answer to a twenty-seven-year-long prayer.

The safe clicked open. On top was a gun; it looked like a .45 to Luke. Woody removed it and uncovered files.

"These are police files," Woody said as he took them out. He opened the top one. "Simon Morgan." Woody frowned. "I know that name. . . . He's Abby's uncle."

"Abby's uncle? He's in prison, isn't he?"

"Ahh." Woody's eyes skimmed the file. "Yeah. At least he was. It was a sore spot with Buck. He and his brother never got along, and when Simon went to prison, Buck wanted to forget him."

"He's in for murder if I remember right."

Woody brought a hand to his chin. "Yeah, the incident is coming back to me. He went up for a minor felony but killed someone there and eventually drew a life sentence."

"Why would Asa have his file?"

"I don't know. He highlighted some names I don't recognize."

"What are the other files?"

Woody set the Simon Morgan file down. "There are a couple of accident reports—hit-and-runs, old ones. This last folder is just notes, looks like Asa's writing. Suppositions. . . . Hmm."

"No smoking gun," Luke interpreted, and the disappointment bit deep.

Woody looked at him. "Maybe not. Or maybe we just have some work ahead of us."

They emptied the safe and found a bag to put everything in. The gun and a hunting rifle Asa owned were to go to a neighbor, who also happened to be a retired cop. Woody was given all of Asa's fishing gear. Asa told Woody he could go through everything in the house, take what he wanted. After Woody finished, he was to call the cleaning lady and tell her to contact Asa's attorney. Asa had left her the house in trust because she reminded him of his deceased wife.

Luke and Woody had flown to Idaho hoping to tie everything up over the course of three days. Their new job in the cold case squad had been scheduled to start next week, though now that was iffy. Luke had a planned weekend away with his daughter set to begin Friday morning so they could spend some time together. He'd been so busy lately, they hadn't been able to do it before she began fifth grade studies. As much as he hated to admit it, Luke had been anticipating this trip to Idaho with Woody more than the trip with Maddie.

Over the past few months the last words Asa had breathed about proof had stuck with Luke. It had permeated his mind that there was a possibility of more answers where his uncle's murder was concerned. He tried to be settled about the crime, to follow the advice he had given Abby often, to trust God's justice. As the hollow feeling of disappointment spread, he realized the hope of concrete evidence was nothing but smoke and what they'd found here would likely not change what they already knew.

CHAPTER

-8-

KELSEY STUDIED THE CONTENTS of the minibar and wondered if any of the alcohol it contained would help calm the head games her mind was playing with her. Though it was often faint, every once in a while her conscience surfaced and bugged, prodded, made her want to stop and get off this path in life she'd taken. She'd said something like that once to Gavin, during a stressful time for both of them, only to have him throw an old cliché at her: "Nice guys finish last."

As much as she hated the phrase, she knew it was true. She'd never have gotten to be a deputy chief by being *nice*. Abby Hart was nice. She was also by-the-book, meticulous, determined, tenacious—all attributes that made her a good cop. But she was naive in a way, parochial, and uninterested in promoting, in having the power to control, give orders, set agendas. Nope, she only wanted the truth, to help the victim.

Slamming the minibar door closed without removing anything, Kelsey moved to the window and looked out over the landscape.

For a kid whose parents were murdered when she was six,

something that should have knocked her off the development rung, Hart had come a long way, and Kelsey had a grudging admiration for the woman.

But it was all of those admirable qualities that were likely to get Hart killed. Who would have thought that she would ever connect with Luke Murphy, a guy whose own uncle was murdered along with Hart's parents? Most of all, who would have expected that their teamwork to find the truth would make Kelsey's boss so nervous, so threatened, that the as-yet-unspoken command to deal with Hart and Murphy in a permanent way hung over her head like rotting mistletoe?

I don't want that kiss, Kelsey thought, *that order to kill, but it will come. I'm sure of it.*

What will I do when it does?

CHAPTER

-9-

"I LOVE THIS PLACE." Maddie beamed and Luke smiled.

"Me too; me too." Guilt nudged. He'd wanted to put off this trip, which had already been rescheduled twice, to pore over the files he and Woody had recovered from Asa Foster's house. They'd not done much in Idaho. In the end Woody promised he'd wait to study them until Luke had the time.

Now, here on the water with his daughter, he was ashamed the thought had even crossed his mind. He loved spending time with his little girl. She was growing up so fast, he didn't want to miss any bit of her childhood.

They bobbed in a small motorboat on Big Bear Lake, both holding fishing poles. It was peaceful and quiet on the water this time of the morning. Two and a half hours from home, it was a world away from the busy city of Long Beach. They'd driven up to the Big Bear area on Friday morning, taking Maddie's lessons with them. Since she was homeschooled, they had that flexibility. Luke had rented a cabin for them amid pine trees, in Fawnskin, a small historic community on the north shore of the lake.

Early Saturday morning, before they'd made their way out

on the lake for the sunrise, Luke had read devotions for them from Psalm 19.

The sunrise over the mountains was breathtaking.

"The heavens sure do declare the glory of God, don't they, Mads?"

Maddie looked up, squinted, and smiled. "The sun is coming out of the tent God pitched for her."

Luke chuckled, heart swelling with pride. Maddie had memorized the psalm. In her translation, the last part of verse 4 said, "In the heavens God has pitched a tent for the sun."

It did his soul good to see his daughter growing strong in faith and applying the Word of God to her life.

It was also a wonder that she liked to fish as much as he did. None of her girlfriends enjoyed sitting still in a boat or on land to try to hook fish. But Maddie seemed to love it, not minding the stillness, the quiet, or the fish guts when they caught something big enough to eat. She didn't even mind the cold. They were both bundled up against the fall chill in the mountain air.

"What do you like best here?" Luke asked.

Maddie let out a big sigh. "It's so pretty. And the smell—I like the way the trees smell. Even the smoke from chimneys smells good. I'd like to live here."

Luke chuckled. "Really? You'd like to live in the forest away from all the things there are to do in the city?"

Maddie nodded. "Any forest with big trees and deer. I think I want to be a forest ranger when I grow up."

Throughout the course of the summer, Maddie had moved from wanting to be a police officer, to a vet, and now a forest ranger. Luke was glad she had varied interests and she was a smart girl; what she put her mind to, she accomplished.

"I like it here too."

"And there's lots to do," Maddie said, looking at her dad. "Biking and ziplining and hiking."

"That there is." He put his hand out and Maddie gave him a high five.

They sat quietly fishing for a minute before Madison spoke up again. "Dad, can I ask you a question?"

"Sure."

"Do you think you'll ever get married again?"

Luke coughed and nearly dropped his fishing pole. *From forest ranger to remarriage?* "Uh, Mads, what makes you ask that?"

"Olivia and I were talking. We decided that you're not too old yet. You could find someone nice if you tried."

"Oh, thanks. It's nice of you and Olivia to think about my love life." He didn't know whether to laugh or cry, but he was certain he didn't want to have this conversation with his eleven-year-old daughter. At least she hadn't said she needed a mother.

"Well, just think about it. Olivia says men need to be married. There are lots of websites to help you."

"Wait; what do you know about dating websites?" Luke was anxious to change the subject.

"Everyone knows about them, Dad," Maddie said matter-of-factly. "I've never been on one, but Olivia's older brother has. That's how he met his girlfriend. It's just a thought if you decide to move forward."

He stared at his daughter from the corner of his eye, vowing to listen more carefully when Olivia and Madison were talking. Holding his breath for more advice, he exhaled with relief when it didn't come.

Abby Hart popped into his mind. Looking out over the lake,

he frowned, and butterflies fluttered in his stomach like a fish on the line. He was attracted to Abby, no two ways about it. But she was promised to another man. When he'd heard they'd postponed their wedding to go through counseling, hope had sprung inside his chest. He'd actually thought about Abby as the woman who would fit in his and Maddie's life. Then guilt bit like a vise as he realized he needed to pray for God's best, and if for Abby that was Ethan, he needed to step back.

Even if Ethan weren't in the picture, Luke remembered how his marriage to Maddie's mother had ended: in a telephone screaming match that concluded with her so distracted she ran her car into oncoming traffic and died instantly. Over the years the horror of that moment had faded, but from time to time he felt a pinch in his heart—guilt, regret, a mixture of both—and embarrassment about how he'd been so wrapped up in himself he'd not seen how his wife needed him, how she was begging for him to hear her.

All he'd heard, all he'd cared about then, was his own ego, his own desires. He'd come home to a motherless daughter and vowed to hear her, to be there for her, and to somehow make amends for the loss of a mother. Would he be different if there were another wife in the picture? Reeling in his line to check the bait, he realized he wasn't sure.

Biting the inside of his cheek, he doubted there would ever be another marriage for him. He couldn't fail a woman like that again. Ever.

CHAPTER

-10-

ABBY ENDED UP STAYING AWAY from work for the whole week. As for the court case she'd been concerned about, the DA and the defense attorney had worked out a last-minute plea, so that was one thing she could remove from her plate. By Sunday, her last day home, Abby was still having nightmares and wondered if she was foolish to rush back to work. During their last conversation on Friday, Dr. Collins, the police psychologist, had suggested she take an additional week off.

"I know that you witnessed a suicide several months ago. You were not required to come talk to me and you didn't, but that was a traumatic event. This second incident occurring in such close proximity is problematic. You have nothing to prove. There is no stigma in saying you just need a little more time to process events."

In the end, though, she didn't heed his advice. Collins was happy with Abby's attitude and the support groups in her life. He suggested she spend time in church, or with the people she played volleyball with, and call him if she had any issues. He also gave her a list of official help groups if she felt she needed that.

While working hard to assure herself, she convinced him she could function. He signed off on her return to work, but her universe felt out of sync, like when you watch a video and the words don't match the lip movement. She still had a grip on normal, but it was far from a firm grip.

The case against Javon Curtis in the murder of ten-year-old Adonna Joiner was strong. But by the end of the week, Abby had heard that while Curtis had made incriminating statements to both Bill and Abby the day he was arrested, once he'd been arraigned and lawyered up, he'd decided to plead not guilty. The lawyer requested a psych exam for Curtis. A trial was a long while away. Abby knew that the inevitable court battle could dredge everything up all over again, but she had time to prepare. This odd, off-balance feeling couldn't last forever, could it?

Protests over the shooting had grown. It bothered Abby when she saw a news report showing the sign-carrying, chanting mob. They wanted her badge without due process. But Abby's union rep had been as supportive as Collins. "You're in policy," he'd said. "By the book. Ignore the media circus and take care of yourself." Abby knew he was right and tried to take his advice. Joiner had fired twice, thankfully both bullets impacting the roof fascia, bare inches above their heads, before her bullets stopped him. She had no obligation to let herself or her partner be shot. But that didn't stop Abby from continuing to second-guess herself. And tomorrow, thirty-five-year-old Clayton Joiner would be laid to rest next to his daughter.

In her nightmares, Abby relived the shooting over and over. It all happened so fast. Her first shooting and she hadn't killed a violent criminal; she'd killed a grieving father.

"I would have done the same thing," Bill told her. He'd had

his hands on the suspect and could not draw his weapon fast enough. *"Joiner could have easily shot one or both of us. I'm glad you reacted so quickly and only sorry that Joiner tried to take the law into his own hands."*

Even the local police beat reporter, Walter Gunther, had called her and, in his cigarette-roughened voice, told her not to be too hard on herself. It was a tough situation, a choice no cop should ever have to face, and he was glad she and Bill weren't hurt.

Abby knew Bill and Gunther told the truth, perceived it in her head, but in her heart she ached. She understood Joiner, recognized the pain and loss that had driven him to do what he did, and wished with all her heart the outcome could have been different. He'd waited three long months to discover that his daughter's killer lived next door and called himself "friend."

The only conversation she'd had with anyone that helped a bit was the brief one she'd had with Luke Murphy, the day he and Woody had left for Idaho. She'd called to thank his mother for the dinner and got Luke as he was putting his stuff together for the trip. The PI seemed to understand her on every level.

"I was involved in a lot of firefights in Iraq; it was war. But one engagement that sticks with me was when a young kid rushed us. He had a bomb vest on. If he'd reached my position, he would have taken out my whole team. I did what I had to do, and you did what you had to do."

They'd spoken only a few minutes. Abby wanted to talk more, but the wanting of more time with Luke left a cloud of guilt over her heart.

Now, though time was supposed to heal all wounds, she felt as if she were still sleepwalking. She fed Bandit, started a pot of coffee, and walked outside to pick up the newspaper. Ethan always teased her about her newspaper subscription.

"Everything is online quicker than on the pages of a newspaper," he said often.

"Maybe, but I like spreading the paper out while I drink my morning coffee."

Today she might agree with him. The only story that had kicked her and Clayton Joiner off the front page was the headline announcing something she knew was coming, but it nonetheless smacked her between the eyes.

Governor Rollins Officially Tosses His Hat in the Ring.

She scanned the story about Rollins's announcement that he was running for a senate seat. It recapped how the governor had bounced back after some bad press related to a cold case, the most famous cold case in Long Beach history, the Triple Seven murders. The story regurgitated how the governor's personal secretary, Gavin Kent, had partially confessed to committing a twenty-seven-year-old murder and then taken his own life. The murky details of the cold case and the stain of Kent's confession had failed to impact the governor and his plans in the least. Abby knew it was likely that the popular governor would be elected to the senate, and that twisted in her gut along with the festering guilt over Joiner.

I could have done without seeing this story, whether in print or online, she thought as she folded the paper and walked outside the house to toss it into the recycle bin.

It was Abby's mother Kent had confessed to killing all those years ago, when Abby was only six years old. Left unanswered was why, and what had happened to her father. Abby had always believed he'd died next to her mother. But a wild theory thrown out by George Sanders, a man in custody for an unrelated murder, had given her a reason to suspect he could have survived. Abby suspected that the governor and his wife were somehow involved with the crime, but so many years later, the lack of proof forced her to back off, try to put everything behind her, and trust God that the guilty would be dealt with, if not in this life, then in the next.

If only Clayton Joiner had been able to do that—trust God and the justice system.

Abby went back inside to poach some eggs. Ethan would arrive to take her to church in a couple of hours and she wanted to be ready. Ever since that first uncomfortable day, when she had avoided speaking with him, Ethan had become extremely helpful. He'd prayed with and for her often and had just been there for her in a way she'd never felt him be there before. A few months ago they'd cancelled a planned wedding date because differences in their individual visions for the future had become glaring. Before the shooting, Abby had begun to think it was over, that they'd never recover and reset a wedding date.

But now she wasn't sure about anything, much less their future.

Ethan was a world traveler, a missionary, and he'd been trying to persuade Abby that the impact they could have in the world as a missionary couple was worth any sacrifice either could make. Initially Abby had bristled that she would be the only one who would have to sacrifice her career and the life in Long Beach she'd come to love.

But the shooting changed a lot. For the first time in her career, Abby felt lost, uncertain. Was Ethan right? Should she quit and follow him?

Abby sat down with her eggs, toast, and coffee. She bowed her head. Prayer did not come easily these days for reasons she could not fathom. Several seconds passed before any words came to mind, and even then, the prayer was brief and to the point.

"Lord, I want to be where you want me. I just don't know where that is anymore. Please help me, and bless this meal. Amen."

CHAPTER

-11-

"YOU'VE BEEN AWFULLY QUIET this morning." Ethan reached across the car and gripped Abby's hand. They were on their way to lunch after the service.

"Just thinking."

"I saw the headline too."

She turned to look at him, but he had his eyes on the road.

"What makes you think that's what's on my mind?"

He gave a half shrug. "I know you. I think the situation with Governor Rollins still bothers you. It's unresolved."

"Of course it still bothers me." She sighed. No, it wasn't the main thing right now, but she had no energy to change the subject. Ethan was generally right on about the present, but he never did truly understand her past. They'd more or less grown up together; Abby met him shortly after she'd moved to live with her aunt in Oregon when she was ten. He was in a youth group her aunt oversaw. Ethan never understood what losing her parents at six and spending four years in the custody of social services had done to her. Even years later, after she'd become a cop and he moved to Long Beach to work with a local church and they'd actually kindled a relationship, her past was a door he didn't want opened. When he'd proposed to her, he'd also asked her to stop looking into her parents' case. "There are so many unanswered questions. Do you really want a man like Rollins representing the state at a national level?"

Ethan squeezed her hand. "I won't vote for him. But you know as well as I do that there is no proof connecting him to anything illegal. The only people who've claimed to know what happened that day are dead, and what they each had to say could be construed as completely self-serving."

He turned at the parking lot for River's End, which was packed. It was a beautiful Sunday, still warm for October. She could see kite surfers soaring in the distance and a line of people waiting to be seated at the restaurant.

For a second she bit her tongue. It was true. Gavin Kent and George Sanders both claimed to know what happened the day her parents were murdered, and after saying so, they both died by their own hands. *Self-serving, selfish liars,* screamed in Abby's head and made her want to stomp her feet and chastise Ethan for reminding her. But that would solve nothing, and Ethan was not the enemy. He just didn't understand her like he thought he did.

"I won't vote for him either, but that's not what's bugging me today. I'm still thinking about Clayton Joiner." She opened the car door and got out, feeling claustrophobic, closed in. She wrapped her arms around herself as a cool ocean breeze hit. It felt good in spite of the shiver it prompted.

Ethan didn't say anything after that, and Abby was thankful. She was certain she had to work this out herself.

He held his hand out and she took it. She did love the solid reliability in Ethan right now. No matter what the problems were that had prompted them to postpone the wedding, Abby could never say that Ethan was not there for her when she needed him.

⎯⎯▸

"I wish you would take some more time off," Ethan said as he settled onto the couch. They'd come back to Abby's with a DVD to watch—one she picked out, an old movie: *The Courtship of Eddie's Father.*

Abby sighed and sat next to him. Bandit joined them a second later, sitting on Abby's lap. "I'm ready to get back to work. You know I hate hanging around here doing nothing when there are cases on my desk." She hoped he didn't hear the indecision in her voice. *It's just butterflies,* she thought. *I am ready.*

"I don't think anyone would hold it against you if you took a few more days off." He pressed Play. "I'm set to be in Butte Falls for that church project I told you about. I want to be sure you're okay before I leave."

"Ethan, I'll be fine," she said more stridently than she meant to. Sitting up, she turned to look at him while the opening credits played on the TV screen. "I'm sorry; that was harsh. I love how you've been there for me lately, but I don't need a keeper. I need to feel useful."

He smiled, but not before she saw irritation flit across his brow. "I like taking care of you. Sometimes I fear that homicide work will destroy you. I've told you that before." He reached out and put his hand over hers. "Maybe this shooting is highlighting a door marked Exit."

He moved his hand to her lips, stifling the protest there.

"I'll be leaving in the morning and be out of your hair. All I ask is that after I go, you seriously consider the possibility, okay?"

Abby held his gaze, seeing the warmth and concern there. Before the shooting, what he'd just said would have had her back up and her anger simmering. But right now she was walking a tightrope of emotion about returning to work and she couldn't spare a thread to lash out at him.

Besides, what if he was right?

She gripped his hand, kissed it, and then said, "Okay, fair enough." She returned to his side and snuggled close as Eddie's father filled the screen, and she let herself get lost in a funny, heartwarming window into romance in the 1960s.

CHAPTER

BLOOD.

"Ouch!" The knife clattered down on the counter as Molly brought her finger to her mouth, the coppery taste of blood hijacking her thoughts, taking them back to another time and place, a time when the knife was at her throat, held by an evil man, and there was nothing she could do about it.

"Ahh." She turned on the kitchen faucet and plunged her finger under the water, watching blood from the cut run down the drain.

She'd worked so hard not to go back to that place, the place the traffic accident had sent her. Tearing off a paper towel, she wrapped it around the cut, hoping that would stanch the blood flow. Squeezing the finger, she stared at her wrists and remembered the cuts there.

Suddenly she was back in the trunk. It was dark. Her wrists burned and bled, and she couldn't get free. When she finally ripped the bonds that held her wrists apart, blood from the cuts on her wrists ran down her hands. And when she scrambled out of the trunk, the blood dripped down her legs and splattered on the dirt as she ran for her life.

She smacked her uninjured hand on her thigh three times, forcing herself back to the present, her kitchen, safety. For a second, the scars were back; her wrists were cut and scabby and painful. Molly pulled her arms to her chest to stop the sobs. They racked her body, burned her throat, and she slid down the front of the dishwasher and sat on the floor, leveled and destroyed by memories that would not release her.

CHAPTER -13-

MONDAY MORNING, as Abby fed Bandit, she was still unsettled about the prospect of going back to work. Ethan had left for Butte Falls at 5:30 a.m. They'd exchanged texts, and he promised to call once he arrived in Oregon. She already found herself missing him but was relieved when there had been no further mention of her return to work. If Ethan had suggested one more time that she take another week off, she might have lost it. She'd convinced the psychologist she was ready to return and he'd agreed. Were they both wrong?

"Should I call him again?" she wondered, pausing to look into the mirror at bloodshot eyes.

Woody had called Sunday evening, after Ethan left, to see how Abby was doing regarding the shooting. He was the only person she'd almost shared her complete indecision with. She danced around the fact that the thought of going back to work made her sick to her stomach.

For Woody's part he seemed to sense something because he'd said, *"It'll do you good to get back into harness, to get back to doing what you do best—fighting to give a voice to the dead. It's like getting back on the horse after he throws you, something you need to do."*

He had to be right, she thought. The PD had been her second home for so many years. It was family she was going back to. That alone should smooth out the wrinkle in her gut.

As Abby drove to the station, she thought of Ethan and his unwavering vision about his place in the world and wondered about her own faltering vision.

"Sometimes I fear that homicide work will destroy you."

Unease swirling inside, part of her feared Ethan was right. The image of the angry, grief-stricken father was seared in her mind. She wanted to pay her respects at the funeral, but the rest of her knew that her presence would be inflammatory. She'd heard that several civil rights attorneys were pressuring Clayton's wife to sue her and the department for wrongful death.

Althea's angry lash out echoed in Abby's mind verbatim: *"How could you take his life protecting that monster?"*

He was only a grieving father trying to make things right for his daughter.

"Whoever sheds the blood of man, by man shall his blood be shed."

Abby jerked as that phrase went through her head. She'd not been able to read her Bible all week and was certain it had been a while since she read Leviticus. If the verse was from that book. She wasn't certain. It was a random thought from a mind that seemed only able to generate randomness right now.

At the heart of her distress was the knowledge that she could have been Clayton. She could have rushed forward to take the law into her own hands.

Worst of all, she still could, if more information came to light regarding her parents' murders. She'd begun to wonder if everyone was right and she was wrong, if her obsession with finding her parents' killers had defined her, consumed her, limited her vision.

Protesters were lined up in front of the station as she drove toward the parking lot. She made no effort to read the signs they waved nor to try to understand what they were chanting. It seemed automatic these days that protesters would spring up after a police shooting. Abby knew in her head that the shooting was in policy. The festering pain she felt was that she couldn't get the head knowledge to soak down into her soul. It was as if her heart beat with a protest of its own: *You were wrong. There should have been another way.*

Abby worked hard to block the indecision and the heart hurt from her mind as she rode the elevator up to her floor.

"Good morning," Bill greeted her when she entered the office. "You're just in time. We got a call."

Abby gritted her teeth. Before Clayton, getting a callout the minute she stepped into the office would have jolted her with anticipation. Right now all she felt was dread. Getting back on the horse.

"What is it?" she asked.

"Looks like a double murder in East Long Beach, just occurred. Suspect in custody on scene."

She deposited her personal car keys, gathered her crime scene kit, and followed Roper out to the parking lot.

Roper stopped her at the door.

"Are you up for this?" His concerned gaze touched her, and razor-thin emotions threatened to slice through. He was a good partner. He deserved a good partner, someone who was firing on all cylinders.

Swallowing, she said, "I'm fine. A little tired, but fine."

He accepted that with a nod and they left the office.

"You're quiet this morning," Roper commented as he merged with 710 freeway traffic, a déjà vu moment of Ethan's observation yesterday morning.

"I have a lot on my mind. Ethan left today for a mini mission trip."

"Is he still asking you to quit and go with him?"

She felt him turn her way, but she kept her gaze out the window. "Not so stridently. It was nice to have him around after . . ."

"I can understand that. If I can do anything for you, anything at all, don't hesitate to ask. My wife would love to have you over for dinner sometime."

"Thanks. I appreciate that offer."

He stayed quiet after that and Abby was grateful. Talking seemed to stir up emotions she needed to tamp down. And working to stay in control made her lose what slim bit of concentration she could muster. She watched the city go by as Bill took the 405 freeway transition and then exited onto Palo Verde in East Long Beach. The address they parked in front of a few minutes later was close to the freeway and not that far from another address in East Long Beach. Luke Murphy lived about a mile away, closer to the college.

Thoughts of Luke were the only ones that didn't seem random. While Ethan had been great the last week, Luke understood all of her, especially her past. He saw through the shields she put up. He was like that one strong, tall tower you could run to in order to be sheltered from the storm.

What would he see now? she wondered. For some reason the

man could read her like a book and she'd stopped being bothered by it. It did, however, bother her that thinking of him tweaked her emotions and sparked a longing in the pit of her soul.

Abby rubbed her forehead for a second before bracing herself and then pushing the car door open. Right now she and her partner owed their attention to this call. *I stand for the dead.* Even a murder with an obvious suspect on scene needed careful investigation, clearly compiled facts that could be presented in court and ensure conviction of the guilty. Her concentration must be on working this case, not on the shooting a week ago and certainly not on a man who wasn't likely to be in her life for any reason now that the case that connected them was essentially closed.

The house was a typical one-story East Long Beach home, with a neatly kept lawn and a short driveway with two cars parked in front of the garage. The entire lot was surrounded by yellow police tape, and curious neighbors gathered in clumps on the perimeter.

The uniformed sergeant on scene stepped up to greet them. "This looks cut-and-dried," he said, shaking his head. "You can thank me for making your life easy today."

"How's that?" Bill asked.

"The wife gave me a spontaneous statement and confessed." He held up a digital recorder. "I have it on tape. I tape everything these days. Anyway, she caught hubby with his girlfriend and administered her own form of justice." He made a gun with his thumb and forefinger. "Boom, boom."

"Where's she at?"

"The backyard. We decided to wait and see if you wanted to talk to her here while she's cooperating. We can transport instead if you wish."

Bill looked at Abby. She knew he wanted her thoughts. The stickiest part of interviewing suspects was getting past the Miranda rights. They needed to be read—Abby had no problem with that—but the hope was always that the suspect would waive their rights and talk. So the timing was the thing. Patrol officers knew never to try to conduct an interview and read Miranda rights if there was any chance the suspect would invoke them and ask for a lawyer. Once a lawyer was requested, there was no interview—period. In general, patrol officers left the advising and the interviewing to the detectives. What the sergeant got on tape, a spontaneous statement, was a gift and admissible in court.

But the question now was, should they advise her of her rights and get a statement while she was talking or risk the possibility that riding to the station in the back of a black-and-white and then sitting in a sterile interview room might make her shut up?

The decision would normally be an easy one for Abby, but she stammered. "Uh, let's . . . let's see what we have here. Where are the victims?"

Bill nodded slowly and Abby wondered if he'd disagree.

"Lead the way, Sergeant."

As the officer led them into the house, Abby immediately noticed the cold air. Since the October weather had been warm, it was no surprise the AC was on, but it was downright frigid in the house.

"Why so cold?" she asked.

"The AC was on its lowest setting. I don't know why. We turned it off, but the place hasn't warmed up yet."

She and Bill followed the sergeant as he led them through

the house to a bedroom. There, a man and a woman lay on the bed, the woman on her back, the man on his stomach. There was an unmistakable odor of blood, a smell that hit hard as she stepped through the bedroom door. As she moved into the room, she could see that both had multiple gunshot wounds to the head and face.

Anger—raw rage—had pulled the trigger here. The blood was fresh, the spatter still moving down the walls in spots.

Abby would have studied the scene, absorbing what it had to tell her. Spatter itself could speak volumes. But it wasn't this crime scene that spoke to her. She rubbed her hands together.

"He murdered my baby!"

The voice was so loud in her head, she turned, only to jerk back quickly, hoping the guys hadn't noticed. They hadn't. Their concentration was where it should be—on the victims. Abby followed their gazes.

It *looked* cut-and-dried, if the suspect had already confessed, she thought as perspiration broke out on her lip in spite of the cool air in the room.

"Who called 911?" she asked, looking at the two bodies but seeing Clayton Joiner bleeding on the lawn.

"Our suspect. She said there'd been a shooting. When I got here, she led me to the room and said—" the sergeant hooked his thumbs in his belt and looked toward the bed—"'The woman doesn't live here; the man does. I shot them both.' I asked her for the gun. It was on the table in the kitchen; she'd put it down to call 911. I didn't ask her anything else. I just had the beat guys take her out to the patio, and I called you."

"I noticed the suitcase in the entryway. Hers?" Bill asked, and Abby wondered how she missed that.

"She told dispatch she'd arrived home this morning from a weekend conference."

"She gets home and immediately shoots two people?" Abby hugged her shoulders as the frigid air cut through her thin blouse, battling the hot flash lingering in her system.

"That's a 10-4."

"No one should bury their ten-year-old daughter," Joiner had muttered while Abby tried to stop the bleeding and they waited for paramedics.

"She's outside?" Abby asked, wanting to shake the flashbacks away.

"Yep." He handed Abby a field information card with the woman's name and information.

"The gun?" Bill asked. "What was it and where is it now?"

"It's been made safe and placed in an evidence bag. It's a 9mm. She emptied a fifteen-round clip."

"I'll go talk to her," Abby said to Bill, gripping the card tight, willing all of her concentration to the present, not on what happened a week ago.

"I'll take you to her," the sergeant said and he showed her to the yard. Welcome warm air hit as soon as she stepped out through the sliding door.

A petite blonde woman sat at a patio table staring at the fence. She wore what looked to Abby to be an expensive gray wool suit, immaculately creased pants, a pale-orange blouse. A matching gray jacket was thrown over another chair. Carla Boston was mostly neat and clean, but for the reddish-brown spots here and there on her nice clothes. Hands cuffed behind her were like the answer to a "one of these things doesn't belong" riddle. Her legs were crossed and on her feet were a pair of high heels. Considering how many times she'd fired the gun at the two people in the bedroom, she was lucky that was all the blood that got on her. Abby was more concerned with her emotional state.

"Mrs. Boston?"

The woman turned.

"I'm Detective Hart. I'll be investigating this . . . situation."

Boston looked at her and nodded. The patrol sergeant was right. She'd shed no tears over this, at least not recently.

Clayton Joiner looked as though he'd cried every day of the last two months.

"Interesting thing to call it—a situation. But then it was an interesting scene to come home to." There was the hint of an accent in the woman's voice. Abby couldn't place it other than to guess it was from somewhere back east.

She sat down at the table and turned on her own digital recorder and advised the woman of her rights.

"Yes, yes, I'll talk." Impatience, resignation, frustration all bled through her tone. "I don't care anymore. I thought he was cheating; I just didn't know with who. Or is it *whom*?" She couldn't raise her hand, so she kind of hiked a shoulder and wiggled her head.

"I came home and caught him with her, of all people. My best friend! He always told me he thought she was frumpy." She spit the last word out. "I snapped. That was his gun I used. I emptied the thing. At least I think I did."

She glared at Abby, her eyes a cauldron of anger and hate, but her voice cold and empty.

"They deserved it. They were cheaters and I killed them. It's my revenge and it's as sweet as a bowl of honey." She stomped one of her high-heeled shoes on the ground, making a sharp click. "I don't regret it."

Abby had arrested gang members, a serial killer, a wife killer, and murderous thieves, but in all her career she'd never seen such vicious, naked hatred. It slapped at her, made her recoil.

Clayton Joiner was consumed by grief.

It took all of Abby's strength not to get up and run from the backyard, but to stay and complete the statement for Boston. She couldn't concentrate.

Abby knew at that moment she needed to get away from work, from murder, until she could sort out the death of Clayton Joiner.

She could miss something critical and let a guilty killer go free.

There was too much of that going around already. She didn't want to be responsible for more.

———■▶———

"Dr. Collins called me." Lieutenant Jacoby stood and looked Abby in the eye. "This is because of the shooting?"

Abby bit her lip, wondering if answering truthfully would label her crazy and eventually get her shuttled to some boring job she'd hate.

No matter what, even with the turmoil swirling inside, she had to be truthful. "I, uh, I think so. It's weighing on me. I know I had no choice, but . . ."

Jacoby watched her. There was no condemnation in his gaze. "I understand. I shot a guy once. He didn't die, but it affected me, and the court case went on forever. Everybody is a Monday-morning quarterback."

She said nothing for a minute, relieved he got it at least on that level. When she'd told Bill, he'd understood immediately. *"Take as much time as you need. I can handle our caseload right now. The one today is cake. You've been through a lot in the last few months."*

Did she need to tell them how afraid she was that she would never be a cop again?

"It's really been a rough couple of months," she admitted.

Jacoby regarded her for a moment. "You're right; it has been. I've signed off on it. File the paperwork with personnel. All I ask is that you keep the line of communication open with Collins. You'll need to follow up with him before you return to work."

With that, Abby left the PD, her home away from home for twelve years. She thought it would be hard, but it wasn't. She needed to get away from Joiner's accusing face, needed to find some way to wipe the blood from her hands.

CHAPTER

-14-

BUT DID IT REALLY HAPPEN?

Molly walked slowly through the market, studying items on the shelf. She was in the cereal aisle. She stepped close, tapping boxes as she read their names, pretending to concentrate on the cereal, but always watching behind. Then furtively checking in front.

They were watching and staring; she knew it.

"She's the one."

The woman with the baby—was it really a baby?

The man stocking shelves.

The old lady in the motorized cart.

Molly felt their eyes on her as if they were pelting her with BBs.

"That's the girl."

She hurried out of the cereal aisle for the dairy products, but that's where a group of teens were staring—everyone was staring.

She turned on her heel and broke into a jog, breath cut off by all the sharp eyes, pounding, suffocating her.

Shoving the bag boy out of her way and ignoring his protest, she fled, hitting her full stride as the doors whooshed open and she was outside.

"She made it all up."

More eyes. She wanted to scream.

She turned left and sprinted, trying to get away from the eyes, but there was the cross. The evangelical church on the other side of the market, with a large cross in the front.

God's house.

This was all God's fault!

God let Molly down in the worst way.

Because of God she was crazy, and now the cross accused her.

Molly's head felt as if it would explode. She stopped and brought both hands to her head, ripping tufts of hair out of both sides.

She screamed and cut right, into the street, away from the cross and in front of the car she never saw coming.

CHAPTER

-15-

"SORRY, BUT THINGS are bottled up right now." FBI Agent Todd Orson sat across from Luke and Woody in a small coffee shop in East Long Beach. "The federal government rarely moves quickly."

"What's the holdup?" Luke asked. He was anxious to start the new job working with Orson, and disappointment bit deep.

"Politics, that's all. One of the sponsors of the squad has some legal issues to deal with. The situation has shelved the squad for the time being. I'm hoping all will be cleared up by November."

"Fine with me," Woody said. "It's a kick working with Luke here. We step into the most interesting cases."

Orson chuckled. "Yep, Bullet filled me in. Watch out for those spry old fugitives."

Luke took the ribbing in stride. "I have no dearth of work to do, but after all the interviews and tests we've taken for the cold case squad, I was really hoping to get started."

"I know. I do have something for you." Orson paused.

"Yeah? What is it?"

"I hesitate to give this to you because I'll be in DC and I'm not certain I'll be able to help much. But this woman who writes a crime blog for the high desert has contacted me. I know her because her husband was a Marine. He got home from Afghanistan only to be killed by an irate boyfriend two days later in Lancaster when he intervened in a domestic dispute."

"Whoa." Luke and Woody spoke at the same time.

"Yeah, it was rough. I knew the kid, met him in country. Anyway, Faye—that's her name, Faye Fallon—blogs about crime and cold cases in the Lancaster/Palmdale area. She sent me a case she's profiled a couple of times, and I wanted you to take a look. There is a bit of urgency because with this case, there's a statute of limitations in play."

"It's not a homicide case?" Luke asked.

"No. It might have been. Ten years ago the victim, sixteen years old at the time, accepted a ride from a stranger. He sexually assaulted her, tied her up, threw her into the trunk of his car, and drove her out to the middle of nowhere. This is out near Mojave. She managed to escape, and the sicko was never caught. The ten-year anniversary was a couple of months ago. Because the victim was under eighteen at the time of the crime, the statute of limitations won't expire until she turns twenty-eight, in a little under two years. . . . Anyway, I'd consider it a favor to me if you would talk to Faye, see if you can help. She can pay you."

"Sure," Luke said quickly, touched by the story and curious. He looked at Woody, who nodded.

"Great. I'll give Faye your number. And I'll try to help if I can, but no guarantees."

After Orson left Luke and Woody in the coffee shop, Woody opened the briefcase he'd brought with him. The booth where they sat was private and quiet, and Luke felt okay to continue the meeting here.

He rubbed his hands together. "I've been waiting to study everything Asa was hiding in that safe."

"Hope you're not disappointed. I've glanced over things and I've seen only theories, no proof or facts. I did see one tidbit that's new. Something Asa sat on. I could slap him. It's something that should have been investigated years ago."

"I'll take everything with a grain of salt."

Woody placed the pages on the table: a file on Simon Morgan, two reports about old hit-and-run accidents, a folder of Asa's notes, and a file of assorted news clippings. Some of the newspaper clippings were old and yellowed, the edges frayed. They were mostly about the Triple Seven, but he did see one concerning a hit-and-run.

"You've looked through everything?"

"Pretty much. Some stuff more in depth than other stuff." He tapped one of the hit-and-runs. "For example, remember the theory that George Sanders floated, alleging that Buck and Rollins stole a car as kids and hit and killed a guy?"

Luke nodded. He hadn't been there when Abby and Bill interrogated Sanders about Buck Morgan and Lowell Rollins's relationship, but he'd heard about it later. Sanders claimed Lowell was driving that night, and he and Buck swore they'd never reveal the truth. Years later, when the Triple Seven partnership was on the rocks and Lowell was ready to throw his hat in the political ring, Patricia Morgan threatened to go public with his secret. Gavin Kent was supposedly sent in to clean up the mess.

"I thought that was all hearsay. I mean, how reliable was Sanders?"

Woody made a face. "Normally, I would trust him as far as I could throw him. But apparently Asa heard that rumor a long time before Sanders spilled his guts."

"From who?"

Woody shook his head. "He doesn't say. But he pulled this report trying to prove it." He held up a report Luke could see was dated from around that time. Luke took it and skimmed the narrative. A man walking his dog had been struck and killed. There was a Post-it note in the center, the message faded a bit but the words still readable: *Impossible to prove.*

"I agree with him," Woody said. "There would be no way to prove Rollins did the hit-and-run even if this were the right one. Besides, I don't want to waste time on this."

"I agree," Luke said. "It sounds like a rabbit trail, a distraction."

He took the report from Luke and moved it to the side. Luke considered that Sanders killed himself so there was no way to pin him down about what exactly he heard and from whom. The whole story was odd.

"Now, as far as the Triple Seven murders go, I read his notes a couple of times. Asa had a theory." Woody held his hands up. "It's just a theory—repeating, he has no proof, but he was closer to things at the time than I was. I'd just gotten married, my second one, so I missed a lot of stuff he saw."

"Spill it. I'm ready to listen to anything."

"Okay. He believed Kent was the killer. But he recognized that Kent could not have acted on his own. Gavin was always more brawn than brains. So Asa's search was to figure out who helped." Woody pulled out a page with some names written on it and handed it to Luke.

Luke read the names and stared at Woody. "Seriously?"

Woody nodded. "He believed some cops helped. He cross-referenced work schedules for that day. He also verified that Kent took off five consecutive sick days after the fire. Claimed he hurt himself water-skiing."

"That punk Sanders said Buck Morgan shot Kent, put some buckshot in his leg," Luke mused. "He would have had to take time off work. But these other names . . ." Luke read them out loud. "Alyssa Rollins, Kelsey Cox, Graham Sophist, Terry Jackson? I don't know those last two."

"They're both dead. Sophist was a friend of Kent's. He was on the PD for a couple of years. Got fired for lying. He died about five years ago, heart attack. Jackson was another bad cop. He was under suspension when he died in a small plane crash. They were both tight with Kent at the time, so that's why they're on the list. But Asa admits in his notes that there is no evidence they were connected in any way to the Triple Seven case."

"But Kelsey and Alyssa? He really thought that Alyssa Rollins was a cold-blooded killer?"

"Well, back in the day, she was nobody's favorite. She was a snob. Rollins inherited old money, but that didn't change him; he was one of the guys. Buck mentioned that to me once."

"You and Buck were tight?"

"We were friends, poker buddies. He and Patricia popped meals for cops. From time to time, he'd sit down and shoot the breeze with us. Asa was still in patrol and my partner then, and the three of us hit it off. Buck was good people. I kinda believe that part of Sanders's story, that Buck and Patricia wanted to buy Rollins out."

"Did Asa find proof that the partnership was floundering?"

"Solid proof, no. Asa says that according to Buck, when Rollins married Alyssa, he stopped being one of the guys. Alyssa felt he was destined for greatness, and she wanted him to behave according to his station in life. That station didn't include palling around with Buck anymore."

"Sounds like she would have wanted to get rid of the restaurant."

"The restaurant was a means to an end. This was before social media. People read about happenings at the restaurant in the daily newspaper. Rollins liked seeing his name mentioned often in a positive light. I think dissolving the partnership was a negative to Alyssa, at least at that time. I'm sure that as Rollins climbed the political ladder, there may have been a point where she would not have cared."

"Just not at the beginning," Luke said, beginning to see a picture in his mind's eye of a calculating and manipulative woman in Alyssa Rollins. "And Cox?"

Woody sighed and rubbed his chin. "Well, Cox and Kent were engaged. And Cox has had her issues. But I find it hard to believe that she would cover up a triple murder."

"I see here—" Luke pointed to the paper—"Asa's cross-reference that Cox was assigned to the Belmont Shore area that day. The Morgan house burned right after the restaurant; she'd have been at one of the fires."

"Right, but I bet the records of exactly where she was aren't that easy to find. Now everything is computerized, and cars have GPS. Back then it wasn't so. She could have said she was one place and been on the other side of the city. No way to know for sure."

"She works for Rollins now."

"Yep, that she does. And that brings up the second hit-and-run report." Woody tapped another file, this one documenting the death of Louis Rollins, Lowell's brother.

"Asa was working the night Louis was killed," Woody continued. "He told me about the crash back then. He thought it was intentional; he didn't think it was an accident."

"He believed Louis was killed to shut him up," Luke said after reading Asa's notes.

"Apparently Asa thought so, yes. He even thought Kent was the one who ran poor Louis down."

Luke set the notes aside to think for a minute. Most of this, except for the names, they already knew because of allegations George Sanders and Gavin Kent had made several months ago.

He pointed to the real unknown. "What about the file on Simon Morgan? What does Abby's uncle have to do with all of this?"

"That's what Asa sat on. According to him, someone saw Buck Morgan after the Triple Seven fire. Simon Morgan's old girlfriend."

"What?" Luke felt his face flush. This was new—way new. "Smoking, meet gun."

Woody nodded. "It took some digging, and like everything else it's all hearsay, but Asa at one time was looking for an old girlfriend of Simon's." He pointed to a name in the margin. "Lucy Harper. Asa heard a rumor on the streets about what she'd seen, that she might have talked to Buck the night after the fire. Asa even took a trip to the prison and asked Simon about her."

"No way. Even Abby didn't know this."

"No one knew it. Asa did it on the down low when he first went to homicide. At that time, Simon was in a prison up north. Asa said Simon played dumb. He thought the con was lying."

Luke had to digest this. "Why on earth would he sit on this?"

"Can't say."

"Have you told Abby?"

"No. I don't think I should tell her anything until she's settled her mind over this shooting."

"Yeah, this might blow her up. Is Lucy Harper still in Long Beach?"

"Asa looked for her, didn't find her. Maybe this is a missing person case you should take on, pro bono."

"Maybe," Luke said, but inside, he wondered if he could do such a thing and keep it from Abby.

CHAPTER

-16-

GIL BARONE WAS CAREFUL. His image was important to him, and he didn't want to do anything that would tarnish it or lead people to the truth his carefully constructed facade concealed.

Because he was so careful, he was sitting here in a business center banquet hall being honored, praised, and considered completely moral and upstanding.

Nothing could be further from the truth.

He smiled with his mouth, but his heart held a sewer of mocking gibes for the people presenting him with the Chamber of Commerce award for business citizenship.

"Mr. Barone is always available to help." Mrs. Waters, head of the Tehachapi Business Bureau, droned on and on. "His expertise with computers has saved us many, many times."

Stroking his beard and offering a humble nod, Gil smothered a smile as a thought came to him. *Wish the old bat would stroke out right here and now. That would make this trip worth it.*

"We're so happy that he is such a responsive and caring member of our business community."

When she finished speaking, she beamed at him as he propelled his wheelchair over to accept the plaque. The room applauded, and he looked over the hall filled with business owners and leaders in the community. It was hard not to smirk.

He'd fully Haskellized them all. That's what he called it. Led them to believe he was one thing when in reality he was another, like the character Eddie Haskell in that nearly forgotten corny television show *Leave It to Beaver*. He was their war-injured techy hero here in town, and fully twisted and depraved in private at home.

After the award was presented and the speeches mercifully ended, Gil's right-hand man, Bart Meechum, grabbed the plaque as Gil released his chair brakes and wheeled toward the door. He kept his fake smile in place until after his chair was safely inside the van and the door was closed. He made the transition to the driver's seat before he broke out laughing, pleased with himself over how he'd successfully and consistently fooled the most distinguished businesspeople in Tehachapi.

Bart was a few seconds behind him, laughing hysterically as he hopped into the passenger seat. They shared a high five, and then Gil started up the van and headed home. After a long day of boring speeches and working hard to be on his best behavior, Gil needed to unwind with a beer and some special movies he and Bart had on tap.

"Life is good." Bart grinned.

Gil agreed as he made the turn onto Tucker that began his drive home. "For us," he said, "at the top of the food chain."

His house sat up on a ridge, overlooking the entire town of Tehachapi. The high desert town known for two things, the Tehachapi Pass Wind Farm and a train loop, was not where

Barone ever thought he'd be living. But his father's death and gift of a house and money changed his perspective.

He'd been living in Northridge when his father died and hadn't expected anything at all from his father's estate. Gil's mother died when he was in his twenties and he and his father, a retired sheriff's deputy, never got along. Gil hated everything his father stood for, hated being a cop's kid. So when Dad died and left his only child such a gift, no one was more surprised than Gil. The old man left a paid-off house and a surprisingly comfortable nest egg.

Gil was happy to take the house and used some of the money to remodel it to suit his needs, even though it meant moving his business and his life from Northridge to what he considered a Podunk, backward town. But he quickly learned that living in Tehachapi, with its population hovering around fifteen thousand people, would allow him to be a big fish in a small pond, something he liked as much as he liked being treated as a war hero.

Confined to a wheelchair after a drunk driving accident overseas, his story when he set up shop in Tehachapi was that he'd been injured in battle, in Iraq. The rubes never questioned him and treated him like the war hero he claimed he was.

He figured his father probably thought that since he was paralyzed from the waist down, he couldn't cause problems or get into trouble, and that was why the estate had been willed to him. Dad had no idea how resourceful Gil was or that he'd meet a person like Bart, a man of like passions, as it were.

He parked the van in his garage and closed the door behind them. He loved the fact that once the door was closed, his life was perfectly hidden. He could see out, but no one could see in. His house backed to a hillside. There was no chance anyone would sneak up from behind.

Right now all he wanted was a trip to his man cave, an addition at the back of the garage. There he had his computers set up, his sixty-inch screen, and it was all surrounded by soundproof windowless walls, totally safe from any prying eyes.

Among other things, Gil was a hacker, and in his world he was the best. While Bart was also good at hacking, and they worked together as a team, Gil had engineered far more serious incursions into computer systems where he had no business than he ever told Bart. With Bart he'd breached a large credit bureau and found a lucrative market to sell the passwords and credit information he'd compromised. For Bart it was all about the money. He went bonkers when he saw the cash they'd netted from that job, cash safely squirreled away in an offshore account. But Gil didn't care about the money. He hacked because he liked it. He was addicted to the feeling of power it gave him. Even customers of his legitimate computer repair business were not immune to his hacking. He knew everything important, and in some cases illegal, about every one of his clients.

But while he hacked his clients to learn their business and because of the power he felt that gave him, he never planned on exploiting them, at least not through hacking. Something his father once said, one of the few times he listened to his father, had stuck with him: smart criminals didn't victimize people in their own backyard. Meaning, as far as Gil was concerned, he'd rip off people far away, never the people in *his* town. But knowing that he could, anytime he wanted to, gave him a buzz like a drag off a big fat joint.

He and Bart had a program running that needed to be

checked. They were attempting a new data breach. It was challenging and time consuming, but Gil was patient and knew they'd be in sooner or later. Then they had a movie waiting for the big-screen TV.

When Gil met Bart in an online role-playing game, it was fate. Gil accomplished a great deal from his chair, but with Bart adding legs and more ideas, he accomplished a lot more. Little Bart could pass for one of the geeks on *The Big Bang Theory*. Small and pasty, horrible with women but a genius with a computer, his harmless appearance, superior computer ability, and complete lack of scruples fit perfectly with Gil.

When they hacked, they sold off the information to people who wanted to compromise the data. Gil and Bart laughed themselves silly over the investigation into the data breach. They had authorities running all over the world, thinking the breach came from some other nation when it was right under their noses.

As Gil checked his computer and the software he'd developed to tell him if anyone was even remotely on his trail, he laughed to himself.

I am the top of the food chain, he thought, *and no one will ever be smart enough to stop me.*

CHAPTER

17

DR. COLLINS WAS HELPFUL. He didn't blame Abby for not taking his initial advice, and he was glad she planned to go home.

"Abby, we talked about this. I know you have in you the ability to be resilient, to move past this. It may take time, and that is no reflection on you. You have a strong base of support—your church, your aunt, your friends. You've been through significant trauma—I would never minimize that—and being honest about how you feel will go a long way in helping you get through this."

She promised she'd call him if she needed to talk. Trouble was, Abby couldn't put her finger on what exactly she did need. Collins had mentioned church, which was Abby's normal refuge. But she didn't want to go there and answer questions about the shooting. Well-meaning people would want to pray, and for some reason the thought of that made her squirm.

It was after noon by the time Abby left work. She went home to change her clothes and pick up Bandit. She thought the expression "cat on a hot tin roof" fit what she felt like at the moment. Unable to sit still, she got back into her car with the dog and drove around aimlessly for a while. At one point she ended up on the Huntington Beach pier. It was windy and a little chilly this close to the coastline, but she ignored the cold and walked out onto the concrete structure. A couple of surfers in wet suits were out on the water, but the swells were small and choppy. No one was on the sand volleyball courts.

Still not sure what she was looking for, or what would help, Abby took Bandit back to the car and drove toward home, this time ending up at Serenity Park. The park had sprung from the ruins of her parents' restaurant, the Triple Seven. She parked in front of the memorial plaque dedicated to her parents and Luke Murphy's uncle. They were the three people thought to be inside when the place was torched. If it hadn't been for Luke's uncle, with his dying strength, getting Abby out, four people would have died there twenty-seven years ago.

For some reason the shooting of Clayton Joiner had brought the case of her parents' murders spewing back up in her thoughts like lava from a volcanic eruption. The revelation that Abby's father could have escaped the inferno in his restaurant twenty-seven years ago, that the body next to Abby's mother was really that of a drug dealer named Piper Shea, had stunned her. In fact, she'd been tased once in training, and that total body hit was not unlike what she felt now. In a painful haze, there were no clear answers for Abby, though she thought she'd made peace with it. She thought she'd finally been able to put the unsolved past behind her and into the hands of God. Her father must be dead; he would never have abandoned her. That's what everyone who knew him said. So she'd left the doubts and the wondering behind her, moving forward with her future in relative peace.

But like the Taser had shattered her composure, the turmoil of the shooting shattered her peace.

She sat on the grass in front of the plaque and tried to pray but nothing came. Like peace, she felt God had left her as well. Why did God let her bullets kill Clayton Joiner?

Why?

She wasn't sure how long she'd sat there, thinking and asking questions to which she got no answers, when someone walked up behind her.

"Hey, kid, how are you doing?"

Even though she'd heard him walk up, Woody's voice behind Abby made her jump.

"How'd you know I was here?" she asked as he knelt in front of her. "Aren't you supposed to be at your new job?"

"New job start got postponed, and I'm an investigator; I followed a hunch. Bill called me. He's worried about you. What's going on?"

Abby sighed. "I took some more time off. I need time to think."

"Is that because of the shooting?"

"Yes and no." Abby's mouth went dry, and she struggled with how to tell her friend she felt like she was losing it. "I . . . I just think I need to get away for a bit."

"It's not about the Triple Seven, is it?"

"No . . . maybe." She threw her hands up. "I don't know, Woody. I just don't know."

He settled down on both knees and for a moment said nothing.

When he did speak again, he asked, "Can I buy you a late lunch/early dinner? We'll talk. It doesn't have to be about this; you can just listen to me."

Abby swallowed the lump in her throat, wanting to hug Woody. He was a good friend, part of her support structure, a big part, but she wasn't certain even he could help her now. A meal might be a good idea. She wasn't hungry but should eat. Maybe it would clear her thoughts to figure out her next move.

"Yeah, that sounds good. I'd like to hear why your new job was postponed."

"Deal."

They stood.

"Hmmm. River's End?" he asked.

"Always."

Woody had been retired for about three months, and Abby missed him more than she thought possible. The few times she and Bill had been called out after midnight were missing something because Woody was not there, not in his patrol car, not on the beat. She'd always looked forward to seeing him on those late-night/early morning callouts.

She knew that if she could open up to him about what was going on in her head, he'd help, and whatever he told her was true, solid, good as gold. What she wrestled with now—the flashbacks, the nightmares—it wasn't because Woody hadn't tried to help.

What I was trained to do: make a hard choice.

Abby rolled the phrase over and over in her mind as she followed Woody to River's End. She knew that nothing in her training would have insisted she hesitate while a distraught man pointed a gun at her in a threatening manner. And he fired two shots. It was pure luck that neither she nor Bill nor their prisoner were struck.

In her heart of hearts she wished there had been something

else she could have done. She understood Clayton Joiner all too well. He'd wanted justice for a loved one who was taken from him in a horrible way.

Don't we all?

She thought about the last thread to her father's case. Woody and Luke had tied that up with their trip to Idaho. They'd closed Asa Foster's house, finished carrying out his last wishes. Woody had been evasive about the visit, and Abby had let him evade. Asa Foster's death was connected to her parents' cold case because he claimed to know the truth. If he did, it had died with him—like everything else about her parents' case, dead or a dead end. She chastised herself for thinking of Asa. His memory brought up the rub about the partial solution to her parents' murders. She had more questions than answers and knew she needed to stop obsessing about it.

She forced her thoughts to Woody's new gig, the cold case squad, and wondered why it wasn't happening right now. Because Woody was still such a hardworking, active cop, she'd been surprised when he retired but not surprised he'd decided to take this new job. Working a cold case was like working a puzzle and Woody liked puzzles. He was also good at seeing the whole picture, which was something Abby often looked for him to help her do.

He and Luke had become good friends, something Abby hadn't seen coming. Whatever happened in the governor's house the day Asa died had cemented their relationship. She was happy Woody had a buddy now that Asa was dead, but that it was Murphy gave her pause. Her feelings about Murphy were so conflicted, and knowing she'd likely see more of him because of Woody chafed.

What about Ethan? She owed him a genuine effort to work through their relationship issues, and it bugged her that this attraction to Murphy grew more intense.

She changed the direction of her thoughts back to the Triple Seven and her old homicide mentor and partner, Asa Foster. Memories of Asa and that horrible day in June when he died and Gavin Kent killed himself reminded Abby of Lowell Rollins and his official bid for the US Senate. She wondered what Woody thought of the announcement.

Suddenly her phone rang. It was Ethan.

"Hey, you're there already?" she said when she answered.

"Yep, I made great time. How's your return to work going?"

Abby braced herself. She'd been anticipating—and to a certain extent dreading—the question all day.

"It didn't go so well. I . . . I, uh, think I'll be joining you. I mean, at least I'm thinking I'll drive up and stay with Dede for a few days."

Silence momentarily and then Ethan said, "I'm sorry things didn't go smoothly for you. But I am glad you'll be joining us. There's no shame in saying you need more time. When do you think you'll be up here?"

No shame. Abby wondered if it was shame she was feeling. Whatever it was, it was unpleasant. "Not sure. I'll call when I am."

They said their good-byes and Abby disconnected. More time with Ethan might help her settle a lot of things. Maybe he was right and this shooting was a door marked Exit. That the thought didn't sting like lemon juice in a cut gave her pause and made her struggle to concentrate on the here and now and lunch with Woody.

She'd parked a couple spots over from him. Working to stop

being so self-absorbed, Abby studied her old friend as he got out of the car in front of the River's End Café. He looked good, relaxed, and healthy. Retirement and no more graveyard hours obviously agreed with him.

She zipped up her sweat jacket as she climbed out of her car. Across the flood control channel from Serenity Park, River's End was on the water in Seal Beach, and the early October evening rippled with cool ocean air. The breeze made her decide to leave Bandit in the car. It was too cold to sit on the patio and no dogs were allowed inside. She gave her little buddy a pat and set him back in the car. Bandit immediately curled up in a ball on the driver's seat.

Woody met her at the door with a hug, and Abby's jittery nerves relaxed. He made her feel safe, gave her back her balance. At least while she was with him, she could put Clayton Joiner on the back burner.

"I just noticed how great you look. Getting regular sleep must agree with you," she told him.

"Never thought I'd like a normal schedule, but so far so good."

They found a table inside. Abby loved the cozy family feel of the place and the smell of comfort food cooking. After they ordered and she sipped on her Diet Coke, she asked Woody to update her on the cold case squad. In the back of her mind, this was also asking him about Luke Murphy.

"We've finished all the paperwork and testing. But the government is stalled. Politics." He made a face. "Agent Orson did toss a case our way, though. Hopefully Luke will find out more about it tomorrow. The victim was sixteen at the time. It's ten years cold now. Sounds like a case you'd find interesting."

"I find all cold cases interesting. They hit close to home. I hope you worrying about me didn't cut your first day short."

"Nah, not much to do right now until Luke gets all the details on this case."

Their food arrived, and Abby looked at Woody.

"Did you see that Rollins is officially in the race?"

Woody gave a dismissive wave. "I saw it. Let that go, Abby. That's one thing Ethan and I agree on. You need to let that go."

Stung, Abby sat back. "I have. The case is closed. I'm just making an observation."

His expression softened. "Don't get your hackles up. I just hate to see you beat your head against a wall."

"I honestly believe I have let it go. But doesn't it bother you that Rollins will most likely be a senator?"

"He's slimy, like all politicians, but there's no proof of anything else, is there?"

Grudgingly Abby had to say no, there wasn't.

"What are you going to do with all your time off?"

"Relax, I hope." She shivered as the question brought her back to the here and now, and turmoil resettled on her heart like an anvil. "I'm driving home, leaving tomorrow or the next day. I might even help Ethan with what he's working on. Maybe being far away for a bit will help me clear my head."

"I hope you're not brooding over Joiner. You did what you had to do."

Abby gave a half shrug, took a bite of her burger. Woody let her think a bit. She knew he would.

"I know I did my job, but those are hollow words when I think about poor Clayton. That could have been me. I told you how close I came to shooting Kent."

"Look, kid, that was a tough deal, no two ways about it. But he forced your hand. Suppose you'd let him shoot the suspect, kill him. Then he'd be sitting in jail and you'd be questioning your judgment the other way."

"I know you're right. I know you are. But—"

"No *but*s. Concentrate on what you know is right; then everything else will fall into place."

CHAPTER
-18-

TUESDAY MORNING found Luke with a large cup of coffee and an open Bible on his lap before the sun came up. Asa's notes and Abby Hart invaded his thoughts and fractured his prayer time. He'd made copies of the notes but had trouble following the man's reasoning. The problem of Lucy Harper nagged at him. The fact that Asa seemed to have found this link almost fifteen years ago and then sat on it irritated Luke. Asa was supposed to be one of the good guys.

As for Abby Hart, it also bothered him that Woody wanted to keep the information from her. Luke didn't believe in secrets, at least not about something like this. True, she had a lot on her plate right now, not the least of which was a fatal shooting. But there was something else that got Luke up and out of bed so early, driving him to the Word for wisdom and guidance.

Abby was off work and leaving to spend time away with Ethan Carver.

Of all the turmoil of the past week—having a fugitive threaten him with a gun, hearing about Abby's shooting, and recovering the hidden files from Asa's safe—this bit of news rocked Luke more than anything. The jealousy that boiled up shook him hard. He came face-to-face with the fact that he'd been hoping that Ethan and Abby would end their engagement and the realization made him ashamed.

"You can't be trusted! You don't keep your word!"

His train of thought trailed off as the memory of one of his dead wife's accusations rang in his ear. He'd promised her he'd talk to her first about reenlisting but then went ahead and made plans to do so. He knew she didn't want him to stay in the Army. At the time he figured he'd reenlist and she'd just have to deal with it. Shame caused heat to flush his face. He'd said he loved her when he married her, that he wanted to share his life with her, but when it came down to it, all he wanted to do was live for himself.

Luke closed the Bible and got up to pace his office and pray. He asked for forgiveness though he knew he'd already been forgiven. He hoped he was a different man now, that he'd changed and he'd never treat a woman that way again. His service to the Army and his unit had usurped any loyalty he felt for his wife and family. Was it possible his job, his quest to find the lost and close cold cases, could do the same thing?

He shuddered with the fear that it could. Abby deserved someone who would keep his word, someone who could be trusted. For her, that was Ethan, and Luke should pray that everything worked out between them. And then, for everyone in his life, he needed to be a trustworthy man. They deserved that. Luke prayed he would be that man, that he would be strong enough to keep his word no matter what, and trustworthy enough to never again make an empty vow.

Later Tuesday, when everyone was up and about their day, Luke got a call from Faye Fallon.

"Thank you, Mr. Murphy, for talking to me."

"No problem. Call me Luke. Cold cases are near and dear to my heart. If I can help, I want to."

"I'm so glad. I've actually heard of you. I saw a YouTube video that really impressed me, but I wasn't certain you'd want to come all the way out to the Antelope Valley to work a case. My foundation can pay, and we can discuss rates."

The woman's voice was musical, calming, and a little sexy. It made him want to say yes immediately. But instead he said, "I'd like to learn more about it before I commit."

"Of course. If you give me your e-mail, I'll send you a case summary. I'll be in Long Beach tomorrow. My cousin lives there and it's her birthday. I'm taking her to dinner. That will give you some time to read the summary and then maybe we can meet and talk it over."

"That sounds perfect." He gave her his e-mail address, and they made arrangements to meet for coffee before her dinner.

"One more thing," Fallon said before they disconnected. "I do have a contact at the sheriff's department. He's said he'll help. He has the authority to give you access to the files. I don't have any quarrel with the sheriff's investigation, but they have so much work, it's hard for them to spend a lot of resources on a ten-year-old case."

"I understand. I have the greatest respect for law enforcement and would never step on any toes."

The case summary was waiting in his in-box when he logged on. Luke opened it and printed it out.

Molly Cavanaugh was their victim in the ten-year-old case. A note at the beginning mentioned California Penal Code 801.1(a) and the statute of limitations pertaining to the situation. She was sixteen when she was kidnapped and raped, and the ten-year anniversary was about four months ago. The dry summary said a lot without hyperbole.

Victim states she was waiting for the bus outside the Antelope Valley Mall at marked, official bus stop. The bus was running late and she states a clean-cut, male white subject driving a late-model Ford Mustang pulled to the curb and contacted her, asking if she wanted a ride. The male subject appeared to her to be in his twenties, and because of his short hair, she thought he was possibly in the service. Tired of waiting, the victim accepted his offer. Instead of driving her home, the suspect drove to an abandoned strip mall where he produced a knife and sexually assaulted the victim, then bound her wrists and ankles with a rough, hemp rope and placed her in his trunk. The victim felt the vehicle move as she struggled inside the trunk and was able to free her wrists and ankles and eventually able to open the trunk lid. Victim cannot say for certain how long she was in the trunk, how far the vehicle had traveled before she got the trunk open. She rolled out of the moving car, found herself on a dirt road she was not familiar with, and ran. Victim believes the suspect chased her, but did not look back. She saw another vehicle and headed that way. Two Air Force personnel were in the second vehicle. They stopped, rendered assistance to the victim, and called 911. Neither saw the suspect or his vehicle.

The summary went on to say that the original investigating officers felt that the suspect was going to kill Molly and dump her body somewhere in the vast emptiness of the Mojave Desert. Though the rape kit recovered a DNA sample and Molly gave a detailed description of her attacker, he was never apprehended.

After dinner that night, Luke shared the summary with Woody.

"Definitely a case for us," Woody said after he read the printout.

"Tomorrow I'll meet with Faye Fallon. Why don't you come along?"

"Sounds like a plan. Are you disappointed about the delay in the cold case squad?"

"Yeah. But I believe being given this case, having the chance to help this young girl, is a great consolation."

CHAPTER

-19-

*"**CONCENTRATE** on what you know is right; then everything else will fall into place."*

Abby tried hard all day Tuesday to follow Woody's advice. She called her aunt and told her about what was going on in her life. Dede prayed with her and expressed excitement that Abby planned on coming home. After their conversation Abby tried to stay busy and occupied, cleaning and organizing her house, anything to keep her mind off Joiner.

By Wednesday morning at seven thirty, she was ready to hit the road, ready to run away. That thought stopped her cold.

Am I really running away?

"Do you mind if I plant things?"

"What?" Abby looked up from the pile of belongings splayed out on her bed and shoved the idea of fleeing from her thoughts, focusing on her friend Jessica Brennan, now also her house sitter. Though Abby was taking Bandit with her, she still liked the idea of someone watching the house and watering the few plants she hadn't yet killed.

"Like flowers and stuff," Jessica said.

"Mind? I don't mind, but you don't have to go to any trouble. It will put me at ease knowing that you're here keeping an eye on things."

Jessica smiled. "No trouble. You forget, I live in an apartment. I can't muck about in the dirt, and I'd like to. You have a blank canvas in your backyard."

Abby hadn't driven to her childhood home in Lake Creek, Oregon, in years. She hated the barren center of the state of California, the hot ribbon of Highway 5 that bisected the Central Valley. It was always a sweltering, dry drive. She preferred the quick, easy, and relatively inexpensive flight to the Medford airport, thirty minutes from Aunt Dede's house.

But she had a dog now and she had no desire to leave him in a kennel, nor subject him to an airplane flight, so she'd decided to drive. Jessica had interrupted the new dilemma she'd created for herself; suddenly what she'd take with her had become an unexpected knot of a problem.

Distracted by her stuff and the offer, she looked at Jessica. "Can I give you some mon—?"

"No, no, no! It will be my pleasure." She redirected Abby to the mess of items strewn on the bed. "Finish packing. Are you taking everything?"

Returning her concentration to the pile of stuff in front of her, Abby chewed on her bottom lip. "I can't decide. When you fly, you can only take so much. Now I have too many options." Another thing she wrestled with was that she really had no idea how long she'd be gone.

She'd gotten up early and should have already completed packing. Her finishing touches were interrupted by a knock at the door.

"You expecting someone?" Jessica asked.

"No," she said, frowning. It was early, an odd time for any visitors. She grabbed her handgun and proceeded to the front door.

Jessica looked at the gun and stepped back into the hallway. "I guess you don't want me to get it."

"Sorry; I'm a bit paranoid with all the protests about the shooting," she said as she peeked through the window and nearly dropped the gun.

Bracing herself, she shoved the gun in a side table drawer and answered the door.

"Chief Cox. And, uh, Governor Rollins," Abby was sure her jaw hit the floor and she did the best she could to recover. "What brings you two to my door this early?"

Lowell Rollins was the last person she expected to see on her porch, and Kelsey Cox was the next to last.

The woman was as close to a personal enemy as Abby had, and the man . . . Abby just wasn't certain about him. Her last meeting with the governor had been surreal; he'd effectively closed the door on the investigation into her parents' death. And the last time Abby had seen the then–deputy chief, she'd accused Abby of killing Gavin Kent, though it was Kent who shot himself in front of them both.

"I retired, remember?" Cox smiled a decidedly fake smile, Abby thought, but she was determined not to be antagonistic and said nothing as Cox continued. "You don't need to call me chief anymore. I work for Governor Rollins now. That's why I'm here with him today; I'm his security chief."

Rollins spoke up as if on cue. "Abby, it's nice to see you again. You look well." His deep voice registered the concern she saw in his face. "You've been through such an ordeal."

He paused but Abby stayed quiet, not at all sure what to make of this visit.

Nodding to Cox, he said, "Both Kelsey and I, we hope we can put any bad blood you may feel is lingering behind us."

"Yes, Abby," Cox said. "What happened the day Gavin . . . Well, that was an emotional day." She swallowed, and for a second the look on her face made Abby feel sorry for her. The woman was obviously in pain. But the expression passed quickly and Cox went on.

"Governor Rollins heard through the grapevine that you had taken a leave of absence."

"And since we were in town on a separate issue, I wanted to stop by and find out if you'd decided to take me up on my job offer." The governor leaned close, taking a conspiratorial tone. "My confidence in you is unshaken by anything I've read in the press. On my team you'll be protected, stood up for."

Abby rocked back on her heels, nonplussed for a moment. Yes, he had asked her if she'd consider working for him, but that was the furthest thing from her mind in any universe of thought. That she'd still be on his radar in such a high profile way after all that had happened surprised her.

"My leave of absence is for personal reasons. I'm driving home. In fact, I was just packing. I plan on leaving in a few minutes."

"Home? That would be to Oregon, correct?" he asked.

"Yes," she answered the governor. But it was Cox whose expression she saw. Kelsey seemed relieved, and Abby wondered why.

"I want you to know that the offer will stay open. You belong on my team. I think you would find that while working for me, your talents would be appreciated, not trashed by uninformed protesters."

"Thanks," Abby said, not really knowing what else to say.

The governor nodded once as if to end the conversation. "You have a safe trip," he said before leaving.

Kelsey smiled as if in agreement, but Abby doubted that. Cox stepped off the porch with the governor, turning back at the bottom. "He's going to win this election, so don't forget what an honor it will be to work for a United States Senator." With that, the pair continued to a waiting car. A shiny, expensive luxury SUV, Abby noted. And Kelsey got behind the wheel. Was the car hers or the governor's?

"Wow, that was *X-Files* weird," Jessica observed as she stepped forward.

"It was, wasn't it?"

"It's like they're checking up on you."

Abby closed the door and moved down the hall to continue packing. "I guess I better hurry up and get on the road so no one else can check up on me."

Back in her office, her eye caught the notebook that contained her Triple Seven investigation. Abby had promised herself and her aunt that she would finally let the investigation go, trusting that the killers, if there were more than Gavin Kent, would face God's justice one day.

But Kent's vague confession left more questions than it answered.

Had he acted alone?

If he did kill her mother, why?

Two men died with her mother. Luke Goddard had been positively identified, but hearsay said that the male next to her mother had been erroneously identified as her father. What about that? What really happened that day?

She probably wouldn't even have noticed the book, or at least given it a second look, if Rollins and Cox hadn't come to the door. Cox had been there when Kent killed himself, so now in Abby's opinion, Cox was part of the investigation.

On impulse, Abby grabbed the notebook and all the information she'd gathered regarding the murder and threw them into her backpack. Maybe she wouldn't look at it, but maybe she would.

She put everything she wanted with her in the car, along with Bandit and all the things he needed for the trip. Her trunk was full, and the ice chest with drinks and snacks went in the backseat. She looked at Jessica, leaning against the porch railing.

"Thanks again, Jessica. I'll call you as soon as I know when I'll be back."

"No rush. Enjoy yourself. Don't worry about anything here."

Abby nodded and climbed into the car. Before she started off, she sent a text to Ethan, letting him know she was leaving so he'd have a good idea about when she would arrive. It was a twelve-hour drive, so she had a long day ahead of her.

She was still pondering Kelsey's visit an hour later as she sat on the 405 freeway in traffic, crawling north out of LA.

Governor Rollins wanted her on his team, he said, but she never took the offer seriously. Even if she thought the offer was serious, she wasn't interested in being someone's bodyguard.

But what am I now? A homicide cop who can't do her job.

CHAPTER

-20-

BEFORE HIS MEETING with Faye Fallon, Luke fielded an interesting call from the Riverside County Sheriff's office. He picked Woody up for the drive to the coffee shop, and his friend noticed the grin right off.

"Don't you look like the cat who ate the canary."

"Remember our old friend Oscar Cardoza?"

"I do. Been watching the news for any indication they found bodies in his backyard."

"Well, I don't know why it hasn't been on the news, but they did. They found three bodies buried on his property, and he was living off the Social Security of all three dead people."

Woody arched his eyebrows. "You don't say. I imagine defrauding Social Security will probably get him more time than the dead guys."

Luke laughed. "Ah, my cynical friend. We collared a serial killer. I think we might be headed to Riverside to testify when the case finally gets to trial."

"Humph."

Laughing at Woody's stoic disinterest, Luke said, "Anyway, they thanked us profusely for our work out there."

"They *should* thank us. We do good work."

They arrived at the Coffee Bean & Tea Leaf early. Faye Fallon was meeting her cousin at a restaurant in the Marketplace, close to the coffee shop, so it was the logical spot to meet. The mercurial October weather had turned cold, and they hoped for an inside table. They were in luck. Woody took a seat while Luke stepped up to the counter to order.

He'd just sat down with two coffees when the door opened and she walked in. Luke recognized her because she had a picture posted to her blog. But the picture did her no justice. Faye Fallon was drop-dead gorgeous. Woody let out a low whistle Luke hoped Faye didn't hear, and heads in the shop turned.

She looked like an actress. Long blonde hair held back in a shiny barrette, perfectly set, she was wearing a pretty dress that accentuated her trim figure. When she headed their way, Luke felt his mouth go dry.

"You must be Luke Murphy," she said with a bright smile, stepping toward the table.

Luke stood, nearly spilling his coffee. Woody also stood.

"Mrs. Fallon." Luke held his hand out.

"Please, it's Faye." She gripped his hand, then looked at Woody. "You must be the partner."

For his part, Woody looked much less affected by Fallon than Luke felt.

"That's me, the sidekick. Nice to meet you, Faye." Woody shook her hand. "Can I get you something?"

"A small black coffee would be great."

Woody moved off to purchase the coffee, and Luke and Fallon sat.

"It's good to be out of the car," Fallon said.

"That's right. You had what, a two-hour drive?" He fidgeted, wondering why a beautiful woman could make him feel like a gangly high school kid again.

"Yes. But I'll be staying over with my cousin, so I don't have to go back tonight."

Soon Woody was back with the coffee, and the three began discussing the case.

"We're in," Luke said. "The summary hooked us. We want to help solve this case."

"Thank you so much." Her smile lit up the whole shop, and for a second all Luke could do was nod and sip his coffee. Briefly he thought of Abby. She was promised to another man; there was nothing to keep Luke from finding out more about this beautiful, dedicated woman sitting across from him.

Woody jumped in. "How did you get involved in doing a, a . . . What do you call it? A crime blog?"

"I've always been interested in writing and crime. My husband was planning on joining the sheriff's department when his enlistment was up." Sadness marred her features.

Luke found his voice. "So sorry for your loss. That had to be tough."

"It was—it is—but doing the blog, feeling like I'm helping others who are victimized, helps."

"I'm not that computer savvy," Woody said. "How does the blog help?"

"I hope it makes people aware of what's going on in the community. And I've become a kind of liaison with local law enforcement. I blog about crime in the Antelope Valley, trends, and good work done by the SD. I record tips from people who don't want to talk to the deputies, and from time to time I highlight cold cases. That's how I met Molly."

"You met Molly?"

"Yes. Actually I first met her five years ago. I've lived in Lake Los Angeles my whole life. I remember when she was kidnapped. So her case was one of the first ones I profiled. I didn't have much reach then, at least not what I have now, so nothing ever came from it. But seeing the way she's lost ground in five years, my prayer is that you guys will be able to find the creep who did that to her."

"How has she lost ground?"

"Well, she was strong five years ago, active in her church, living on her own in Lancaster. She wanted to be an EMT and was in school. Eventually she graduated and went to work for an ambulance company. But as time has passed, she's been having some problems. PTSD they think."

Luke nodded. "I know the syndrome. I've served with people who are suffering."

"Yes, I met some of the guys from my husband's unit who suffered with dreams, flashbacks, sometimes so debilitating they have difficulty functioning." Her eyes held his for a moment, and Luke felt a connection click into place.

"I can see that you understand," she continued. "As for Molly, the trauma seemed to drop right back in her lap like a lead ball with the ten-year anniversary. She began to cut herself, trying to re-create the marks on her wrists from the bonds. Then there are the flashbacks, and she wonders, because the guy was never caught, did she imagine the whole thing? At one point a couple days ago she stepped into traffic and was hit by a car. Her leg and wrist were broken. She's had to take a leave from her job and move back in with her parents in Tehachapi."

"That sounds bad," Woody said. "Are you thinking that solving the case will change things for her?"

"I don't know. That's my prayer. And I believe that seeing her attacker caught and punished should help."

"I agree. I bet it will," Luke said, thoughts now bouncing back to Abby and the Triple Seven. "I'd like to meet her."

"That's touchy. I haven't completely convinced her mother that we aren't giving her false hope. I'd like you to review the files, develop something, before I bring you to meet Molly. Is that okay?"

"Of course. The last thing we want to do is traumatize her further."

Luke found himself fervently hoping they could find something new. He knew firsthand what false hope could do to people. He also found himself wanting to spend more time with Faye Fallon, and that kind of surprised him.

CHAPTER

21

DURING THE LONG DRIVE NORTH Abby tried to think about anything but police work and the shooting. Ethan had texted once, but he was busy and she didn't expect texting at rest stops would be any kind of diversion.

Praying was still elusive. She tried but felt as though a barrier popped up every time she started a prayer. There was heaviness on her soul, an oppression she didn't know how to crawl out from under. She turned the radio up, stopped often to get out and walk Bandit. It was on one of these stops that she noticed the car. A nondescript rental agency type car—and she was certain the driver was watching her.

Fear perked her up in an instant. Would a protester be after her? She looked away and acted nonchalant, idly following Bandit as he sniffed the pet area bushes. The hair stood up on the back of her neck, and she wished she had her gun with her, but she'd left it in the car. The feeling quickly passed and she chastised herself for being paranoid.

Bandit did what he was supposed to, and she scooped it up and put it in the trash, glancing toward the dark sedan. The car was still parked, but the driver was nowhere to be seen. Sighing and shaking her head, she got back in her car with Bandit and left the rest area. A short time later she saw the sedan coming up behind her fast. Her heart rate skyrocketed and she moved over, only to watch him fly by, traveling at least fifteen miles per hour faster than she was.

"My goodness." She patted Bandit and took a deep breath to calm down. The sedan disappeared from view and she felt incredibly foolish to be so jumpy.

The rest of the drive passed without incident. Abby stopped for a stretch and a snack as it got dark, picking a fast-food restaurant in Redding, about three hours from home. She went through the drive-through and then parked and ate some fries in the car just because she didn't want to leave Bandit. Her gaze roamed the darkening parking lot, and she stopped herself when she realized she was looking for bogeymen.

"What is wrong with me, Bandit? There's no reason for anyone to be following me."

It was late when she pulled off the highway onto the Lake Creek cutoff. Her aunt lived in a rural setting to be sure. The Lake Creek grange building followed by the historical society and a general store across the street constituted the downtown. A huge, thirteen thousand–acre private ranch took up much of Lake Creek, but there were smaller parcels dotting the unincorporated area. Dede's place was about four miles away, close to a historic covered bridge, and she presided over a forty-acre spread. Abby yawned as she turned onto the gravel driveway that led to her aunt's house.

Aunt Dede had raised Abby from age ten. The driveway, the shadows of trees in the darkness, took Abby back to that time. Coming here after living in foster care in Los Angeles was like dying and going to heaven. Lake Creek was as far removed from Long Beach as possible. Dede's two-story Craftsman-style home sat overlooking a creek-fed pond that had year-round water.

Lights were on in the kitchen, and she knew her aunt had waited up for her. The driveway circled around, passing the house, coming to a vintage barn Dede had remodeled into a guesthouse. As she made the circle around the barn, she passed the chicken coop and the livestock pens. Dede had a couple of horses, a few head of cattle, some goats, and a few chickens.

Abby completed the circle and parked under the carport next to her aunt's Jeep. She remembered the first morning she'd woken up in her new bedroom. When she looked out the window, she saw deer feeding on vegetation near the pond. She thought she'd found paradise.

Warm feelings filled her as she yawned and turned off the ignition, but the oppression didn't lift. Could she really be healed and refreshed here? She and Bandit climbed out as Dede and her Australian shepherd, Scout, came out the kitchen door.

For a minute Abby worried about how Scout and Bandit would get along. Her fears were allayed when the two dogs began circling and sniffing each other with wagging tails.

Abby sighed, so happy to be home, she hoped she didn't start crying.

Dede hurried to her and enveloped her in a tight hug. "It's good to see you, Abby."

"Ditto." Abby closed her eyes and smiled, not wanting the warm hug to end too soon. She could smell the fresh night air and her aunt's perfume, and the warm feeling of being home, in

119

a safe place, calmed her angst, for a moment masking the darkness. Yes, she'd made the right decision to come home.

"Are you hungry?" Dede asked, pulling back and then linking her arm in Abby's to draw her into the house. "I've got a pot of venison stew on the stove."

Abby smiled and let her aunt pull her toward the house, mouth watering at the thought of a meal she'd not enjoyed in years. The shadowy car stayed in the back of her mind, but she was still hard-pressed to think of any reason anyone would have to follow her.

━━━●▬━━

Abby forgot about the shadow car as the next day unfolded. She was too tired. Sleep had eluded her as flashbacks of the shooting invaded her thoughts, keeping her from winding down and shutting off. From the nightstand she retrieved her phone and saw two messages from Ethan waiting. She wrote back that she was tired; she didn't feel like talking to anyone, not even Ethan at the moment.

Bright Oregon sunshine pouring through the upstairs window hurt her eyes. The familiar surroundings did have a minuscule calming effect. Her aunt had kept her room here for her all these years. Dede had spent years overseas as a missionary, and she knew it was important to have a place to come back to. She wanted to be certain Abby knew she had that place here in Lake Creek.

Bandit wagged his tail as she stretched, and Abby knew that the little dog wanted to go out. She pulled on some sweats and then the two of them went downstairs. In the kitchen Abby found a note on the coffeemaker.

Had some things to take care of in town. Coffee is ready
to go; just press Start. Bacon and eggs in the fridge,
or granola fresh from the mill. There are Oreos in the
cookie jar, but eat breakfast first! Be back around noon.
Dede.

The Oreo comment brought a wry smile to her lips because
that was exactly what she felt like eating. The tasty cookie was
her one big vice, her ultimate comfort food. *I don't feel like eating
breakfast first,* she thought as she picked up the granola. There
was a historic flour mill nearby and they made the best granola,
but she set the cereal down. She pressed the Start button on the
coffee, then walked to the back door to let Bandit out. The house
had a wraparound porch, and Abby stepped outside with the dog,
shivering a bit as the morning air hit. It was much cooler here
than at home. Fall was unequivocally in the air.

Abby walked around the porch as Bandit sniffed here and
there. There were a couple new rocking chairs and a large swing-
ing bench overlooking the pond. Abby noted them, but a yawn
brought with it the desire to eat and then lie down. After a few
minutes Bandit trotted back inside. She bet it was just a little
too chilly for him.

Last night it had felt so good to be home, but now the angst
had returned and a nagging thought had her mind in a vise: *I
can't stay here forever and run away from what's waiting for me
in Long Beach. What if I can't put the shooting behind me and go
back to work?*

Abby fed the dog, then poured a cup of coffee and took a
container of yogurt from the fridge. After a couple of bites her
hunger was sated and she almost put the half-eaten container

back. Bad form, she thought and forced herself to finish. She tossed the empty carton away to concentrate on the coffee. Her favorite beverage didn't taste very good this morning, and she gave up after a half cup, pouring the rest down the drain. She grabbed a handful of Oreos and marched upstairs again, Bandit at her heels.

Feelings of failure seemed to weigh her down, and after she finished the cookies, Abby crawled back into bed and pulled the covers over her head.

CHAPTER

-22-

KELSEY COX GOT THE CALL early Thursday morning—but she hadn't been asleep, so it didn't bother her.

"She did go home, if home is some godforsaken place in the middle of nowhere. Not much is anywhere near."

Kelsey sighed and bit her lip before responding. "Where are you now?" she asked.

"A fast-food place in an area that vaguely resembles civilization. You don't want me to stay with her, do you?"

The tone of his voice bugged her. He was being paid enough to do whatever she asked without whining.

"No, she's not a threat there. But I do have a couple more errands for you regarding Hart." She carefully outlined what she wanted from him. "Be discreet. Understood?"

"My middle name. Anything else?"

"You need to check up on the other one, Murphy." Kelsey had a good idea about Murphy because of his association with Woody. She kept tabs on police department gossip through a friend still working, and that friend also knew Woody. But her hired guy could specifically pin the man down, and she needed that.

Briefly she told him what she knew about Murphy's current situation and what to watch for. The man's attitude improved.

"Ah, back to civilization. I'm on my way. I'll take care of the first thing. Then give me a day to be in position for the other."

"Not a problem. Just call me when you are."

She ended the call and walked across the room to look out the window of her hotel. They were in San Francisco for a fundraiser. She missed Gavin. It was an ache that never went away. She reflected on the fact that it was Abby Hart and her family who had squashed any and every chance of happiness she and Gavin might have shared. Twenty-seven years ago Buck and Patricia Morgan, by their stubbornness, caused the cancellation of the wedding she and Gavin planned. Gavin's involvement in the Triple Seven fire had changed their relationship, damaged it almost beyond repair, because at the time Kelsey was still idealistic and appalled that a law enforcement officer could have been involved in anything shady.

It took years for the idea of "nice guys finish last" to soak in and for Kelsey to realize that she didn't care about methods or involvements; it didn't matter what Gavin had done. And just when they were reconnecting, rebuilding their lives together, Abby ruined everything by forcing Gavin to take his own life. Ironically, in death Gavin had helped Kelsey more than he had while alive. The dream job she now enjoyed and the place of importance to which she'd ascended were hers now only because he was dead. It was with a bittersweet heart she whispered, "Thank you, Gavin."

Lowell Rollins would be elected to the senate, she was certain. Then he would go to Washington, DC, and so would she. She smiled at the thought of the power, the prestige.

Her phone chimed, interrupting the dream, and she frowned when she saw who it was. Her boss would want a report about Hart and Murphy and would press to make sure Kelsey was doing her job. This was one fly in the ointment Kelsey wanted to be rid of. She would figure out a way to stomp this fly, but it would take time. Right now she needed to be patient.

Sighing, she answered the phone and in a professional tone gave the report.

After she hung up, she relaxed and began another daydream, this one about ridding herself of the fly and stepping into place at the governor's side as his equal, not just his employee.

CHAPTER

-23-

FRIDAY MORNING Luke and Woody headed to Lancaster to review the Molly Cavanaugh case. They'd gotten the call late the night before that the case information was assembled, and they had an appointment with Faye Fallon's contact, a sheriff's deputy assigned to the Lancaster office. He promised to walk them through the boxes of evidence and reports pertaining to Molly's case and answer any questions he could. The drive would take them around two hours, so Luke picked Woody up while it was still dark.

They'd been on the road for about twenty minutes when Woody spoke up.

"Abby's been in Oregon for a couple of days now."

"Hmph," Luke said, not sure where to go with that. He was worried about Abby but certain he had no right to be. The shooting coming so close on the heels of no real answers regarding the Triple Seven was definitely messing with her head, and Luke wondered if Abby was suffering from PTSD. That thought brought him to Faye Fallon, and his mind went meandering, wondering how much time they'd spend working together and if that was a good thing.

Realizing Woody had gone quiet, Luke shifted gears back to Abby. "You think she's still having a hard time about the shooting?"

"I don't know. She shouldn't. It was in policy and downright awesome she reacted as quickly as she did. Women—I don't understand them. Probably why I was married three times and couldn't make any stick."

Luke chuckled at that. For the rest of the drive Woody told him about all his marriages and the women who had broken his heart.

By the time they reached the sheriff's station in Lancaster, Luke was shaking his head in wonder. He'd never known Woody to talk so much and was amazed at the amount of information he'd received in the two-hour drive.

Detective Steve Jones met them in the lobby. "So you two are going to help Faye with this case."

"That's the plan," Luke said as he shook the outstretched hand.

"I wish I could have done more for her," Jones said, his tone regretful. "Unfortunately the resources just aren't here right now."

"Well, I hope we can help," Woody said.

Jones took them to a conference room, where one wall was stacked with document boxes. "Here you go, gentlemen." He swept his arm toward the boxes. "That's all the evidence and reports we have on the Molly Cavanaugh case."

Woody whistled and for a minute Luke lost his voice. He knew there'd be a lot to go through, but he wasn't prepared for all this. They'd be sifting through documents for a week.

"It's stacked with the most recent paperwork closest to us. We did a due diligence review every year. I did the last one, so I can bring you up to speed."

"Thanks," Luke said as he took a seat at the table. "That would be great. You said on the phone that you worked the case ten years ago."

Jones nodded and sat across from Woody and Luke. "Yep, I was in uniform then. I talked to a lot of people, followed up on tip line leads. We had a dedicated tip line running for two months. But when tips began to dry up, so did the department's interest. Phones stop ringing, and there was no reason to have people sitting on their butts waiting." He clicked his teeth. "We really thought we'd catch the guy. I can't believe it's been ten years without a peep from him."

"You don't think it was his first rodeo, do you?" Woody asked.

Jones shook his head. "Molly told us he was prepared with tape and rope. He wasn't hesitant or unsure; he knew exactly what he was doing. Like I said, I did the due diligence review on the ten-year anniversary."

He got up, walked to a box, took out a file, and brought it back to the table. "You guys know as well as I do that teenagers, especially teenage girls, go missing all the time."

"You bet," Luke said with a nod.

"Well, Molly was victimized in May of 2005. Back then we pulled all missing reports for the year in order to find any similarities—you know, did anyone else go missing from the mall? Stuff like that."

He opened the file and took out three missing reports. "At the time, we had a lot more than three, but nearly all of them have been resolved in one way or another, except for these three. Two are from 2005, February and March, while one is from December 2004. All the girls were sixteen at the time of disappearance, and all of them were supposed to be taking a bus home."

"You don't say," Woody said as Jones slid the reports toward him.

"You'll notice that the girls disappeared from different areas in the county—Palmdale, Agua Dulce, and Acton. And all three of them had running away in their past. One was thought to have been taken by her father out of the country, but that was eventually disproved. The only connecting item is the bus angle. They may not be connected at all—" he threw his hands up—"but I decided I'd toss it in the mix."

"Nothing recently?" Luke asked.

"Lots of missings and runaways, but none that I'd categorize as close enough. Bottom line, I think the guy picked girls up before Molly, and they weren't as lucky as she was. As to why he stopped, well, that's anyone's guess. We have DNA. Molly's description was very clear and corroborated by another girl at the mall who says the guy tried to pick her up as well. But we never caught him."

Luke and Woody studied the missing posters. Luke was struck by how all three girls were similar in description to each other and to Molly.

He looked up at Jones, who was watching them. "Thanks. I appreciate all your hard work."

"You want to thank me? Catch him. I've got a daughter now. I don't want this creep out there. And it would be nice to give Faye a victory. Her husband wanted to join the sheriff's department. He called and talked to me about the job two days before he lost his life."

He left Luke and Woody to their work.

As he sifted through documents, a thought popped into Luke's head. "If he is a serial rapist and killer, why'd he stop?" he asked, half to himself.

"He could be dead," Woody said with a shrug. "To me that would be just. He could have moved elsewhere and is still active. But ten years is a long time. I can't imagine a puke smart enough to be doing this kind of stuff that long without being caught."

"Look how long it took them to catch the Green River killer. He started killing in the eighties and wasn't stopped until 2001."

"Yeah, but his victims of choice were prostitutes, women who lived transient lifestyles."

Luke started to protest about the value of everyone's life, but Woody waved a hand at him. "Don't get all bent out of shape over that. It's just the way of the world. I'm not saying it's right, but a lot of those girls had no one who cared enough to worry about them or push for a resolution to the crime. He kept killing—that's why he was caught."

"You're saying that if this guy were still active, snatching young girls like Molly off the street, he'd have been stopped by now."

"I believe that, yeah."

"Do you think he killed these three missing girls?" Luke held up the flyers.

"It's a possibility. I'm not a psychologist—I don't even play one on TV—but from what I've heard so far about this sick groundhog, I don't believe Molly's abduction was his first. And someone as deviant as our mutt would not be able to just stop."

Luke folded his arms and looked at the faces of the three missing girls. He looked back up at Woody and said, "Then where is he and what is he doing?"

CHAPTER

-24-

ABBY WASN'T SURE how long she'd been in bed when she heard her aunt calling out to her.

"I'm upstairs."

Dede poked her head into the room a few minutes later, a worried frown scrunching her brow. "What's the matter? Are you sick?"

"No, I was just tired. I ate breakfast and went back to bed."

"Abby, you've been here for two days and in bed most of that time."

Abby just grunted, hoping her aunt would leave, but Dede didn't take the hint.

"Ethan called. He was going to come over for lunch, but I told him you were still asleep. It's past lunchtime now. You're not going to sleep the day away, are you?"

The last thing Abby felt like was getting out of bed. But the look on her aunt's face made her reconsider.

"I guess I should get up and take a shower."

"I'll fix lunch, so come down as soon as you're ready." Frown still in place, Dede closed the door and Abby heard her head downstairs.

Abby got up and felt like lead. It was all she could do to get herself into the shower. She stood under the hot water for a long time. When she finally made it downstairs, her hair was still wet and she wore comfortable sweats with only socks on her feet.

Abby noticed the strange look on her aunt's face and ignored it. Dede had made sandwiches and set out a colorful salad. When Abby sat, Dede said a blessing. "Thank you for the food and your many blessings, and for bringing Abby home for a visit." She smiled and squeezed Abby's hand.

Abby made it through half of her sandwich and some salad before she wanted to excuse herself, but Dede stopped her.

"Abby, if I thought that you were tired from your drive, I would let this go. But this is not like you."

"I am tired from the drive. I just want to go back to bed." She started to rise.

Her aunt held a hand up. "Wait; I have something for you. I wanted to give it to you last night. Before you run off to hibernate, I'll give it to you now."

Abby sat back down and felt irritated at the comment about hibernating. Was that what she was doing? Did it matter? She'd not had any dreams since she went back to bed, where it was safe, warm. That was where Abby wanted to stay. No thinking, no talking, just sleeping.

"Remember Uncle Simon?" Dede asked.

Abby frowned. "Remember? I never knew him. He's in jail. He killed a guy."

"Yes, he's in jail. He's also come to faith. He started corresponding with me about a year ago. I knew him when I was a kid. He and your father were both wild young men. Unfortunately Simon's wild streak landed him in jail and . . . well, you know the rest."

Abby did know the rest. Not because anyone had told her, but because it was an issue she'd researched as she investigated her parents' murders. Since her dad had disowned his brother after Simon was convicted of homicide, one theory was that Simon ordered a hit on her parents from prison. It was a theory that went nowhere, and she'd never even felt it necessary to speak to him.

"He's asked about you, wondered how you were doing. Of course he's read about you and the Triple Seven investigation."

"Lots of convicts claim to have jailhouse conversions." Abby was not at all certain she wanted to get to know an uncle who would be in prison for the rest of his life.

"I know that. But he seems sincere, and he'd like to meet you." Smiling despite Abby's look of disbelief, Dede went on. "In his letter from a couple of weeks ago, he told me he'd read about the situation with Gavin Kent and the governor and you. Remember, he grew up with Lowell Rollins just like your father did. He enclosed a note for you. I've prayed about the right time to give it to you. That time is now."

"I don't know what to say." This was an avenue Abby had never examined, a line of investigation she'd never even considered pursuing. And it opened up an old sore: what was the truth about her parents' homicides?

"I know that he and your dad had their issues, but read the letter. Maybe visit him. It can't hurt to talk to him, and it might even help you with the picture you have of your dad." Dede pulled a letter from her sweater pocket. She held it out, but Abby didn't immediately take it. "He is family. And he knew your father. Part of your angst about this shooting may have something to do with all that nonsense about your dad still being alive."

Abby said nothing.

"No strings if you don't want to see him," Dede said when Abby finally took the letter. "He enclosed a visitor form. You have to sign it and send it back. Once you're approved to visit, he'll call and tell you. Of course, if you don't want to have anything to do with him, don't sign the form."

"I'll read it and think about it," Abby said, holding the correspondence but not really knowing what she wanted to do with it. Why was it so hard to think?

Dede got up to clear plates and do the dishes. After a few minutes Abby opened the envelope and took out the letter.

Abigail . . . that's a pretty name. It was my grandmother's. Did you know that you were named after your great-grandmother? I have had so many years to think about what to say to you, and now that I'm finally writing, I'm at a loss. We've never met, and there's no reason you would want to meet me. Except you are the only family I have now, aren't you? I'm doing my time in Tehachapi State. If you're ever in the area, I've signed a visitor form. Fill out your portion and mail it back if you want to talk.

Uncle Simon

Abby stared at the form with her uncle's signature on it. She noted the part she must fill out to be approved for visitation.

Dede said she'd been exchanging letters with him. She knew him when she was a kid.

What could it hurt?

Abby read the note a couple more times before putting it down. Dede had left a pen on the table. Abby picked it up and filled out the visitor form. She put it into the envelope and sealed it, setting it on the table.

There was no way to know how long it would take for her to be approved for visiting. It could take months, knowing the state of California. A lot could happen between now and then.

"Great! You decided to sign it." Dede picked up the envelope. "I'll put a stamp on it and get it in the mail."

Abby sat back and thought about her uncle. He was a year older than her dad would have been, but he'd been in prison for longer than her dad had been dead. What was Simon like? Was he like her dad? Was he a typical convict? The fog in her brain lifted for a minute as she pondered this new wrinkle. But it was only for a minute and then Abby returned to bed.

She got away with spending most of her time in bed until Saturday. That morning Dede burst into her bedroom early. "Okay, okay, enough of this. It's time to get up."

Abby grimaced and squinted against the light of a bright sunrise. "I'm tired. I don't want to get up."

Dede faced her, hands on hips. "Abby, I'm not going to allow this. If you want to hide from the world, you can do it at your house."

"Are you kicking me out?"

"If I have to. Right now you need to get up. We're going visiting. We're going to see what Ethan has been up to."

"What if I don't want to go visiting?"

"You're not going to sleep your life away in my house. If I have to kick you out, I will."

"I'm not a child."

"Then stop acting like one. It's time to get to the bottom of what's bothering you, and you can't do that hiding under the covers. I'll pray with you, I'll listen to you if you want to talk, I'll take you to talk to a pastor if that is what you need, but I won't watch you do this."

Abby flung the blanket off, furious with her aunt. "You have no right to treat me like a silly teenager! You don't know what I've been through."

Dede held her ground. "No, I don't. But I know that you've been through a lot of bad stuff in your life. You've never faced any of it by hiding. That will solve nothing. Problems have to be faced; that's the only way to solve them."

For a second they stared at one another.

"I'm putting the dogs in the car. You have twenty minutes to shower and get dressed. If you can't do that, then you can pack up and get ready to go home. I won't watch you hide."

Dede turned and left the room, leaving Abby staring at empty space.

Abby went to the bureau and grabbed her suitcase, intending to pack and leave, fuming that her aunt was so insensitive. Self-pity swirled inside and boiled over. So much for home being a safe place.

I've been through trauma upon trauma.

She should understand.

I'll show her.

She is mean and heartless.

She shoved her clothes into the case and then reached for

her Triple Seven notebook. She was about to toss it into her backpack when the verse she'd written on the cover caught her eye. It was her work verse, Hebrews chapter 4 verse 13:

And no creature is hidden from his sight, but all are naked and exposed to the eyes of him to whom we must give account.

You can run but you can't hide.

It was a verse she'd always felt applied to criminals, to the evil people she hunted.

How can it possibly apply to me?

She looked at the bed, still mussed and unmade, and knew that it did apply to her right now. She was hiding; she didn't want to face all the issues knocking on her heart: the shooting, the lack of clear closure regarding her father, and her own attitude right now.

It isn't fair. God isn't fair, and this is all his fault.

Pierced, she sat down on the bed as tears started. Something seemed to break inside, and the oppression she'd felt for the past few days lifted.

Dede is right. I've run and now I'm trying to hide.

Holding the book close to her chest, she let the tears fall, crying for Clayton, Althea, Adonna, and a little bit for herself. She wasn't sure how long she sat there, but after the tears ended, she felt drained and brittle but somewhat better.

Grabbing a Kleenex, she stood, put the book down and her clothes back in the bureau, and hoped Dede hadn't left. Blowing her nose and stepping to the window, she saw that Dede's Jeep was still there. Abby hurried to shower, dress, and catch up with her aunt.

CHAPTER

-25-

SATURDAY MORNING Woody hit the button to start the coffee brewing. He stretched and then sat at the table to peruse the paper while awaiting his caffeine fix. For nearly thirty-five years he'd worked graveyard or afternoon shift and loved it. He'd never wanted to work days. Now, retired and out of uniform, he found he loved the feeling of normalcy and looked forward to meeting up with Luke to work more on the Molly Cavanaugh case.

His phone buzzed and he frowned. It was a PD extension; it would be Abby if she were there, but he knew that she was still out of town.

He answered the call, surprised to hear Bill Roper on the other end.

"Bill, what's up? Anything wrong?"

"Yes, as a matter of fact. I got a call from a patrol unit on my day off. Abby's house was burglarized last night."

"What? She's not there. She's—"

"I know. She's out of state. She had her friend Jessica Brennan house-sitting."

"Jessica? I know Jessica. Is she okay?"

Bill chuckled. "She is. In fact, I bet the burglar is worse off. Apparently she woke up and confronted him. He was going through files in Abby's office. She says he was as surprised to see her as she was to see him."

"He knew Abby was gone."

"Yep. The short story is, Jessica got in some well-placed kicks and the guy fled limping and bleeding. Officers were out fast but didn't pick up his trail, and nothing is missing that Jessica can see."

"She's okay?"

"A little shaken, and she might have sprained a finger, but she's okay. The reason I called is, well, she doesn't want to tell Abby until Abby gets back. She doesn't want to ruin Abby's vacation. That doesn't sit well with me. I'd want to know, if it was me. But you know Abby better than anyone. What do you think?"

The coffeemaker beeped. Woody rubbed his chin. "Give me a minute to think."

He poured a cup of coffee and left it steaming on the counter before responding. "Offhand, if nothing is missing and Jessica is okay, I'd say let it go. Abby will be mad when she gets back, but she'll get to enjoy her time off. Did Jessica get a good look at this guy?"

"Not a great look, but she's working with a sketch artist. She did bloody his nose, so there is DNA, but . . ."

His voice trailed off and Woody knew why. No loss, no one hurt—the department would not pay to have the DNA analyzed. Woody poured his coffee and took a scalding gulp.

"What bothers me," Bill continued, "is that he was obviously looking for something. What if this is related to the Triple Seven?"

"I can't see why it would be. But I understand why you'd think that. The Joiner case is hot—hot enough that people would burglarize Abby's house?"

"The protests have been loud, but mostly confined to the main station, so I doubt this is related to the shooting."

"Let me talk to Luke. He's got a stake in the Triple Seven as well. I'll call you in a couple of hours. You can hold off a decision that long, can't you?"

"Yeah. But I can't promise anything if Abby happens to phone or text and ask how things are going. I'll tell her."

"I doubt she'll do that. If she's smart, the last thing she's thinking about right now is the PD. And Abby is smart."

CHAPTER

-26-

DEDE WAS LEANING against the Jeep, looking down at Scout, when Abby hurried out of the house. Arms folded, Dede looked up. "Are you okay?"

"I don't know." She held up the package of Oreos she'd grabbed on the way out and tried a weak smile.

"I've been waiting for over an hour. I thought maybe I was too hard on you."

"Maybe," Abby said. "What you said stung. But it also made me realize that I wasn't finding any answers in bed." Abby shook her head. "I still want to crawl into a hole and never come out. I've never felt this way before, but maybe you're right—it's no way to solve a problem."

Dede stepped forward and held her arms out. Abby fell into a tight hug. "So glad to see a little light in your eyes again," she whispered in Abby's ear.

"So much is jumbled in my mind right now, I can't even pray. Maybe I need to think about something else for a while." Abby pushed back from the hug. "We're going visiting?"

"Yeah, hop in. I think you'll be impressed by Ethan's project." Dede wiped her eyes and jumped into the driver's seat.

"A church over in Butte Falls burned down a few months ago," Dede explained as they drove. "So a lot of other churches in the valley have come together to rebuild a sanctuary. Since Ethan specializes in building things in the mission field, he's running the show, and he's doing a great job."

Ethan had been born and raised in Butte Falls. Abby had met him in a small church there before getting to know him better in youth group.

"Have you been working with Ethan?" Abby asked.

"There's a lot to do. I've been helping a little and will be more involved next week."

When Abby said nothing, Dede clarified. "We haven't been talking about you, if that's what you're worried about. He's excited about you taking time off but worried about you at the same time."

Abby sighed. "I've had a lot of time to think about our relationship. I wonder . . . maybe Ethan is right. Maybe I should just marry him, quit my job, and be a missionary wife."

Dede slowed the Jeep as they passed through minuscule downtown Lake Creek. She grunted her displeasure. "You go to the mission field because you're called, not because your life hits a hard patch."

"But maybe this is a sign that I am called."

Dede laughed. "Abby, you get married because you love someone and you desire to raise a family and be together for life. I've known Ethan since he was little. He's always known he was called to travel, to build and plant. You never were. I've wondered about the attraction, but I do believe that if you are both committed to God and each other, everything would eventually work out for the best. To travel the way Ethan travels on the mission field, you need to be called and totally committed."

"What if I can't be a cop?"

"Abby, you don't go on the mission field because you can't do anything else. Stop using today's strength for tomorrow's trials. Give yourself time."

They reached the building site about thirty-five minutes later. The place was active and busy. Work trucks were everywhere, and two cement trucks were lined up behind a third that was pouring concrete into the mold for the foundation.

"I don't see Ethan right now. Let's go meet Pastor Cliff."

Dede led Abby to a man on crutches, who was missing the lower half of one leg. Around him were several children and a woman holding a baby.

The man smiled. "Dede, glad you could make it."

"Wouldn't miss it. Pastor Cliff, I want you to meet my niece, Abby, up from Long Beach for a visit."

"Ah, Ethan's friend." The pastor smiled broadly as he shook Abby's hand. "He speaks of you often. It's my pleasure to finally meet you."

Introductions were made all around. Abby learned that Pastor Cliff and his wife had four children. He was a man full of hope and enthusiasm, despite having a body crippled from a car accident that cost him his leg.

"Ethan is meeting with the main contractor, firming things up for next week when we plan to push hard to finish everything."

Pastor Cliff excused himself and stepped away from Dede and Abby to talk to the concrete men.

One truck left and another pulled in. Abby learned from Dede that the small congregation Pastor Cliff served could not pay him a living wage even when they'd had a set meeting place. After the church burned, they'd moved from place to place and attendance had dropped. He'd taken a part-time job to supplement his income and was extremely grateful for the help with the new building.

Already partly finished, the foundation would be completed today, and then framing was scheduled to start next week. An army of volunteers would descend on the site and get the building up and enclosed in record time.

"This is the most important phase," Pastor Cliff said when he returned. "The foundation." He looked at Abby. "The foundation is a vital part, whether it be your foundation in faith firmly set in Christ or the foundation to build firmly set in concrete. That's why I wanted to be here, to pray and watch the hard work that goes into it."

Abby looked away from his perusal and wondered why his words seemed meant specifically for her even though he was speaking to many people.

Dede retrieved some papers. She was coordinating the meals and needed a head count and a shopping list. After she had the papers, she and Abby left.

As they drove away from the site, Abby watched the men work the concrete pump, admired the coordination and concentration she saw as they spread the viscous gray substance. The image stayed with her for some time as she pondered the importance of a solid foundation, concrete or otherwise.

CHAPTER

27

"BURGLARIZED?" Luke stared at Woody. They were about to set out for the Lancaster sheriff's office to formulate a plan of attack on their cold case. Because they'd been given the okay to work through the weekend, they decided to divide the workload and hoped to be able to comb through everything pertinent by Monday. Then the plan was to pool what important information they'd each pulled out and determine the most useful tidbits, see if they had a handhold and a place to start.

"No harm, no foul. Apparently Abby's friend Jessica was house-sitting and she scared the guy off. Bill called me this morning." Woody fastened his seat belt.

But Luke stopped the car in the driveway. "Does Jessica know what the guy was after?"

"She caught him in Abby's office. As far as she can tell, nothing was removed."

"What does Abby say?"

"I told Bill not to tell her."

"What? Is that a good idea?" Luke was beginning to wonder if Woody was going overboard on the "protect Abby" angle.

"I don't want her rushing back for no reason. Do you think we should call her?"

"Uh . . ." Now Luke stammered with the ball in his court. "I guess I'm not sure. I want her to get the rest and relaxation she needs away from all the bad stuff here, but . . ."

"When she calls Jessica to check in, Jessica will tell her."

Luke had to be content with that response. He put the car into drive and they started the long trek to Lancaster. Traffic was light, and for the first part of the drive they bounced possible reasons Abby's house was burglarized. It all circled back to the Triple Seven.

But who still had a stake in that investigation?

They talked themselves out after an hour and rode the rest of the way in silence. It wasn't until they'd parked in the SD lot that Luke's mind fully returned to the task at hand.

"Where do you want to start?"

In the conference room they had before them all the materials pertinent to Molly's case.

"I'll take the official police reports," Woody said. "I'll be able to read between the lines and sift out what is important."

"Good idea." Luke nodded. "I'll go through the tip line files and the follow-ups."

They sat for several hours and got through a good bit of the paperwork. After lunch they took a break to go over what they'd found so far.

The first step in opening a cold case was reconstructing the investigation from the beginning. So they'd drawn a time line of the investigation on the whiteboard. Point one was the date of the attack, and the last point was the most recent due diligence review done by Steve Jones on the tenth anniversary.

The due diligence reviews were extremely helpful. Many of these reviews were brief, noting only another check with CODIS, but it was useful to know that the case had not been buried away and never reviewed.

Luke stood in front of the board. The first point was the bus stop where Molly and her assailant had their fateful meeting. Also on the board was a map of the entire area, with pushpins of all the relevant locations in place: the Antelope Valley Mall, the strip mall where the assault occurred, and the road where Molly got away. Additionally they had a box of various reports, pages from the tip line logs, and all the follow-ups to the initial investigation. There were also pages of notes written by the investigators regarding Molly herself.

It was as important to understand the victim as it was to understand the crime. The original investigators had looked at Molly to ascertain her veracity and discovered that she was the proverbial good kid. She had no history of running away or fights or problems with high school classmates. She was an average student, on the swim team, and the day she was abducted, she'd had permission to be at the mall.

Particularly interesting to Luke were the girl's references to God and prayer. The investigator asked her how she got out of the trunk.

"I prayed and prayed for God to help me with
the rope. It was really tight at first, but the more
I prayed, the looser it got. When my legs got loose,
I thanked God and kicked something and it released
the latch. I believe Jesus opened the trunk. He
saved me."

When Luke looked over the photos taken of Molly and saw the marks the tight ropes made on her wrists and ankles, especially on her wrists where the securely tied bonds had broken the skin, he didn't have any problem entertaining the thought of a miracle freeing her. He wondered, looking at the reports on the girl's struggles now, what had destroyed her faith over time, since it was obviously very strong ten years ago even after the horrible rape and kidnapping.

"Well, I'm not sure." Woody studied the board. "As far as the crime scene or scenes, the strip mall where the rape occurred is no longer there, and there's a big-box store there now. But it looks like not much else has changed in the area."

"Yeah," Luke said. "Not sure we could learn much from the mall even if it were still there. And the two servicemen who saved Molly were interviewed three times. Their stories were consistent. I'm not sure we need to recontact them."

"Good call. They seemed squared away and innocent."

"I'm drawn to a couple of other things," he said, tapping on the table. "The most interesting stuff I found revolves around the composite drawing of the suspect." He taped the picture up on the whiteboard. "I think the guy looks like Johnny Depp with short hair. All he needs is a little mustache."

"I'll take your word on that," Woody said. "You think by focusing on this picture, maybe seeing if we can get it rebroadcast, we'd find the guy after all this time?"

"Maybe. The tip line logs document a call from a woman convinced she knew the guy. She said he looked exactly like her old neighbor, even named him. I'd like to connect with her, find out why she was so certain before we run to the media with the photo. My instincts are telling me this is our best bet."

"Didn't the original guys follow up?"

"Yeah, but it's not clear what they found." Luke pulled out a piece of paper. "See, here's the guy's name and address and a note that says *Iraq*, with a question mark."

"Did you ask Jones about that?"

"I did, but he wasn't familiar with it. He remembered the tip, that it went nowhere, but doesn't recall exactly why. Other than this tip sheet, I don't find any more references to this guy. Does his name ring a bell with you?"

"Nope, I didn't see this name in anything I looked at. Maybe the note 'Iraq' means he was serving and it wasn't possible for him to be our guy."

"I thought that, so I asked Orson to check enlistment records. Once we hear back from him and know one way or another, I'll have a better idea of the next step I want to take."

As if on cue, Luke's cell phone rang and he answered. It was Orson.

Luke put the call on speaker. "Speak of the devil, we were just talking about you. Were your ears burning?"

"Only if you really sit around and think of me as the devil. I have info for you. I got no match on that name you gave me. The guy never served."

"Thanks; that helps."

"Is he a suspect already?"

"Just an avenue to investigate. There's a question as to why he was crossed off the list ten years ago."

"Cool. I'm glad to hear it. If you do a great job on this case, it may clear the bottleneck no matter how the sponsors' legal issues play out."

"Sounds great. Thanks again for your help." Luke hung up

and looked at Woody. "Not in the service. I think I need to ask Faye if she's heard of this guy." He ignored Woody's raised eyebrow and the flush he felt in his own face at the excuse to talk to Faye again.

Luke had spoken at length with Faye about Molly, and at the same time he learned more about the victim, he also learned a lot about Faye. He could tell she was still hurting over the loss of her husband. But she had strong faith and a strong sense of purpose, and Luke found that very appealing.

He cleared his throat and got back on track. "She might know something not in the notes. And I'm going to set up an appointment with the tipster. Her name is Brenda Harris. I'm pretty sure I can find her."

"Tell Faye I said hello when you talk to her," Woody said with a smile in his voice.

Luke ignored him and phoned Faye to ask if she remembered the tip from a woman who was certain she knew the face in the composite.

"No, I don't. Did she have a name to put to the face?"

"Barone. Gil Barone from Northridge."

"I don't remember that, and if someone had mentioned that to me five years ago, I would have remembered." Her voice turned hopeful. "It sounds like you're already making progress. I'm impressed."

"I don't want to get your hopes up. This may just be a miscommunication, but I will set up a meeting with Harris if I can find her."

"Well, miscommunication or not, I can tell you're working hard. Thank you for that."

"It's what we do. Thank you for the time you put into this

before us." He wanted to say more, but Woody was watching, and there really wasn't more to say. So he thanked her again and said good-bye.

Turning to Woody, "She doesn't remember the name."

Woody nodded, pensive. "That Faye sure is a looker. Too bad I'm not twenty years younger."

"This from the guy who's been divorced three times?"

"Not thinking of me, thinking of you. She took a shine to you. I could see it."

Luke was sure his face flushed crimson. "Ah, Woody, don't try to be a matchmaker here."

"Just saying. I've been working with you for a while and you seem to live like a monk. No reason for that when there are women like Faye out there worth dating." He held his hands up as Luke started to protest. "I'm a trained observer. I know what I see."

"The woman still misses her husband," Luke said, trying to ignore the "she took a shine to you" comment.

"Maybe you could give her a good reason to move on."

Shaking his head, Luke tried to change the subject. "I did some poking around about Lucy Harper. She graduated from Jordan, so I talked to some people I know from church who were in her class. She was Simon's girlfriend, on and off, from what the two people who remembered her said. I've also been searching the Web, but the name is common, and she could have married and now have a completely different name. Not sure if I'll get anything anytime soon."

"I wish I could help, but I didn't know Simon at all. He didn't hang around with his brother, and his actual arrest was in San Diego."

"I'll find her, I'm sure. That's what I do."

"I have faith in you."

"I still think we should let Abby in on this."

"Not unless we get something solid. Trust me, she'll need a solid connection, not another wisp of smoke like she's gotten all these years."

Luke said nothing and prayed that Woody was right.

CHAPTER

-28-

WHEN THEY GOT BACK TO DEDE'S, Abby wandered out to the porch with her Bible. She sat on the porch swing. She'd been out there for only minutes when Aunt Dede joined her.

"Ethan will be here for dinner," she said.

Abby nodded. "That sounds good."

Dede had a fleece throw with her and sat down next to Abby and arranged the throw over both of them. She reached over and put a hand on Abby's. "You've had a rough summer. I know that. I've been praying for you."

Abby felt a lump in her throat and it surprised her. People praying for her when she couldn't seem to pray for herself touched her deeply.

Dede patted her hand. "Feel like talking?"

For some reason the thought of baring her soul to her aunt brought the threat of tears. Dede might not understand her as well as Luke, but she was always a source of comfort and guidance.

Swallowing the lump, she said, "I feel so off-balance right now. This shooting has thrown me into a tailspin. I'm not sure I can go back to work. That's what makes me want to hide." Her voice broke and she grabbed a Kleenex, unable to stop the tears.

"Give it time and prayer. I can't imagine going through what you just did. Confusion and second-guessing is human. You work a job that requires you to make hard choices." Dede leaned over and pulled Abby into a hug. "I haven't always agreed with your choice of profession, but I do know that you are good at it."

"But I'm just not sure of anything anymore. Not my job, not my life, not anything." The words came out in a tumble she couldn't stop. "I shot an innocent man. Before that I let a guilty man shoot himself in front of me. And the worst of it is, I almost shot that guilty man in anger, not because he was a threat to me. I only wanted justice, for things to be put right, and everything has gone wrong. I feel like God doesn't listen to me anymore." She hated the whine in her voice. Her fist clenched on the Kleenex as she ran it under her nose.

"God always listens." Dede sat back but kept Abby's hand in hers, gently patting it. "And I'm listening. But I don't think that's what's at the root of your angst. Tell me about the man you shot."

Abby turned to stare at Dede and saw love and understanding in her eyes. She'd been trying to forget Clayton, had been overjoyed that she slept the night before without dreaming of him. Now Dede wanted to hear about that awful day? "Why do you want to hear that story?"

"It has everything to do with why you feel off-balance, as if God has forsaken you. Which, by the way, is something he would never do."

"I don't want to talk about it. I've talked it out with the PD psychologist. We've spoken several times." Abby looked down at Bandit sitting at her feet.

"Did that help you get your balance back?"

Abby couldn't answer. The talks with the psychologist had been impersonally clinical. He was a nice man, and Abby had nothing against him, but no, he hadn't helped her get her balance back.

"Indulge me," her aunt insisted. "I promise, it may be painful, but it will be like tearing off an old bandage, letting fresh air into the wound to heal it."

Abby looked away and took a deep breath. After a long moment, she mustered up the best cop voice she could and dispassionately told Dede about the death of Clayton Joiner.

Dede listened without interrupting.

When Abby finished, she turned to her aunt. "It was the worst day of my life."

"I believe that. And even though you know you did the right thing, it still lacerates your heart." She gripped Abby's hand with her right and squeezed, holding tight.

"I can't get the image out of my mind." Abby sniffled as tears ran down her face again. "That's why I took the leave. It was interfering with my work, with my ability to do my job. Am I finished as a cop?" The last sentence tore at Abby's throat, and she fought to keep from sobbing. This was her biggest fear.

"Like tearing off an old bandage." It stung to realize the real fear she had that her career was over.

"I can't answer that question; only you and God can. But I will tell you what I believe." Dede let go of Abby's hand and placed an arm over her shoulder, pulling her close again as the bench swung gently. "Your parents' case defined you, dictated your choices for most of your life."

Abby flinched to pull away, but Dede held her tight. "I'm not condemning. You know I never wanted that case to be an obsession for you. You became an officer because of it, and a dedicated one, with a single goal always in your mind: find the killers. Now you've come to the end, the final chapter in that horrible case, and it only brought more questions, not the black-and-white answers you wanted. Your foundation was sand, and the sand has washed away."

Abby sagged into her aunt. "You're saying I'm done?"

"No, I'm saying you need to go back, set your life on the right foundation, first and foremost. Pastor Cliff told you how important a foundation is for a building . . . and for your faith. Once your faith foundation is firmly set, then I think everything else in your life will become clearer."

Abby couldn't argue with that. It made a lot of sense. But she'd always thought her faith was strong. Had she really let it get so weak?

Abby felt somewhat better when Ethan arrived for dinner; at least she felt normal enough to converse with and listen to Ethan. He was excited about the church build and equally excited about his next mission trip. In a couple weeks he was headed to Malawi.

"There's so much to do there. I'm teaming up with an organization that is working to build chicken farms."

"Chicken farms?" Dede asked. "Not churches?"

Ethan shook his head and swallowed his bite before answering. "No, the need there is for food. There's been a severe blight to many crops and people are in danger of starving. They need food sources, and right now they love the idea of chickens and chicken farms."

Abby wondered if Malawi was a place of unrest, of war and persecution. She didn't remember if she'd read about it in the news. She knew that the threat of danger wouldn't stop Ethan, and she realized she was clearly seeing his heart. He loved to travel and build and help those who really needed the help. He never feared, even when the papers were filled with stories about bad things happening where he planned to go. He trusted God and he went.

She thought of what Dede had said about the mission field, about being *called*.

Ethan was definitely called.

Until now I've always believed I was called to police work, Abby thought. She felt a little uncomfortable. She did love Ethan, but in her heart of hearts she wondered if she could ever have a passion, a calling, for foreign mission work.

"What did you think of Pastor Cliff?"

"What?" Abby realized Ethan was speaking to her. "Oh, sorry; I was daydreaming."

He repeated his question.

"Inspiring. I really liked the guy."

"Do you want to help with the build?"

"I don't know anything about construction."

Ethan put a hand on hers. "There will be a lot of professionals there. It might be mostly grunt work for you. It's up to you, but it might be a good change of pace."

Abby thought for a minute.

"I agree," Dede said. "I think that you need a change of pace."

Finishing her Diet Coke, Abby looked from Ethan to Dede. "Yeah, I guess you're right. I'll help."

As they went back and forth about plans for Monday, Abby toyed with her dessert and pondered the day in a different way. *I do need a change of pace, a real test,* she thought. *Maybe while helping with the building project, something will click and I'll find my calling. It's possible that I just haven't opened the right door.*

But even as she said yes, a tiny bit of unease rose. The unanswered questions about the Triple Seven murders, her father's fate, and Luke Murphy all crossed her mind at the same time.

Finally a clear, strong prayer came to her mind. *Lord, I need to know, beyond a shadow of a doubt, where you want me. At Ethan's side or back in Long Beach fighting for those who no longer have a voice, and finally uncovering the truth in my parents' murders.*

She was certain she'd get an answer soon, one way or another.

By Sunday night, the conversation she'd had with her aunt had played over and over in her mind seemingly a hundred times. For Dede the answer to every life issue was in the Bible. Talking with her, Abby realized that she had stepped away from that belief. Through most of her career she trusted in herself, her education and training, and her own abilities.

I've prayed, she thought, *and if you'd asked me, I would have told you that I believed in prayer. But in all honesty, I never thought God worked fast enough or that he was even listening all the time.*

But it was Dede's comment about the foundation of her life that caused Abby the most angst. She remembered the biblical parable that the idea of a firm foundation came from. It referenced building a house on different foundations. Any foundation other than obedience to God would wash away at the first sign of trouble.

Abby picked up the Bible and found the passage in the book of Luke. Jesus was telling the parable. She read the verses before going to bed.

Everyone who comes to me and hears my words and does them, I will show you what he is like: he is like a man building a house, who dug deep and laid the foundation on the rock. And when a flood arose, the stream broke against that house and could not shake it, because it had been well built. But the one who hears and does not do them is like a man who built a house on the ground without a foundation. When the stream broke against it, immediately it fell, and the ruin of that house was great.

Tears threatened. *I've always considered my foundation firm, my belief in God strong. Why am I so shaken? Why do I feel as if everything has been washed away by the storm of the shooting?*

Abby knew that in investigative work when a case looked as if it was going nowhere, you went back to the beginning, started over with the basics to be certain nothing was missed.

My life looks like it's going nowhere, she thought. *Maybe I need to go back to the beginning, review the basics of my faith.*

Where to start? I've always taken faith for granted. I believe, God should hear, and that's the end of it.

What am I missing?

The question stayed on her mind as she closed the Bible and lay down to go to sleep.

CHAPTER

-29-

BUTTE FALLS WAS A SMALL but beautiful place, surrounded by forest. It was a town of less than five hundred people with a rich logging history.

When they arrived at the site Monday morning, Abby was amazed at all the people already there. The group was gathered around the new foundation. Framing was the next project. All around were piles of lumber and stacks of plywood. Everyone was dressed for work. As Dede parked next to a pickup truck with the logo for Sure Foundation Construction, two men got out and waited for Dede and Abby.

Ethan waved to them and Dede led Abby that way. "I want you to meet a couple of guys from my church, those two with Ethan. They're also part of the mission team." She pointed. "This is Jon and Pete. They've been here since the beginning."

Jon was about six-two with a thick red beard and a broad smile. From the laugh lines around his eyes, Abby bet he smiled a lot and she knew she'd like him. Pete was a bit taller than Jon and a beanpole. He also sported a beard but it was not as thick as Jon's. They were obviously father and son, and she guessed Pete was her age and Jon was her aunt's age.

"Great to meet you." Jon beamed and gripped her hand in both of his. She felt engulfed by two baseball mitts. "I've heard a lot about you. This is my boy Pete."

"Nice to meet you as well."

"Let's go join everyone else," Ethan said, pointing to a forming circle, then taking Abby's hand. Abby waded in after him, meeting many other people and being swept away by the atmosphere and the work.

⸻

Luke stopped at the corner to tie his shoes. He'd seen the dark car before and knew it didn't belong in the area. But that had been a couple of weeks ago. When it left the neighborhood, he thought maybe he was being a tad paranoid. Ever since two men had attacked him on the bike path next to the flood control channel several months ago, warning him to stay away from the investigation into his uncle's death, he'd paid extra attention to his surroundings. He'd installed a state-of-the-art security system at home and a camera to watch the front of the house. Though there'd been no suspicious characters around the house lately and things seemed to be returning to normal, he'd not let his guard down.

Now the sedan was back, and he was certain that it wasn't one of his neighbors'. It looked like a government car or an unmarked police car, but there was no government license plate on it. He'd taken to jotting down license plate numbers of strange cars, so he knew he had this one written down in the house.

He stood and continued his jog. No one else was home, so he wasn't worried about the occupant of the car messing with his family. And if the guy wanted to mess with him, well, he was prepared. He left the neighborhood and headed east on Willow Street toward the flood control trail. The dark sedan shadowed him a bit but turned left on Studebaker.

Briefly, Luke wondered if it were wise to take the flood control route, since he'd been ambushed there once before. Thinking it through, Luke kept going. The car couldn't follow him on the jogging path there, and he wouldn't stay on it long.

Once he was off the street and on the trail, he took his cell phone out of his pocket and punched in Woody's number. Since it was Tuesday morning he knew Woody would be up and about, looking to see if it would be possible to contact the Air Force personnel who rescued Molly. Luke himself had a meeting scheduled with Brenda Harris. When he answered, Luke told him about the dark sedan.

"Where are you at?" Woody asked.

"Southbound on the flood control bike path." He came to a stop under a bridge and worked to regulate his breathing.

"You want me to call a black-and-white to check out a suspicious vehicle?"

"I'm not sure where he is now, so you wouldn't know where to send them. I was hoping you can come pick me up, drive me back to the neighborhood to see if he's still there. Maybe we'll get the chance to confront him, see what's up."

"I'm game. Where do you want to meet?"

"I'll hotfoot it up to College Estates, cut over toward Studebaker there. Why don't you meet me over that way? We'll drive back to my house. If he's still there, we'll try to talk to him. If not, I've got his license plate. We can call Bill and have him run it."

"On my way."

Luke put the phone away and picked up the pace to be where he'd told Woody to meet him. Briefly he wondered if the dark sedan was heading to Seal Beach to the same place the two men had jumped him months ago and threatened his daughter. One of those men was dead. The other, Alonzo Ruiz, was wanted; there was a warrant in the system for him. A former Orange County deputy fired for beating a man to death, he was well known to the sheriff, and he even had a faraway connection to Gavin Kent. Luke always wondered if it was Kent who hired Ruiz and his buddy to watch his house and jump him on the flood control trail. *No way to know now,* he thought, *unless I catch this guy and it turns out to be Ruiz.*

He jogged through a neighborhood and made it to Studebaker quickly. As he continued north on Studebaker, he saw Woody's car coming south. Woody made a U-turn, and sweating and breathing hard, Luke hopped in.

"I drove by your house on the way over, saw a dark sedan."

"He went back to my house?" Fury coursed through Luke.

"If it's the same car," Woody said as he accelerated. "Anyone home?"

"No, my mom took Maddie on a field trip to a museum in LA and my dad is on a job in south Orange County." He opened his fists and fought to calm down. He'd earned his nickname Bullet in the service because of his temper but tried hard to keep it in check.

"You want to call a unit?" Woody asked.

"Not yet. Let's see if it is the car. If it is, I want to talk to this guy."

When Woody turned onto Luke's street, Luke saw the sedan, parked two doors down from his house.

"That's the car," Luke said and Woody stopped, pulling in behind the vehicle.

Luke turned to his friend. "Why don't you call communications and ask them to run a records check on the plate. I'm going to walk to my house and see what's going on."

"It's broad daylight. You really think this guy would try something now?"

"I don't know. All I know is he watched me head for the flood control, then doubled back and parked by my house. I need to know what he's doing."

Woody nodded and tapped his phone. "Anything hinky with the license plate, I'm asking for a patrol car code 3."

"Fair enough."

Luke got out of the car and wiped perspiration from his forehead. For a minute he stood on the sidewalk, deciding the best course of action. He was at a loss as to what this guy could want and whether or not he was as dangerous as the pair from the flood control months ago. Ruiz had shot at him after Luke threw a punch at his friend.

Luke knew his neighbors were at work, so he walked across their lawn, intending to stay close to the front of their house and then cross over to his and creep around to the garage.

Worry nagged as he made his way slowly toward the corner of his house. There was more cover on the parkway, where mature jacaranda trees stood, but that wasn't the best path to be sneaky. And there was a Brazilian peppertree on this side of the house he could use as cover in a pinch. He strained to hear anything. If this guy was here to break in and had tampered with the security system, there should be noise, but he heard nothing.

If I were breaking in, I'd go to the back, he thought. *Is that where this guy is?* As he reached the corner of his home—he'd have to go across the front lawn to get around back—he saw the man coming from the side of the garage, carrying something in his hands.

He burglarized my house!

Before he could speak, the man saw him and skidded to a stop. He looked at Luke, then toward his car.

I know him, Luke thought, but the context of the meeting stymied his recollection.

"Hey," Luke yelled and tensed to block his escape. A sort of stalemate formed, the man inching slowly to his right and Luke bracing himself to act quickly and cut the man off. He noticed that the man had tape over his nose and two black eyes. Realization dawned.

"Alonzo Ruiz!"

The man threw what he had in his hands at Luke. Luke ducked to avoid being hit. When he faced Ruiz again, there was a gun pointed at him.

"It wasn't in the order to kill you, so get out of my way."

"Whose order?"

The man cursed and raised the gun to fire. Luke dove out of the way behind the only cover available, the peppertree. Bullets impacted the tree, spraying bark and wood in his face.

He rolled behind it and was trying to clear bits of dirt from his eye when he heard Woody.

"Stop! Drop the gun!"

Fear replaced the anger in Luke's gut as he heard a volley of gunshots. He prayed. *Oh, Lord, please; I pray that my anger didn't get Woody killed.*

CHAPTER
-30-

WOODY WAS FINE.

Luke thanked God for that, but the investigation and police officers soon overran his yard and home. He'd cancelled his appointment with Brenda Harris and promised to reschedule as soon as possible. Luke stayed outside the perimeter tape and watched for his mom's car. He stepped out to the parkway when he saw it. He'd called her and his dad and explained what had happened. His front lawn was still encircled in police tape, and the shooting investigation had not yet finished. Alonzo Ruiz was gone; paramedics had transported him away, and Luke heard he died at the hospital.

Maddie was out of the car quickly, and Luke knelt down to envelop her in a hug.

"Look at all the police officers," she exclaimed. "Is Bill here?" Bill was Luke's best friend, and Maddie was used to him being around.

Grace had stepped around to Luke. Unlike Maddie, whose

expression was pure excitement, Grace's brow was scrunched in worry. Then James's truck pulled up and Luke's equally worried stepfather joined them.

"No, Bill's not here, Mads." He stood and faced his mom. "Why don't we all go out to eat and talk about this elsewhere?" He looked at James, and his stepfather suggested Hof's Hut on Bellflower.

"Are you sure you're okay?" Grace asked.

"Yeah, Mom, I'm fine. Woody saved the day. He's left for the station to give a formal statement. The alarm system is toast." He shrugged. "I'll have to find another one."

"That can be replaced; you and Woody can't," Grace said. "I'm so glad that the two of you are okay, but this really unsettles me." She turned on her heel to get back into the car.

One of the uniformed officers stepped to where Luke and Maddie stood and told him that he was free to go and that they would be off his lawn shortly. Luke thanked him, and the officer gave Maddie a junior police badge. She was happy with the sticker.

When the officer went back to his duties, Maddie looked up at Luke. "Why is Grandma mad?"

"It's not that she's mad. I think she's a little scared."

Maddie frowned. "About Woody shooting a man?"

"Yes." He looked up at James, who nodded as if to say, *"I'll take this."*

"She'll be okay, baby," James told Maddie. "She just needs time. Let's get in the car and go have lunch."

Maddie hesitated. "But Woody wouldn't have shot the man if the man didn't have a gun, right?"

"That's right."

"I'd rather have Woody shooting a bad guy than a bad guy shooting Woody, wherever it happens."

Now James looked to Luke as if to say, *"You can't argue with that."*

"Me too, Maddie. Me too," Luke said, knowing that eleven-year-old logic would not go very far in mollifying his mother. He prayed for some wisdom to help him to that end.

As the next few days progressed, Abby spent time reading the Bible every morning, restoring habits she'd admittedly let go. She came across a favorite passage, one she'd not read in a long time, and it brought tears to her eyes. Psalm 10:17-18 were the first verses she'd memorized after coming to live with her aunt.

> Lord, you know the hopes of humble people. Surely you will hear their cries and comfort their hearts by helping them. You will be with the orphans and all who are oppressed, so that mere earthly man will terrify them no longer.

She'd seen herself in the verse—an orphan, oppressed—and she'd been comforted by knowing that God would hear her cries, feel her pain at the loss of her parents and her life. Truly she'd slipped from her foundation when she'd forgotten this verse and the promise it contained. She recommitted it to memory and vowed not to forget ever again.

Ethan led the construction group in prayer every morning. Abby didn't get much time alone with him, but that was okay. She knew she had to work out the issues plaguing her on her own. And she needed to watch Ethan, clarify in her own heart if the life he was called to was really where she was called as well.

In any event, she appreciated the reverent atmosphere of the group and the sense of family. Bandit and Scout came with them every day, and Abby marveled as Bandit followed the big dog around and seemed to love the outdoors and the lifestyle change.

The workdays were intense and busy. There was no time to wallow in self-pity or to do anything other than work. During the day Abby helped wherever she was needed, carrying wood, hammering nails, cleaning up after someone used the saw. Dede headed up the kitchen staff. There were other groups of builders in addition to those who came from Lake Creek, so she was busy all day as well. The goal was to have the structure up and roofed in a week, so there was plenty of work for everyone all the time.

Abby worked hard, used muscles she didn't know she had, slept well every night, and began to feel her balance return.

By the fourth day on the job when everyone broke for lunch, Abby gave in to her craving for Diet Coke. The church provided a hearty lunch with water, punch, and iced tea, but Abby needed a jolt of caffeine.

"Do you mind if I run to the general store for a bottle of Diet Coke?" she asked Dede.

"Not at all." She handed Abby the keys. "You can bring me back one," she whispered with a conspiratorial smile.

Abby took the keys with a chuckle and hummed her favorite hymn, "Trust and Obey," on her way to the Jeep.

The general store was in the center of what made up downtown Butte Falls, which wasn't much, and about ten minutes from the build site.

Abby parked next to a beat-up camper resting on a big, equally beat-up Chevy dually with California plates. The fact that the license plate tags were expired caused her to shake her head. Nothing she could do about it. When she got out to walk into the store, she paused, thinking she heard someone crying. As she continued around the front of the truck, she realized that someone was crying inside the camper.

Frowning, she paused again as all of her cop instincts seemed to jump at once and the hair rose on the back of her neck.

I'm being silly, she thought. *Crying doesn't mean a major crime has occurred. A child could be crying because they didn't get their way.*

A favorite Woody phrase popped into her mind: *"Not my circus, not my monkeys."* Smiling at the echo of Woody's voice, she continued into the store.

But she paid attention to everything once she entered the store. There was an older, heavyset woman behind the counter. Her back was turned as Abby entered. Abby followed her gaze and saw one other person in the store. A bearded man with a stringy brown- and gray-streaked ponytail trailing halfway down his back was at the refrigerator section, perusing beer. Walking that way, Abby took note of the man, mentally making out a field interview card on him: male white, 5'8", 140 pounds, gray-brown hair, black headband, scraggly beard, between fifty and sixty years old, wearing dirty blue jeans and a black T-shirt.

He smelled like stale sweat and cigarettes, she noted as she opened the refrigerator two doors down from him and removed two Diet Cokes. Carrying the drinks to the cashier, Abby observed now how uneasy the woman at the counter seemed.

Butte Falls was a small town. Abby had no doubt this woman knew who was from around here and who wasn't.

"How are you doing today?" Abby asked as she slid a five-dollar bill across the counter.

"Not too bad," the woman said, eyes flitting from Abby to the ponytailed man and back again. "I'm vertical at least."

"Always a plus." Abby smiled and took her change and sodas.

She stepped outside and considered waiting for the man to leave before heading back to the church.

Her curiosity got the better of her. After putting the sodas in the Jeep, Abby ignored the "curiosity killed the cat" phrase running though her mind and sidled up to the camper and listened. The windows were covered with plastic or something opaque, so she couldn't see inside. She looked back at the door of the store. Ponytail was nowhere to be seen yet.

"Is someone in there?"

Sniffles, whispers, rustling.

"If there's a problem, I can help."

More rustling, but nobody said anything and she couldn't hear crying anymore. Sighing, thinking she was overreacting but still feeling uneasy, Abby decided to make one last try.

Leaning close, she said, "I thought I heard some—"

"Get away from my rig!"

Abby jerked around as the ponytailed man lurched toward her. He set a bag on the hood of the dually and continued toward her, fists clenched.

She stepped back and reflexively settled into a position of advantage, a well-balanced stance learned in weaponless defense training.

"I thought I heard someone crying."

"None of your business." He spat out the words through rotting teeth that told Abby he was a meth head. He moved close, trying to intimidate her, but he was shorter than she was and she wasn't intimidated, only angered.

Abby glanced around to make sure she had room to defend herself if he was more than just a verbal bully.

"Is someone in there hurt?"

He exploded in curses, called into question her lineage, and then said, "Ain't no one in there, and even if there was, it would be none of your business."

Abby would have backed off, realizing she had nothing to go on since no one had answered her, but Ponytail pulled a knife from his back pocket.

Opening the blade, he jammed it toward her, but she was ready. In a much-practiced move, she grabbed his wrist and used his own momentum against him, pulling down and then jerking his wrist back, forcing the knife to fall. He squealed as she twisted him around and set the reverse wristlock, leaning with her back against Dede's Jeep and holding him in complete control.

Over his shrieking, Abby yelled for the woman in the store to call the police.

The cashier stepped out of the store, phone in hand, breathless. "I already talked to them. I think he stole some things. You need help?"

"No, I got him," Abby said, feeling strangely euphoric at catching a bad guy. "Can you check out the camper? Someone was crying in there, I'm sure."

The woman nodded. After a moment Abby's euphoria increased. The counter woman helped three young girls out of the camper, all with varying degrees of bruises. They all claimed to have been held against their will.

A bad guy indeed, Abby thought, tightening her grip and eliciting a whole new round of howls and denials.

CHAPTER

-31-

"MY HEART FELL in my chest when I saw all those sheriff cars around the store." Dede smiled across the table. "I should have known you'd have everything under control."

Abby shrugged, a little uncomfortable with all the praise she'd been receiving, but still gratified her instincts had led her to catch a bad guy.

The only one who'd been quiet was Ethan, and Abby guessed she knew why. But she preferred to have the conversation with him in private. Right now they were in a small Mexican restaurant on the highway, Abby to eat the lunch she missed and the others to eat dinner. By the time the deputies had finished with Abby at the Butte Falls market, it was dark and dinnertime. Jon knew the deputies who had responded and stayed behind to get more information out of them.

Ethan, Dede, and Jon had come looking for Abby when she didn't return to lunch. By the time they'd arrived at the store, three Jackson County sheriff's deputies were on scene to deal with the man and the girls. Abby had called Dede, but the church build was noisy and busy and Dede didn't hear the phone right away.

"I'm just glad I was in the right place at the right time," Abby told everyone.

It turned out that the ponytailed man had a felony warrant in the system for assault and kidnapping. The three girls were all from California, runaways who'd encountered something they never expected: a guy who said he would help them find real jobs but instead forced them into prostitution. Once they saw their captor in handcuffs, they opened up about their ordeal, which had been going on for between six and eight months.

Before Abby had a chance to say anything to Ethan, Jon joined them at the table. They'd been waiting for him to arrive before ordering.

"I just finished talking to the deputy who stayed behind to tow the camper," Jon shared. "Apparently the guy you tangled with planned on taking those girls to Portland."

"Why'd he stop in Butte Falls?" Ethan frowned. "That's out of the way if you're going to Portland."

"He said he needed some gas money. The deputies don't believe that story and are working hard to get the truth. Will Bascom promised to stop by the build tomorrow and let us know what else they find out."

"You know, Abby," Dede said, "this part of the country might not seem as dangerous as where you work, but we do have our issues, and being a corridor for human trafficking is one of them."

"Sadly true," Jon said. "I was born and raised in Medford. I've done a lot of work in this area as well, and I've seen and heard things that sometimes make me wonder if the big bad city isn't invading our peace and quiet."

"Sin has no boundaries," Dede said.

Abby nodded in agreement and noted how close Jon and Dede seemed. To Abby's knowledge her aunt had not dated since her husband died, many years ago. She was happy if after all this time Dede had finally found a match.

Abby picked at her dinner, jazzed about the arrest of the ponytailed guy. Woody was right; getting back on the horse and catching bad guys was powerful medicine. Clayton Joiner would always be with her; she couldn't run away from that. But she could move on and do her job again.

"I'll give you a ride back to Dede's," Ethan said to Abby after they finished dinner. From his demeanor, she knew it was time for the conversation that had been brewing since she intervened with the ponytailed man.

"Sure, that's a great idea." Abby was not one to put things off. She felt stronger in a lot of ways, more clear on where she wanted to go, and Ethan deserved to know how she felt about things.

"You're upset, aren't you?" she asked as he drove out of the restaurant lot.

"A little. Abby, you could have been killed."

"Ethan, I know how to handle myself. I couldn't ignore those kids crying."

"I'm not saying ignore." He glanced from the road to her and back again. "You could have just called the local police. You didn't have to put yourself in danger."

"Things happened. I won't apologize for saving those girls."

He pulled over and stopped the car, turning to face her. "I'm not asking that you apologize. All I'm asking is that you think carefully before you act. I was actually praying that by taking more time off from work, you were considering other, safer avenues."

Abby sighed and took Ethan's hand. "I love my work. It's my mission field. We've been down this road so many times. You travel to dangerous places, and I trust your judgment. Why can't you trust mine?"

"Didn't all the work we accomplished this week inspire you?"

"It did. It was great. I feel privileged to have been part of it. But it's not my calling."

"What about being with me?"

Abby held his gaze, pain tugging in her heart at the sadness she saw in his eyes. "Ethan, I love you and I'm committed to working on this relationship; believe that."

After a minute he smiled. "I do believe that," he said, "and I am too." Ethan squeezed her hand and drove back onto the road.

———■▶———

The day after her ponytail man confrontation, Abby saw Deputy Bascom when he arrived at the work site. She waved to the stocky cop as he wandered around the chaos. She guessed he was looking for her.

"Just the person I wanted to find—Detective Hart, the homicide investigator from Long Beach up here on vacation who cracks human trafficking rings on her lunch hour," he said with a smile when he saw her.

"Hello, Deputy Bascom." She shook his outstretched hand. "Do you have more news?"

He ducked his head. "I sure do. We eventually peeled down to the real story and it had nothing to do with gas money. We found two more girls held against their will at a spread in Butte Falls, with a man waiting to buy one of the young ladies you freed."

"Buy?" Abby's eyes went wide, and she was amazed that something criminal could still surprise her.

"Yep. He's in custody. Two more girls are free, and we also shut down an active meth lab. Thanks again for the intervention. By the way, how are you enjoying your working vacation?"

Abby chuckled. "Actually, I'm having the time of my life. This has been a great experience."

Will nodded. "I've been involved with two church builds. It's a great feeling to help those who really need it. Thanks again for helping some kids who really needed it as well. Great observation on your part." He shook her hand one more time before saying good-bye.

She couldn't help but notice Ethan watching Bascom as he climbed into his vehicle and drove away. Ethan had been avoiding her since their conversation last night. He'd asked when she planned on going back to Long Beach. She said she didn't know and at that time she didn't. But now she knew she was ready. She meant what she said when she told him she was committed to working on their relationship, but a thought nagged: *How can we truly be a couple when our hearts take us in different directions?* Abby did love Ethan, but she knew she'd never join him on the mission field. Could he live with that if they were married?

Could she?

"I'm glad we can help Pastor Cliff," Abby said to Dede as

they drove from Butte Falls to Lake Creek at the end of the day. "What a nice family he has."

"He's a great guy. He and his family deserve some good times after all the hard they've endured."

And it did me good to help, Abby thought. *I'm okay. I'm back. I can return to work. I need to return to work.*

CHAPTER

-32-

BY FRIDAY, Woody's shooting had been officially cleared as self-defense. That part was a no-brainer. Ruiz had a gun, and he'd fired at Luke and Woody before Woody dropped him. There was still a lot of investigation into why Alonzo Ruiz had broken into Luke's office, and there was no reason to believe answers would be coming anytime soon. Luke and Woody sat down with Lieutenant Jacoby Friday morning.

"Of all the people to be involved in a shooting, Woody, you surprised me." Jacoby looked from Luke to Woody and shook his head.

"You're not the only one. After all the years of range work and nothing else, I'm glad to say that my training kicked in."

"Me too," Luke said. "That guy had me cold."

Happy the department had cleared Woody quickly, Luke was able to hash everything out with his mother in terms of the shooting. He could understand her gut level fear for him. He felt the same way about Maddie. That his home had been violated struck him at a visceral, personal level.

The shock of seeing that Ruiz was the man following him

was almost as great as the shock of the shooting itself. The Triple Seven was front and center again. The incident was a powerful impetus for Luke to expedite his attempt to locate Lucy Harper, shake her, and uncover why Asa had her in his notes as a possible smoking gun. But he couldn't go off half-cocked. Even with Woody being cleared, the shooting and subsequent investigation had delayed their work on both the Cavanaugh case and his search for Lucy Harper.

Luke was glad that since the dead man was suspected for another crime, Jack O'Reilly and Ben Carney, the LBPD detectives who responded to the shooting scene, were sharing the investigation with Orange County Detective Fred Wright. He'd investigated the incident on the flood control path several months ago, when Ruiz and the other man had confronted Luke.

Wright was trying to determine where Ruiz had been staying and who he was working for, while O'Reilly and Carney investigated the shooting and completed an inventory on a bunch of high-tech surveillance equipment located in the trunk of his car. There were cameras, listening devices, and tracking devices neatly organized in the trunk. It was likely they could find the vendors and maybe in a backdoor way discover who, if anyone, Ruiz was working with. There was no evidence that he'd used the equipment in any kind of surveillance of Abby or Luke, but it was problematic that he had it at all. Luke thought it creepy that Ruiz could possibly have been listening in on conversations, recording his movements. Another carrot dangling in front of him, urging him to get to the bottom of things.

CHAPTER

-33-

WHEN FRIDAY ROLLED AROUND, Abby realized she'd been gone for over a week and she hadn't checked in with Jessica. True, Jessica had told her not to worry, but she felt like she should have at least called once before now. When her friend didn't answer her cell, Abby dialed her own home number but nearly disconnected when a familiar, but completely unexpected voice answered the phone.

"Hello?"

"Um, hello?"

"This sounds like Abby. You're probably wondering why I answered your phone." It was Luke Murphy, and there was a bit of a smile in his voice.

"Yeah, I guess I am. I expected to speak to Jessica. It's comforting at least that I didn't dial the wrong number. What are you doing there?"

"Well, it's a long story and one you weren't supposed to hear until you got home. But somebody broke into your—"

"Broke into my house? Is Jessica okay?" Abby stood, tense and angry.

"Yes, Jessica is fine. In fact she gave the burglar a bit of a thrashing. He got away with nothing to show for his trouble but a broken nose."

For a second she couldn't find her voice. She remembered the dark car she thought had been shadowing her.

"Are you still there?" Worry shaded his voice.

Sighing, Abby pinched the bridge of her nose. "Still here but not believing what you just said. Can you tell what he was after?" She didn't have many valuables; her most important was her laptop, and that was with her.

"Jessica isn't sure. She caught him in your office. As far as she could tell, nothing has been removed. The doorjamb was destroyed—he jimmied it open to get inside—and I had some time on my hands, so I came over to fix it. We didn't want to ruin your time away since, at the time, it seemed to be a no harm, no foul situation."

Abby almost laughed out loud when Luke used a Woody-ism like "no harm, no foul."

Luke went on. "The back door will be good as new, and Woody wants me to install a camera like one I put up at my house. That's where Jessica is, with him picking one out."

"You guys shouldn't go to so much trouble. A camera? Aren't you overreacting?"

"Uh, first, it's no trouble, and second, it doesn't hurt to be cautious. Anyway, I'm sorry you had to find out this way."

There was something in his voice. Abby heard it and knew there was more. "Was the guy caught?"

"In a manner of speaking."

"What manner would that be?"

"Abby, I think all this can wait until you get home. Woody didn't want to ruin your trip and neither do I."

Abby felt anger rise. "I'm not fragile. What is going on down there?"

"I know you're not fragile. We just wanted to give you time to heal."

"Tell me please," she said firmly.

She heard Luke blow out a breath. "The guy who broke into your house was Alonzo Ruiz."

"Ruiz?" Abby frowned as the name and the memory of that name and what he'd done came roaring back to her mind. "The man who shot at you on the flood control trail?"

"The same. He paid me a visit as well. That was where we stopped him."

Questions exploded in Abby's mind. "You stopped him? He's in custody? Who is he working for?"

"We can't ask. He's dead. He had a gun and Woody had to shoot him. And before you ask, Woody is fine."

Words wouldn't form, and Abby felt like all the air had whooshed out of her lungs. She had to sit down to digest this news.

"Tell me everything," she was finally able to say.

Luke told her what had transpired at his house.

She took deep breaths as the fear for Woody subsided, along with an overwhelming wave of protectiveness that extended to Luke Murphy as well.

"So he'd tried to remove all your notes on the Triple Seven?"

"Yeah, that's what he chucked at me on the front lawn. And just when we thought that was all settled. We know Ruiz was the same man Jessica confronted at your house because his nose was broken. Bill took pictures to Jessica and she was able to positively identify him. He also had a ton of state-of-the-art surveillance equipment in his car, and he bypassed my alarm system like it was nothing."

"What kind of car was Ruiz driving?"

"A black Ford Crown Vic. Why?"

Abby told him about the dark car she'd thought had shadowed her to Oregon.

"Could have been him. He'd have had plenty of time to get back down here, break into your house. He knew you were gone if he followed you all the way to Oregon. But why is anyone following you? Look, bottom line, it's okay here. Woody is good. We're sidelined for a bit while the shooting is officially investigated, but I'm sorry if I've ruined your vacation."

"You didn't ruin anything. I was already thinking that it was time to come home. I settled a lot in my own mind about the shooting. It's time for me to get back to work."

———➤

"I'm glad I came along, glad I could be a part of this." Abby put her arm over Dede's shoulder as the two took in the sight of the newly constructed sanctuary. Ethan was going over some last-minute arrangements with Pastor Cliff, so he'd said he would miss this final group prayer. They'd talked earlier.

"So you're going home, back to work?" he asked.

"I'm going home, and then I have to talk to the psychologist. I'm assuming he'll let me go back to work. How long will you be tying up the loose ends of this project?"

He shrugged. *"A week maybe."*

"Then you leave for Malawi."

Nodding, he took her hand. *"Yeah, and I'll be gone for a*

month. But I'll be back in LB for a few days before that." He held
her gaze and the sadness in his eyes broke Abby's heart.

"And I'm sure that we'll talk on the phone before that."

He nodded. *"Call me when you get home so I'll know that you
got there safe, and promise me something as you go back to work."*

"Anything."

"Be careful."

Now it was late Friday afternoon and almost everyone who'd
taken part in the build was gathered at the new church to pray
and dedicate the building. The sun dipped low by the time
workers and volunteers finished, joined hands for prayer, and
then packed up their belongings to leave.

"I'm glad too," Dede said. "It was wonderful reconnecting.
Are you sure you're ready to go back into the lion's den? It's only
been a week."

"On one level, not really," Abby said honestly. She bent down
and picked Bandit up, wanting to hug the warm, furry body. A
part of her still found the idea of hiding from the realities waiting for her in Long Beach appealing, especially if she was going
back to again face the brick wall that was her parents' murder
investigation. "But I was already thinking it was time, and now,
hearing about Woody's shooting . . . Well, I want to know what's
happening."

"I understand. Keep me up to date, and let me know if you
visit Simon."

"I will." She hugged her aunt and together they drove home.
Abby packed and prepared to leave first thing in the morning.

CHAPTER

-34-

FOR A MOMENT when Abby pulled into her driveway, she thought she was at the wrong house. Even in the fading evening light, she could see the color exploding across the front of her house. All kinds of flowers in various colors blended together to make the porch and walkway look like something from a gardening magazine.

"Wow, Bandit, Jessica has been busy."

As if on cue, Jessica stepped out the front door, a huge grin on her face.

Abby turned off the car and got out. "You outdid yourself."

"What do you think? The house has real curb appeal, huh?"

"It's gorgeous. You must have spent a fortune." Hands on hips, she shook her head. "You have to let me pay you."

Jessica frowned and waved her hands back and forth. "No way. I had fun doing it, and you have done more for me than I can ever repay. The only thing I ask is that you water or have someone install a drip system."

"Of course, of course." Abby gave Jessica a hug. "Thank you. What a wonderful sight to come home to." She stepped back, her tone changing. "Are you sure you're okay?"

Jessica looked bewildered for a minute. "Oh, that." She laughed.

"I'm glad you find it amusing. Confronting a burglar isn't really a laughing matter."

"Sorry; I can't help it. I spent so much time training to protect myself, learning so much I wish I'd known when I was married to that wife beater Rory, that finally having the opportunity to put it to practical use, and being successful, makes me smile." She shrugged. "You get to do heroic cop stuff all the time; this was a first for me and it felt great."

She pointed to Abby's car. "Can I help you unload?"

"Sure," Abby said as she opened the car door to let Bandit out. Between her and Jessica they had the car unloaded in two trips. Abby fed Bandit and then Jessica took her into the office to see what she'd caught the burglar doing.

"He had your file cabinet open." Jessica pointed. "I had my bat. He tried to take it away from me but I got him with my elbow, right in the nose, heard it crunch. He gave up after that and ran." Jessica smiled.

Abby couldn't help but chuckle. She stepped to the cabinet and looked carefully around the room to see if anything was missing. "I can't imagine what he wanted. Even if he was after my Triple Seven file, which I had with me—" she held it up and put it back in its place on the bookshelf—"it has no new information in it."

"He tried to steal Luke's notes as well. Maybe he just wanted to be certain everything was finished, you know? Tie up loose ends?"

Abby cocked her head, thoughtful. "Too bad we can't ask him. But I am glad that he's no longer a threat to me or to Luke Murphy."

"Me too," Jessica agreed. "And I'll house-sit for you whenever you need me. It's so quiet here, much better than the apartments where I live. Even after being burglarized, I actually got good sleep here."

"I'll take you up on that. I may need you in the near future. But I might have to leave Bandit as well. Would you be okay with that?"

"Of course!" Jessica said. "Are you planning another road trip?"

"I am, and I can't take the dog." She told Jessica about her uncle Simon. "When I go to visit him, I think I'm going to spend the night in Tehachapi. It's not that I can't do the drive in a day; it's just that traffic is unpredictable. I don't want to get stuck on the 14 freeway for hours and miss visiting time."

"That makes sense. When are you going?"

"Not sure. I only mailed back the visiting form last week. According to my aunt, Simon will call me when I'm cleared. It may be a few weeks; it may be a few months."

"Can't you just go as a cop?"

"I don't want to. I just want to go as his niece."

Jessica shrugged. "I guess I can see that. And don't worry about the house or Bandit. I love staying here. I wish I could afford a house in this neighborhood, so I'll house-sit anytime. But I'm glad you're home. We missed you at volleyball."

Abby yawned, the long drive hitting her all of a sudden. "I missed playing. Can't help but feel completely out of shape."

After Jessica left, Abby settled on the couch with Bandit, bowl of popcorn in hand. In the DVD player was *The Maltese Falcon*. She felt the need to veg in black-and-white. She was about to hit Play when the phone rang.

It was Ethan.

She'd forgotten to call and tell him that she arrived home okay.

"Hi, Ethan. Sorry; I forgot to call you." She explained about Jessica and the new landscaping. But she left out the break-in. After all, nothing was taken. Did Ethan really need to know about a "no harm, no foul" situation?

"That's great; just glad all is well down there."

"Yeah. The drive was fine, and I am glad to be home."

They chatted for about twenty minutes. It was a good conversation, but there was a sad undercurrent to Ethan's tone that Abby couldn't ignore.

The week had gone well—her trip, working with him, being away. She'd come home feeling like her old self.

But the vast chasm between their visions for the future was becoming clearer to Abby the steadier she became. After Ethan hung up, for the first time, she wondered if he was seeing that as well. He'd be back in Long Beach in a week for three days before he left for Malawi. Abby prayed he'd have a safe, productive trip and that the next time they talked face-to-face, the future would be clearer to both of them.

Bandit yawned on her lap and Abby laughed. Together they padded into the bedroom, and Abby fell asleep as soon as her head hit the pillow. No dreams.

CHAPTER

35

BY THE TIME ABBY ARRIVED back in Long Beach, neither Carney and O'Reilly nor Fred Wright had uncovered any more information about Alonzo Ruiz. They hadn't discovered where he was staying or, most important, whom he was working for. She planned on meeting with Carney and O'Reilly as soon as they had time for her.

While Abby was glad Woody had been cleared, she was ecstatic that neither he nor Luke Murphy had been injured. But on Sunday, the day after she returned, she was at her friend and mentor's house for a solemn reason. The older of his two dogs, Ralph, had suffered a stroke and had to be put down.

"I feel like a sissy asking you to come with me," Woody said as Abby entered his house.

She gave him a hug. "You're not a sissy. Ralph has been a good dog for a long time. I know you'll miss him."

Her heart broke when Woody wiped his eyes. "True that. He's a great dog." Tenderly Woody picked the big dog up. Ed, his other Lab, whimpered and looked up at them, tail between his legs.

Gently Abby pushed Ed into the house. "We'll be back, sweetie. I promise." The dog whimpered but stayed inside, and Abby closed the door, throat thick as they walked to her car.

She opened the door for Woody to sit with Ralph on his lap. She drove to the vet, sniffling as Woody held the ailing dog and talked to him, telling him what a great dog he was. A vet tech was waiting for them when they arrived and led them to an exam room. There was a blanket and pillows on the floor, and Woody laid Ralph down and sat next to him. Abby took a seat on the other side of the dog.

"The doctor will be in in a minute," the vet tech said before she left them in the room.

Woody cradled Ralph's head, gently caressing him. Abby scratched the dog's ears, noting the gray muzzle and remembering a younger dog following Woody everywhere with love and devotion.

"Do dogs go to heaven?" Woody asked, voice thick.

The question took Abby by surprise. She'd prayed for Woody for years. Once when she'd tried to talk to him about salvation, he'd made the request that she leave the subject alone until he asked. This was the closest he'd come to asking since then.

What do I say, Lord? Abby prayed quickly before answering.

"I believe they do," she said, swallowing a lump. "I believe heaven is a place where we'll be perfectly happy, and I've learned, after having Bandit for only a few months, dogs make us happy. I imagine we'll see them again."

Woody nodded. After a couple minutes, the vet came in. He offered his condolences and shortly after that, Ralph peacefully took his last breath. Abby cried many tears at the loss of the dog and the pain in her friend's eyes.

Abby convinced Woody he needed a condolence lunch. River's End was crowded, but the day was beautiful. Sunny, seventy degrees, with a gentle ocean breeze tickling the skin. Abby and Woody sat on an outside bench to wait for a table. They had picked up Ed on the way, deciding that he needed to share in the consolation.

"That was as painless as possible, I guess," Woody said.

"Yes, it was. It's good he's not suffering."

Just then his phone rang. From Woody's side of the conversation, Abby guessed that the caller was Luke.

The thought of Luke mixed up her emotions like a blender. She wanted to talk to him about the burglary at her house and his own confrontation with Ruiz. As much as they both tried to put the Triple Seven behind them, Abby had a sinking feeling that that would be impossible.

She wondered if Woody would invite him to lunch. As if reading her mind, the next thing Woody said was "Why don't you join us at River's End?"

Abby felt her face blush, and she turned toward the ocean, hoping Woody didn't notice.

"Yeah, we're here, waiting for an outside table. Come on down." After signing off, he disconnected.

"Is he coming?" Abby asked.

Woody nodded. "He's close. Probably be here before we get seated. He's still working a missing case, was actually in Sunset Beach checking an address."

A short time later, she looked toward the parking lot as Woody's name was called. Their table was ready, and there was Luke Murphy striding toward them.

He was amazingly good-looking, had a movie-star quality with his strong jaw and his alert, expressive gold-flecked hazel-brown eyes.

Abby's breath caught in her throat as she stood, wondering what in the world she was going to do about these feelings that were getting harder and harder to ignore.

CHAPTER -36-

"SORRY TO HEAR ABOUT RALPH," Luke said to Woody as they were all led to an outdoor table. He leaned down to scratch Ed's head as he took the seat next to Abby and tried to ignore the fluttering in his stomach. He'd faced down a crazy pimp with less anxiety than sitting next to this pretty cop. And he realized it had to stop. Abby was engaged, off-limits, involved with another man.

"He lived a good, long life," Woody said as he too gave Ed a pat.

"Are you sure you're okay, Luke?" Abby asked. "Burglary and shots fired at your house has to mess with your head."

"I'm fine. Glad my partner is proficient with firearms. And grateful no one else was home at the time."

"He didn't take anything but your Triple Seven notes?"

"Nope. He tossed my office, but that was all that he removed."

"Lots of guys are looking into both crimes," Woody said. "They'll shake something loose."

Sandy came to take their order. She asked where Woody's other dog was.

"I prefer to believe that he's in heaven," Woody said.

"Oh! I'm so sorry," Sandy said as she frowned and gave Woody a hug.

"All dogs go to heaven," Luke said, winking at Abby and smiling at Woody.

"Hear, hear," Woody said, raising his water glass. They all toasted Ralph.

"How goes your case, the girl in the high desert?" Abby asked.

"We've been sidelined because of the shooting. Hopefully, first thing tomorrow, we'll be back at it," Luke said, leaning forward and catching Woody's eye before turning to Abby. "We're set to drive to Tehachapi to meet her on Wednesday. We'll be there a couple of days." He almost said they'd also be making a trip to Bakersfield to talk to a Lucy Harper but thought better of it. Nothing was certain; nothing was concrete. *I'm not going to give Abby false hope.*

"Luke's got a line on a possible witness."

"Really?" Abby asked. "For a ten-year-old case?"

"It's a maybe." Luke told her about Brenda Harris, the tipster who was certain that the rapist was an old neighbor. "We're meeting Tuesday. I'm praying it's a great lead."

"I'll join that prayer," Abby said.

Luke looked into her beautiful green eyes, saw the sparkle, and felt like he could drown there.

Woody brought him back to earth. "Will that blogger, Faye Fallon, meet us in Tehachapi?" he asked.

Luke nodded. "She's heading up there tomorrow. She's spending a couple of days with Molly because she's not entirely sure Molly will talk to us." For a moment Luke struggled with the fact that the attraction he felt for Faye made him feel disloyal to Abby. Abby would be happy for him if something came of his relationship with Faye, he was certain.

"You're going up there without being certain your victim will talk to you?" Abby asked, bringing Luke's focus back to the victim, where it should be.

"I'm hoping she feels up to speaking with us. We have a lot to do before we meet with her anyway." Luke shared with Abby the work they'd done so far and where they planned on starting. For a couple of minutes the back-and-forth reminded him of when they were furiously working on the Triple Seven investigation. They clicked, they jibed when they talked about stuff like this, and it made him want more.

Woody interjected here and there, but he seemed distracted, hurting about Ralph, Luke thought.

"Why is the victim so reticent to speak to you two?"

"Faye thinks it's PTSD. And the victim's mother doesn't want us to give her false hope." Luke knew Abby was not nearly as frail as Molly, but he still couldn't bring himself to mention the trail leading to Lucy Harper.

"I understand that." Abby gave a knowing nod. "You should be certain about your facts, and exactly how firm her foundation is, before you sit her down. Don't string her along with vagaries."

"I would never do that," Luke said, holding Abby's gaze and loving that he saw strength and balance there, so much better than the uncertainty he'd seen right after the shooting. He wanted to reach across the divide and grip her hand.

But their food came, and instead he said a blessing, mentioning comfort for Woody and his loss.

Abby spoke up when he finished. "Sounds like you've got the bases covered with your case." She looked down at her food, and Luke got the distinct impression she had something else to say.

"What's on your mind?" he asked. "You think we missed something?"

She shook her head. "No, you guys are thorough. Listening to all of this has made me think that I'd like to help. If Dr. Collins can't get back to me right away, I may have a few days before I go back to work. Would you mind a little company?"

Luke and Woody exchanged glances as Luke's heart jumped in his throat. She'd read his mind. There was nothing he wanted more.

"We'd love your help. Molly might feel more comfortable talking to a woman, especially one who can totally empathize. When will you know about Collins?"

"I'll call him again first thing in the morning, then let Woody know. Sound good?"

Both Woody and Luke nodded in agreement.

"I have some other news. I don't know when—it could be a couple of months or more—but I'll eventually be making my way to Tehachapi on some family business. My uncle is in CCI up there. I'm waiting to be approved for visiting."

Luke felt his jaw go slack and saw that the news got Woody's attention as well. Simon Morgan's file was where the information on Lucy Harper was. Would he know about her possibly seeing Buck after the fire? Would he tell Abby?

"Simon?" Woody said, putting his sandwich back on the plate. "In the prison at Tehachapi? I thought he was in San Quentin."

"He was, but he calmed down and stopped being a problem

some time ago, apparently. He was moved to CCI about three years ago."

Luke was truly nonplussed. "What, uh . . . what made you decide to visit him?"

Abby sighed and Luke thought he saw a hesitation in her eyes.

"I don't mean to get personal . . ."

Cocking her head, she said, "It's not that. It's just that my aunt convinced me that I needed to talk to my uncle. He knew my father. He might have insight about him that could help me put any doubts to sleep."

"Doubts about whether or not he's alive?" Woody asked, and Luke shot him a glance. He really hadn't thought Abby would still struggle with that. The idea that she did gave him pause.

"Maybe a little." Abby hiked a shoulder, gaze thoughtful. "But I have gotten past it. Going home was good for me. Visiting my uncle is just a way of connecting with a long-lost family member and learning what he remembers about a dad I barely knew."

"You do sound as if getting away was just what you needed," Luke said.

"It was. I feel as though I'm on a firmer foundation now." She smiled and raised her glass. Luke did likewise with his tea, and Woody followed suit. The three toasted one more time.

"To the future," Abby said. "And catching bad guys and putting them in jail."

CHAPTER

-37-

MONDAY MORNING Luke found his thoughts drifting to his conversation with Abby after she returned home from Oregon. She'd called him after the lunch with Woody, assuring him that she was serious about wanting to help with the Cavanaugh investigation, and that surprised him. He also realized that no matter what was happening in either of their lives, they would always be connected by the Triple Seven.

"I'm sorry I ruined your time away, made you rush home."

"You didn't. I was already thinking it was time to come back."

"You'd only been gone a little over a week."

"Yeah, but I was running away. Anyway, don't worry about it. Woody sounds at peace with his shooting. I know how unnerving such a thing can be. How are you doing?"

"Like I said, I'm glad Woody is a good shot."

The sound of her chuckle, though subdued, was music to his ears.

"But why anyone like Ruiz," Luke said, *"or whoever he was working for, would be following me or burglarizing you is still a mystery."*

"Because it involves both of us, you know it has to be connected to the Triple Seven."

"Why would anyone care about that case anymore? It's closed, isn't it?"

"Tight, according to the chief, and I'm okay with that."

Luke almost shouted hallelujah when Abby made that statement: *"I'm okay with that."* She'd said it before, but this time he felt she meant it.

She'd also voiced what he'd been thinking, but neither of them could come up with any reason why.

"I highly doubt that Ruiz was working on his own."

"I agree."

"Look, Luke, in the past I've been accused of obsessing over the Triple Seven, but I'm not. I do trust that no one will escape justice, nothing stays hidden. That being said, I think someone else is still worried about being found out."

"I agree. Ruiz got orders from someone."

"I think we need to find out who. Quietly. I don't even want to say anything to Woody. This involves only us."

He'd agreed with her, seeing wisdom in keeping any poking around they did quiet. It bugged him. Who would have any reason to be worried enough about what they had in their personal files to hire a burglar? Abby went on to ask if this disturbing new development meant that Kent had lied about his role in the murders and only covered for the real killer. Abby's calm query surprised Luke because he thought she was still eager to dig and find answers.

Digging for the truth appealed to him more now than it had in a long time. The attack at his house had changed the dynamic for Luke, and when he shared that with Abby, she totally agreed and understood.

"This is just all too personal for us and the people close to us."

"Hey, Luke, you listening?"

Luke looked up and felt his face redden. "Sorry; what did you say?"

"You rethinking carrying a gun?" Woody asked.

Luke shook his head. "Not right now. I can't imagine being in another situation like that ever. If I see a tail in the future, I'm dialing 911 and stepping back."

The quiet while the shooting investigation was going on had left Luke champing at the bit to get out to the high desert and to meet with the tipster, Brenda Harris. He was tempered only slightly by the knowledge that the woman could be another dead end. Her tip went nowhere ten years ago, and it would be the wildest stroke of luck to think that it would go anywhere now. But paying attention to details meant he had to check.

———■———

Detective Carney had an opening for Abby on Monday morning. She stopped by the station to look over what he and O'Reilly had on Alonzo Ruiz.

"Was he recording things?" Abby asked after she read the report they'd filed about all of the high-tech equipment in Ruiz's car. "I'm almost 100 percent certain it was him following me. With all this stuff, he could have been tracking, recording . . ."

"He could have." Carney nodded. "But we've found no indication of any recordings, and the trackers were never activated. Of course, he could have been recording and downloading the stuff straight to someone."

"To who?" She met Carney's gaze. "Someone connected with the Triple Seven? That case is closed according to the chief."

Carney shook his head. "It's the only investigation that involves you both. And so far you two are the only ones referenced in Ruiz's sparse notes."

The notes had creeped Abby out. Ruiz had tracked her for a week after the shooting, noting when she came and went, when Ethan was there, and when Abby was alone.

"We're trying to figure out who he was working for," Carney continued. "And if he was working alone, why."

They were both silent for a moment.

"I'm just glad Jessica, Woody, and Luke are okay," Abby said.

Carney snickered. "That lady is a tough customer. Were you missing anything?"

"No, it just looks like he riffled through my files. I had my Triple Seven book with me if that's what he was after."

"We'll figure it out. Don't worry."

Abby smiled. "I'm not worried. You guys are the best."

"Are you coming back to work?"

"Yes, I am. But I'm not sure when Dr. Collins can fit me in. I have to talk to him before my return, and he's in the middle of a crisis today."

CHAPTER

-38-

KELSEY GRABBED the bottle of Advil and shook out four tablets, hoping they'd be enough to stop the pounding in her head. Nothing right now could help the feeling that she was losing her grip, she was hanging by one weak finger. She swallowed the pills without water and walked to the window of her hotel room. Years ago she'd learned the hard way that if you wanted something done right, you had to do it yourself. That had, in fact, been Gavin Kent's motto.

If only I had made it my motto and lived by it, she thought, opening the wet bar refrigerator to get a bottle of water. The Advil was stuck in her throat.

After a swallow of water, the pills went down, and she worked hard to develop a plan to dig herself out of the pit Alonzo Ruiz had dug for her. All he was supposed to do was keep track of Hart and Murphy, make sure they weren't opening doors they shouldn't. His interpretation of that order not only got him killed, it threatened to expose everything. She hoped against hope that there was nothing in his possessions to connect them. She'd already disposed of the phone she'd used to speak to him.

The only bright spot in the situation was that her employer was too involved in scheduling fund-raising events and kissing up to prospective donors to have heard what had happened.

Kelsey hoped, as she always did when Rollins made appearances and took questions from the press, that no one would ask about the Triple Seven. She knew the opposition was already considering running ads about the cold case and Gavin Kent's involvement to hint at some shadow over Lowell Rollins. So far, he'd been able to deflect, and it hadn't affected his approval numbers. If the subject came up in any interview, the governor always dodged, but it set Kelsey's boss off like a cherry bomb. The boss had even threatened to send a personal aide, Quinn, a man Kelsey hated, to help her keep a lid on the Hart problem.

I don't need anyone breathing down my neck about this, she thought, rubbing her shoulder. *Especially not a gorilla like Quinn.*

Kelsey believed she had time to clean up Ruiz's mess, but was loath to look for someone else to take his place. Ruiz had been Gavin's friend and contact. Gavin loved him because of his wizardry with electronics. There was no time to vet someone else. She had a short list of trustworthy people but hesitated to use it. After all, Ruiz had been the best as far as Gavin was concerned and he'd messed up. What if the next guy was worse?

She did what she learned to do as a cop: she organized all the information available to her and tried to map out her next move, always with the objective in mind to stop Hart and Murphy from opening any doors that needed to stay closed and keeping her boss placated and Quinn away.

If Hart weren't already back in Long Beach, Kelsey was certain the shooting would bring her back. Ruiz's bonehead move gave Kelsey a major migraine. She'd heard from her contact on the PD that Woods and Murphy would be heading to the Antelope Valley, and eventually as far as Tehachapi, on some cold case. She still didn't believe Murphy posed any threat at all to her employer, particularly out in the high desert, but she knew better than to say that, especially in light of what happened with Ruiz.

As much as Kelsey hated to admit it, she wasn't able to handle the situation herself. She needed eyes on Murphy, and she needed eyes on Hart. She couldn't be two places at once. She had to find someone she could trust. A name came to mind. He wasn't on her list, but he'd retired to the high desert and he liked cash. She knew him because he'd been a sheriff's deputy. He'd gotten into serious trouble in Long Beach a long time ago, when sheriff's deputies had been assigned to patrol North Long Beach during a budget crisis in the city, and she'd done him a favor. That favor had helped him keep his job and eventually his retirement. Kelsey made a point of keeping track of people who owed her. She was certain she could persuade him to do a little freelance surveillance. He didn't strike her as someone who would be careless like Ruiz had been.

The Advil finally kicked in. Kelsey found the man's number in her book and punched it in on her new burner phone.

"Jerry, I need a favor," she said after they caught up on old times.

"I figured. There's no reason for you to be talking to me unless you were calling in a marker."

His voice was not bitter; rather there was resignation there. Kelsey was certain she'd made the right choice.

"I need some surveillance out your way, discreet, with regular reports about what's happening." She detailed the situation for him.

"Hmm," Jerry said, then went quiet.

After a long minute while Kelsey held her breath, he said, "I can do that for the right price."

Kelsey exhaled and relaxed. Money wasn't an issue. They decided on a price and a method to connect with one another. He'd get a burner and text her. Headache gone, she disconnected and collapsed on the bed.

I can and have handled this. It will all work out in the end.

CHAPTER

-39-

AFTER THE WEEKEND, dealing with Ralph, then Monday's meeting with Carney, Abby found herself with nothing pressing to do but walk Bandit. She'd left a message over the weekend with Dr. Collins's answering service that she was home and was hoping for an appointment. They'd asked her if she had an emergency and she'd told them no. They advised that Dr. Collins was involved in a crisis and would call as soon as he was able. So far, she hadn't heard anything.

Abby thought about Luke and Woody's investigation and remembered Luke had a meeting with the tipster. The investigator in her felt a little pang of jealousy. That could be a good lead and she would have loved to be asking the questions. Once she and Bandit returned from the walk, she decided she'd try the doctor again. She called and was told Dr. Collins was almost free and would call her back as soon as he was able.

She wanted to return to work and had already spoken to Bill about their caseload. They discussed their double murder case; Carla Boston claimed temporary insanity. Bill still insisted Abby take her time.

"You handled things for a while without a partner. I can do the same until you're 100 percent sure about what you want."

At this point Abby wasn't 100 percent sure about anything but that the opportunity to try to help Molly was appealing. Her thoughts drifted to the girl often. Abby had looked up PTSD, or post-traumatic stress disorder, and realized it might even be applied to her, if she hadn't gotten past the turmoil over shooting Clayton Joiner. It was a disorder that affected some people after they saw or lived through a dangerous event. Even though Molly's event had happened ten years ago, it still affected her.

Abby ached to help the girl. Luke had e-mailed her a summary of the case, and she knew that Molly had faith, but right now it was fractured, something Abby could relate to. She reread the summary and had just finished when the psychologist returned her call.

"I'm doing much better," she told him in answer to his first question. "Going home helped me put things into perspective."

"Glad to hear it. Are you ready to discuss returning to work?"

"Yes, I am."

"It may not be right away, but I'll do my best. I'll need to set up an appointment to meet with you, and this week is full. Make an appointment for first thing next week. I'll give Lieutenant Jacoby an update and explain the scheduling. Is that fair?"

"Fair. Can I ask you an unrelated question?"

"Sure, I have a minute."

Abby told him about Molly and her desire to help since she believed that they both struggled with the same thing.

"Abby, it's laudable that you want to help, but you're not a mental health professional."

"I know that, but I am a detective. I'd like to help with the crime, see if we can solve the case and give the girl closure. That might be a big step forward for her, to see the rapist caught."

"Yes, but giving the girl false hope when the crime might never be solved would not be a good thing. Do your thing, investigate, but encourage the girl to find her validation in the here and now, the people who love and support her. Agreed?"

"Totally," Abby said, understanding and feeling an odd connection to the girl who'd been through such a tough event.

Collins rang off after she set up the appointment for the following Tuesday. She doubted Molly's case could be solved in a week, but at least she'd be able to talk to her and maybe help in a small way. She was on a firm foundation again, felt confident. Jacoby might even call and talk to her, and she'd tell him what she told the psychologist. She was ready to go back to homicide and be an advocate for those who could no longer speak for themselves. She also wanted to head out to the Antelope Valley and see if she could help a hurting girl.

She picked up the phone again to call Woody. Though she'd only heard about the girl through Luke and Woody, she felt she knew her.

Bad guys need to be caught.

The phone rang before she punched in Woody's number.

"Detective Hart, please." The voice was formal, clear.

"This is she."

"One moment please."

Abby realized that had been someone's secretary and she was being transferred. After a click, a deep baritone voice came over the phone.

"Detective Hart? This is Marcus Freeman. I represent Althea Joiner."

Abby's heart caught in her throat. How did this man get her phone number? She knew very well who he was. He wanted her fired. He was threatening to sue her for violating Clayton Joiner's civil rights, for wrongful death, and she forgot what else.

"This is Detective Hart. I'm not sure we should be speaking."

"I've cleared this conversation with the chief of police. I have a request from my client."

He paused, and Abby wondered if he was waiting for her response, but after a couple of seconds he went on. "Mrs. Joiner would like to meet with you. She has something she'd like to say and a few questions to ask you."

"Uh, I don't know what to say. . . ."

"I know this is irregular. It was not my suggestion. It's not a trap or a ploy; it is my client's wish, and I'm obligated to relay my client's wishes."

Abby got the distinct impression he wanted her to tell him to pound sand. And that was her first impulse. But she was too curious to pop off with the first thought that crossed her mind.

"Can I ask what she wants to talk to me about?"

"I'm not at liberty to say. I will say that the meeting is to be just the two of you. Are you familiar with Grounds Café on Spring Street?"

"Yes, I know the place."

"Mrs. Joiner would like to meet you there tomorrow morning."

"That's quick."

"Yes, it is. Shall I tell her you decline?"

This guy did not want the meeting to take place. *I must be obstinate,* Abby thought, *because just knowing he doesn't want me to meet with Althea makes me want to be there.* Before the shooting, Abby had liked Althea and thought that they had connected on one level. Althea had trusted her to find her daughter's killer, had even prayed with Abby and Bill a couple of times. A tinge of guilt bit Abby's gut as the shooting flashed in her mind, and she heard Althea's accusations.

I want to talk to her as well, she thought.

"Detective Hart?" Freeman sounded impatient.

"No, you can tell her I'll be there. What time?"

———▶

Althea's lawyer's request wasn't the only surprise of the day. Uncle Simon phoned that night as well.

Abby was prepared for the collect call. California prison inmates could not be phoned; they could only make collect calls. She'd expected her uncle would be contacting her once he knew that she submitted her visitation application. She accepted the charges. After a couple of clicks, she heard his voice.

"Hello?"

"Hello, Uncle Simon?"

"Yeah, wow! I'm so glad you agreed to talk to me and that you want to visit."

Abby swallowed. "I think we probably have a lot to talk about."

"You're right; we do. I'm not sure how long your approval will take, but I turned in the form. I'm so looking forward to your visit. You are all the blood family I have left."

He explained to her how visiting worked. She could walk in on a Saturday or Sunday or set up an appointment online.

"I'll let you know as soon as I know. I have a few minutes. How are you? I read about the stuff going on in your life."

"I'm okay. I—" For a second she fumbled, not sure what to say to a man she'd never met.

He read her mind. "Kinda funny talking to someone you don't know. You've probably only seen me in decades-old photographs."

Abby laughed. "That's true. From those, you looked a little like my dad."

"A little, but he was always better-looking. I lost my hair by the time I was thirty. Buck's hair was always thick and full. We corresponded for a time before he died, you know."

"No, I didn't know." This was a surprise to Abby. She'd always been told her father disowned his brother.

"Yeah, he kept it quiet because his partner didn't want any connection to a convict to overshadow the restaurant. I guess I can understand that." There was some noise and clanging in the background.

Abby wanted to ask him more questions, but he asked her to hold on for a minute.

"I have to go," he said when he returned. "I'll call again, maybe read you some of your dad's letters if you'd like."

"Yeah, I would like that. I really would."

"Okay, good-bye, Abby. It's really great to talk to you."

The call ended and Abby stared at the phone for a minute. Letters from her dad, his actual writing. She didn't know what to say, but the knowledge that such things existed made her feel warm and hopeful.

CHAPTER

40

AS LUKE DROVE TO HIS MEETING with Brenda Harris, he thought about their conversation when he'd initially found her. She was skeptical about him and about the investigation.

"That was so long ago. How can you still be interested in that tip?"

"The crime has never been solved. The young victim is having a difficult time. I'd like to give her the peace of closure."

Concern for the victim seemed to allay Harris's reticence, and they made an appointment to meet.

Luke recognized Brenda right away even though all he had was a driver's license photo. Brenda Harris could be an older version of Molly Cavanaugh. The petite blonde woman entered Panera a little after eleven thirty.

"Mrs. Harris?" He stepped toward her. "I'm Luke Murphy." He handed her his ID. "Can I buy you a cup of coffee?"

She looked at the ID, then looked at Luke and shook her head. "No, that's okay. I don't drink coffee. I just picked a nice crowded public place to meet you."

Luke smiled and motioned to a table where they both sat down.

"You're not an LA County sheriff. Why are you investigating this case?"

He told her about Faye Fallon, her blog, and the cold case.

"If you really think you can solve this, why are you talking to me? I thought Gil was in Iraq at the time of the crime; he couldn't be your guy."

"I couldn't find any record of him serving in Iraq. Who told you he was there?"

Her brows scrunched together. "I don't remember now where I heard that. It must have been from one of the original investigators." She looked down and rubbed her forehead. "Yes, I think that's who told me, a long time ago. I was so sure it was Gil, and he said that it couldn't be. But it did surprise me that Gil joined the armed forces. He never seemed the type."

Luke considered that, wondering if this was a waste of time. "Well, we're starting over from the beginning. There were many tips, but yours was one of the few who left contact information. And you were convinced the composite was Gilbert Barone. I wanted to show it to you again and ask what made you so certain. Do you remember?" He slid the composite across the table.

Brenda took a deep breath and slid it back. "Unfortunately I will never forget. That guy was my personal nightmare. I lived next door to him—rather, his parents—in Northridge." She shuddered. "It was a wonderful place to live at first. His parents were really nice people. His dad was always helping me out. I'd just moved to California from Utah, got my first engineering job in the valley. His mom was a saint, but she got sick.

That was when Gil moved back in. He was in his twenties, I think, twenty or twenty-one. There was some nasty gossip in the neighborhood that he got kicked out of college for some perverted reason, but that's just gossip. Anyway, Gil was very good-looking. I noticed him right away. Because his dad had been so nice, I just assumed the son would be the same." She shook her head.

"Not a chip off the old block?"

"Not at all. One day I saw him out in the yard and engaged him in conversation. I guess he thought I was coming on to him. Next thing I know, he's knocking on my back door. It scared me half to death because I had a fenced-in yard. I answered the door, and he's asking me if I want to get high with him. I told him no. I was a working person. I had a job that did drug tests. I didn't get high. But the way he looked at me was so disturbing, like he was imagining me without my clothes on."

"I take it he didn't like being turned down."

"You got that right. That was when the nightmare started. I swear he stalked me. He prowled around in my backyard at night trying to peep in my windows, he vandalized my car, but the worst . . ." Her voice trailed off and she took a deep breath. "The worst was when he broke into my house. I know it was him. I came home and found all my underwear spread around my bedroom and in the center of the bed some of the most graphic, disgusting pornography. I'd never seen anything like it and I hope I never do again."

"You're sure he did all of this? You called the police?"

"Of course I did. But I had no proof it was him. I just knew—I can't explain how, but I just knew. Anyway, after that, I packed up some things and left. It was a rental, so I just moved out. When I saw the composite . . . Well, that's Gil. It's as if he posed for it."

"Did you ever talk to Gil's dad about his son?"

She shook her head. "That poor man. His wife was dying. I didn't have the heart to say anything."

"Do you remember what college he went to? Where he was kicked out?"

"I think Long Beach State." She frowned. "But if Gil was in Iraq when the rape happened, why do you even care about any of this?"

———■▶

Luke thought about Gil Barone on the drive back to Long Beach. The college was near his home, so he made a stop there to see if the man had been a student. The only information they would give him was whether or not he had been enrolled. Barone had been a student from 2000 to 2001. What classes he took or why he left was information Luke could get only with a subpoena.

When he got home, he did a computer search for Barone and laughed out loud when he found a match. A Gil Barone owned a computer repair shop in Tehachapi. He clicked on the website for the store. There was a head shot of Barone, but this man was bearded and it was impossible to compare the small square image with the composite. But the details fit: Barone would be the right age, and the name was not all that common. Luke felt confident this was the man he was looking for. Even more so when he saw a small paragraph that said Barone had moved from Northridge five years previous. The blurb was from an endorsement page, a customer raving about the service he got, driving all the way to Tehachapi from Northridge whenever he had a computer problem, being worth the time and money.

Luke read every comment on the endorsement page. Customers loved Barone. But then he certainly wouldn't put negative comments on his website. He couldn't wait to tell Woody. They'd add visiting Barone to the list and, he hoped, hit pay dirt.

Luke was sure he was at least Brenda's old neighbor and quite possibly a vicious rapist. And maybe even a serial killer.

CHAPTER

-41-

"IT'S NO PROBLEM AT ALL, Mrs. Gentry. It was an easy problem to fix." Gil Barone smiled his best smile. Gil knew it was pleasant and disarming no matter what was going on in his mind.

"Oh, but you had to take time out of your day. Please let me pay you."

He shook his head. "Nonsense. It was my pleasure."

"Well, I'll be baking this weekend. Maybe I can bring by a pie?"

Gil grinned. "Now *that* I would never refuse."

The woman nodded and picked up her laptop. Gil had reformatted the drive and added security software after the woman had picked up a virus and crashed her system. While he thought the woman was an idiot, she was the wife of the mayor, and Gil knew it paid to have friends in high places.

"I'll see you on Saturday then."

The phone began to ring. Gil wheeled himself over to answer it.

"Gil?"

"Yeah, that's me. Who is this?" Gil did not recognize the voice.

"It's me, Jerry G."

Gil recognized the man now. He was an acquaintance of his father's, not really a friend because his dad had never liked him. Jerry G. had issues. He was into kiddie porn. Gil had erased a hard drive for him once when Jerry came to him terrified that the police were going to seize his computer.

"Sure, I remember you, Jerry." Wary now, Gil wondered what the creep was up to. "What can I do for you?"

"I know that I owe you, and I may have something that will go a long way toward clearing that debt. I have a little work to throw your way, if you're interested."

"Computer work? Sure."

"Not computer work. This is easier. I just need you to keep tabs on some people who are going to be in your neck of the woods."

"That's not my line of work." *How is this paying the debt?* Gil wondered.

"I'll make it worth your while. Ever heard of that blogger, Faye Fallon?"

Gil made a rude noise. "Who hasn't? She's easy on the eyes."

Jerry told Gil about some private investigators coming to Tehachapi at the request of Fallon.

"My employer just wants to know where they are and what they do. I'll send you a brief description of everything, and like I said, there's money here, a lot for little work."

"Give me a minute to think about it." Gil set the phone down on the counter and scratched his beard. His legitimate computer business did well, and so did his illegitimate business. He wasn't wanting for money. He'd also branched out into security systems, camera systems, and any miscellaneous technology problems he could solve. He wanted his adopted hometown of Tehachapi safe and sound.

If this was just surveillance on out-of-towners, he wouldn't be fouling anything. And it sounded as if the job wouldn't take much energy. It might even be entertaining if it involved the looker Faye Fallon. The man on the other end of the phone had been a cop, a crooked one. Growing up, Gil had hated cops because he'd hated his father. He'd always worked to avoid them. But now he saw them as a new challenge to manipulate. Sometimes they were smarter than the average guy, but not often. And Gil loved to pull one over on a cop. He knew firsthand that Jerry wasn't the sharpest knife in the drawer, but the fact that he wanted someone watched and it involved an adult skirt made Gil curious.

Yeah, it might be worth his time to find out what this little job was all about. He picked up the phone.

"Sure, Jerry. I'll help you out. E-mail me the specifics." Gil gave him an untraceable e-mail address and disconnected.

He turned to his laptop and looked for the Fallon blog. What was it called? He tried to think. He knew the woman was a Holy Roller. The title of her blog was like a Bible saying. He gave up and just punched in her name.

The blog popped up right away, and he scowled.

Justice, a Joy to the Righteous—A Blog for Safety-Minded High Desert Dwellers

What a stupid name. But he knew she had a lot of readers, even here in Tehachapi, though she wrote primarily for the

Antelope Valley. People were always talking about her blogs on the state of crime in the area.

"Cold Case Warriors Set to Visit the Valley" was the title of her latest entry. He read the piece through, and for the first time in a long time, he felt fear bite.

Closing the laptop and pushing his chair back from the counter, Gil stroked his beard and took a calming breath. He was smarter than they were. Even with the DNA there was no way they'd ever connect him to that crime. No way.

CHAPTER

-42-

"I'VE GOT A FRIEND who works for Cal State Long Beach police,"
Woody told Luke after being updated on what Brenda Harris
had said. "He's been there for thirty years. He'd know if there
was a complaint filed against this guy, Barone, through the campus PD."

They were in a rental car office waiting for their ride to be
brought up from the lot. They had decided to make the trip to
Tehachapi in a rental, figuring a full-size sedan would look more
official than Luke's pickup truck or Woody's beat-up Saturn.

"Can you get ahold of him?"

"I'll call him right now." Woody activated his phone. "He
might have to research it a bit. I'm not sure how long it took
campus police to get everything computerized. In 2001 LBPD
was still lagging behind in that area."

Woody phoned his friend and left a detailed voice mail message. "Sheldon is a good guy. He'll come through." He put the
phone back on his belt as the rental car guy waved them out
to a vehicle.

Luke and Woody started their trip to the Antelope Valley

with a plan. They wanted to be familiar with the area in which the crime occurred, and they wanted an idea about the timing involved. Luke wasn't sure he liked that he was getting used to the drive along the 14, the Antelope Valley freeway, through Canyon Country, Acton, and assorted dry, high desert communities. The Antelope Valley, or AV, specifically the Palmdale/Lancaster area, was considered high desert. It was actually part of the Mojave Desert. He knew from his research that the Tehachapi and the San Gabriel mountain ranges bounded in part the western end of the Mojave Desert. The Tehachapi range was ahead of them and the San Gabriel behind. The desert itself was huge and ranged between three thousand and six thousand feet in elevation. It generally received less than six inches of rain a year. That made sense to Luke. It was just desert, barren and kind of ugly.

Known chiefly for Edwards Air Force Base, the area had had its share of housing booms and busts over the years. Affordable housing boomed in the eighties and nineties, then crashed with the housing market. The commute from Palmdale/Lancaster to LA was a long nightmare, and when the job market crashed in LA, thousands of houses went into foreclosure in the Antelope Valley. Luke remembered reading conflicting accounts about whether the community had fully recovered from the 2008 crash. He knew the valley primarily from driving through it on the way to fishing and skiing in Mammoth Lakes. All along the 14 freeway, they passed through brown canyons sparsely dotted with homes, and he wondered how anyone could consider this a great place to live.

"Makes me thirsty just to look at all this dryness," Woody said as if reading Luke's mind.

"Me too. It reminds me a bit of Iraq, just no sheep or shepherds. Or bombs."

"I worked with a kid for a little while who liked it out here. Said his money would buy him a much nicer house than he could get in Long Beach. He ended up quitting the PD and getting a job out here somewhere."

"Hope he's happy." Luke knew that if he lived out here, he'd miss the ocean and the beaches he was close to now.

They'd been on the road for two hours when they dropped down across the LA aqueduct and into Palmdale. The mall was on the west side of the freeway, and they exited on Rancho Vista. Ten years ago Molly and her family had lived on the other side of the Antelope Valley freeway, off Pear Blossom Highway, about fifteen minutes from the mall. They moved to Tehachapi after the crime, not only because of the incident, but also because Molly's father got a job at a school there.

After circling the mall, checking out the bus stop, and getting their bearings, they started out for the area where Molly was assaulted. Woody drove as Luke timed the trip from the Antelope Valley Mall to where the sexual assault would have occurred, a location close to Highway 138. They knew that the defunct mall was gone, replaced a few years ago by a big-box store.

"Molly said that before the assault, after they left the mall, the man was nice and polite." Luke held a copy of the police report in his hands. "She and the suspect were talking about a band. Molly was wearing a Switchfoot T-shirt; the suspect said he'd seen them in concert. It was a few minutes before she realized he wasn't following her directions. He wasn't taking her home; he was traveling the wrong way."

He turned the page, looking up and noting that it took

fifteen minutes for Woody to reach the spot where the strip mall would have been.

"He apologized and pulled into the parking lot as if he was going to turn around. But once he was around back, his entire demeanor changed. Molly said it was like he yanked on an evil mask. He produced a knife, forced her into the backseat." Luke bit back his anger and skimmed this part. "She begged him to let her go. He slapped her several times, saying, 'You can't stop me. I'm the top of the food chain and you're just an afternoon snack.'"

"Definitely a sick groundhog who needs to be stopped," Woody said, turning to Luke with a frown. He'd pulled over to the side in order to be certain about what direction to travel next.

Luke shook his head and continued. "Once he was finished, he bound her hands and feet and tossed her into the trunk. He told her that where they were going, no one would hear her scream, so stay quiet and save her strength." He looked up. "From here, she was pretty sure he turned left. And that makes sense if we are to reach the spot where she was rescued after escaping from the trunk." Luke pointed to the map. It was out in the general direction of Rosamond.

Woody nodded and headed that way, traveling on Highway 138 for a few miles before turning onto 140th Street West.

Molly told police officers at the time that it felt as if the man drove for an hour before she managed to free her hands. There was no way to know the exact route the rapist took. Woody followed the path that the sheriff had indicated to travel. He drove the speed limit, angling for the spot on the map where Molly was rescued. While Palmdale and the area around the mall had been dense with development, it was not so out here. Palmdale gave way to a part of Lancaster, full of tumbleweeds and scrub brush. Luke remembered reading that the Air Force personnel who found Molly were driving around looking for a safe place to do some target practice. There would be few other reasons for anyone to be out here. Woody had spoken to them on the phone, but neither was able to shed any more light on that day in the desert.

Luke settled back in his seat. For the entire time the suspect drove, Molly worked to free her hands. Luke glanced down at the pictures taken of her when she was in the hospital. She sported a black eye, and both wrists were bloody and rope-burned. The deputies who responded said that if it did take a whole hour to get to where Molly was found, the suspect was taking his time. Luke wasn't surprised by the discrepancy. He imagined that for Molly, brutalized and tied up in the dark trunk of a predator's car, any amount of time probably felt like an eternity.

He watched the scenery go by as development thinned out into empty spaces. From the map he could see several small airfields out here and a whole lot of nothing. One of the responding deputies had thought perhaps the suspect was heading to Tylerhorse Canyon, a canyon actually located on the Pacific Coast Trail, and considered to be in Rosamond, which was in Kern County, not LA County. But that was pure conjecture; there was no way to be certain. Luke couldn't imagine what Molly went through on this hot and dusty drive, and he thanked God she'd survived.

At least it was cool today, Luke thought, not desert hot. Fall temperatures reigned; he guessed it was about seventy. Woody crept along, and Luke read weathered signs that advertised a new housing subdivision. Letters were missing but Luke guessed the place was to be called "Quiet Oasis" with homes priced from the low $200,000s. Obviously the project never materialized. They eventually reached vague dirt roads and pads for the houses, but too many years had passed since anyone had done anything with them, and they were fading like sand structures under the onslaught of the waves.

Luke cringed at the thought of sixteen-year-old Molly, barefoot, half-clothed, and scared to death, running out here looking for someone to save her. Thank God the Air Force guys had been here. The landscape was desolate.

Woody stopped the car, and he and Luke climbed out to look around, more to stretch than expecting to find anything.

"He could have been planning to dump her anywhere. Probably had a shovel in the car," Woody said, hands on hips, surveying the area.

Luke nodded. "Yep. Deputies looked, but this is the middle of nowhere." He turned at the sound of an approaching vehicle. "I guess not quite nowhere. I wonder where they're going."

A large SUV was headed for them and slowed to a stop when it reached them.

The driver's window rolled down, and a bemused woman poked her head out. "What are you guys doing? Is the housing project going to be restarted?"

"Nope, not by us," Woody said. "We're conducting an investigation into an old crime."

"Oh, okay. Did something happen that I should be aware of?"

"It happened ten years ago." Luke gave her a brief recap and one of his cards. "Are you familiar with the area? Ever seen anything strange?"

"I vaguely remember that case. I've lived here all my life. But now the only strange and sad thing I see are dumped animals. People lose their house and can't take their dog to an apartment, so they find a remote spot and leave them. That's about the only reason people drive to this area. I'm with the local dog rescue. Maybe if the housing project was revived, dumping animals would happen less in this spot."

"You find a lot of dogs?" Woody asked.

The woman rolled her eyes. "Too many."

"What happens to them when you find them?"

"We evaluate them, get them medical attention if they need it. Find them foster homes and place them with new families if we can."

"I love dogs. Just had to put one of the best dogs ever down. He was a seventeen-year-old Lab."

"Oh, I'm sorry for your loss. Here's a card." The woman held out her hand with a business card in it. "I'm Carol. We have a website. If you're looking for another dog, consider rescuing one. I'm sure we'd find one that would be perfect for you."

"Thanks." Woody took the card.

"I'm looking for a pregnant Lab mix. Have you seen any dogs?"

Both Woody and Luke said no.

"We've seen no signs of life so far," Luke said.

"We'll keep our eyes open," Woody said as he put the card in his wallet.

"I hope you solve the case," Carol said before she rolled the window back up and drove off over the dirt road.

"I guess we've done all we can do here." Luke looked at Woody.

"Agreed. Let's get going to the next stop."

As they climbed back into the car, Luke's thoughts went to the next stop, lunch with Faye. He looked out the passenger window and smiled with anticipation, truly looking forward to spending time with the beautiful, compassionate blogger.

CHAPTER

43

AFTER RETRACING THE CRIME, Woody and Luke finished their survey and made the hour drive to Tehachapi, arriving a little after one. They checked into the hotel Faye Fallon recommended, and Luke sent her a text.

"She wants us to meet her at a deli," Luke told Woody. "That place we drove by, the one you thought looked good."

"Great. I'm starved."

Luke agreed, and a few minutes later they ordered a late lunch and joined Faye at a table in a wonderful-smelling German deli.

"So did the two of you find anything on your tour of the valley?" Faye asked. Luke couldn't help but notice how casually beautiful the woman looked wearing jeans, a light-green sweater, and a baseball cap, her long blonde hair pulled into a ponytail and sticking out the back of the cap.

"Unfortunately, no," Luke said. "But we have perspective."

They went over their reconstruction of the crime, the time line, and their investigation so far.

Faye looked over their notes. "Thanks. You guys are doing

a great job. You sifted through so much in such a short time. I'm not at all worried about the statute of limitations expiring before you stir up a good lead."

Their lunch came and for the next few moments everyone concentrated on their meals.

Luke swallowed a bite of his ham sandwich. "Yesterday I did get a chance to talk to the person who called that tip in ten years ago, the one I asked you about." He told her about his meeting with Brenda Harris.

"It's odd that the tip would have been left hanging. I certainly never heard anything about it."

"Not really so odd," Woody said. "I've been on task forces, big deals where there's a tip line open. So much information is generated in a short period of time. It wouldn't surprise me if someone made a note of 'Iraq' and meant to follow it up, but never got back to it for one reason or another. I hate to say it, but cops are human; things get missed."

"It would be nice if that pans out." Fallon frowned.

"What's the matter?" Luke asked.

"That name, Barone. Ever since you called, I've been thinking. It's vaguely familiar."

"I found him. He owns a computer shop here in town."

"Here?"

Luke nodded.

"That's not it. I see a tech guy in Palmdale if I need help." She made a face of frustration.

"From the crime file?"

"No, I can't place it." She shrugged. "It will come to me. I'm afraid I have bad news as far as Molly is concerned."

"She's not ready to talk to us."

"No, not at all. I think I told you that she was hit by a car a week ago and is working through some pain and being slightly immobile. She's not up for any company. Sorry."

"Don't apologize. I understand. But I'd like to throw a new wrinkle into the mix." He told her about Abby, her offer of help, and her background, why she might be the right person to talk to Molly. "If we call her, she'll be here as soon as she can. What do you think?"

"I've read about Detective Hart, I know her story, and I think that's a great idea. I'll talk to Molly's mom tonight and text you. Is that okay?"

"Perfect. We have some other things to work on—I want to talk to Gil Barone for one—and then we're doing some work on another case. It will be great if Molly changes her mind and talks to Abby."

After lunch, Woody excused himself to go to the restroom and left Luke alone with Faye.

She smiled warmly. "I can't thank you guys enough for coming up here and looking into this case."

"Even if nothing pans out?"

"I'm an optimist. I'm praying something will pan out. And—" she paused—"in a way, something has panned out: I've met you and your partner. We have a lot in common, I think."

Luke nodded, appreciating the optimism. "We do. We all want to see justice done."

Her expression mellowed, saddened for a minute. "Yes, it was my husband's greatest desire to be a police officer, to help people who were victimized by criminals. You remind me a lot of Jared. I wonder why you didn't enter a career in law enforcement."

Luke explained to her how he'd started at the police academy but dropped out after he realized how much time he'd spend away from Maddie. "It's worked out. I love what I do now, and I still get to spend a lot of time with my daughter."

Woody came back and Luke and Faye stood.

"Thank you both again," Faye said. Pausing, she looked at Luke. "I hope when all this is over, we can sit down and talk more about the cold case squad and life in general."

Luke felt his heart warm and looked forward to that sit-down.

CHAPTER

44

THE BELL OVER THE DOOR JINGLED, and Bart walked in.

Gil nodded toward him. "News?"

"Yep, it was pretty easy. Fallon is here. I don't mind following her around." Bart leered at Gil. "She's staying at the La Quinta, and she just met with two guys I never saw before."

"What is she doing here, anyway?" He'd not told Bart the whole story; he'd only said there was money in keeping an eye on Fallon and a couple other people. Bart was, after all, his legs, the one who could sneak about without being obvious.

"She's all worked up about a cold rape case, like the guy said. I bought some coffee and listened for a little bit while she talked with the two guys. Apparently they're private investigators here to work on the case. I left when they started eating lunch. Got the license plates for both cars, like you asked." Bart handed him a sticky note.

"A cold rape case?" Gil took the paper. "Fallon is always on about crime in her blog. Why this cold rape case?" Gil wanted to know if the reason that the case was being investigated now was because of a new lead. He didn't think that was possible—in fact, he'd bet good money this was just a shot in the dark—but he'd like to know what the people were saying.

"I don't know. Something about the statute of limitations. You know that chick—it's always about crime and victims." Bart made an L with his thumb and forefinger and held his hand up.

Gil agreed. Faye Fallon was a loser in one respect, but not in another. He bet every red-blooded American male in the AV knew Faye Fallon. Gil loved to fantasize about him and Fallon, what they could do together if he still had two good legs. But the money phrase was "statute of limitations." That was why the case was being reinvestigated. There were no new leads.

"Bart?"

"Yeah, boss?"

"I'm going to go home for a bit. Can you handle things here?"

"Sure. Anything wrong?"

"Nah, just need some downtime. Be back in a couple hours."

Gil rolled out of the store and into his van. The fear was gone, replaced by calculation. He needed to know everything there was to know about these "cold case warriors." Jerry had e-mailed him quite a bit of information. He doubted they'd ever get remotely close to him, but if they did, he'd show them what he was made of. Along with hacking, Gil was proficient with weapons and explosive devices. He could also make their electronic world a nightmare if he chose to. And if worse came to worse, with his knowledge of electronics, it would be a piece of cake to set up some kind of device on a timer or a remote and blow those two investigators to bits. Whatever he did, he'd plan it carefully.

Once home and safely locked inside his man cave, he powered up his personal computer, set up with an Internet connection that was more secure than the Pentagon's.

Luke Murphy was easy to find, YouTube videos and all. Gil sneered. For such a proficient PI, he wasn't that computer savvy. He had some safety protocols on his home computer, but in half an hour Gil was through them, and he knew everything there was to know about the private investigator. Still lived with his mommy and daddy. Hmm, he had a pretty little daughter.

Gil checked out the kid's electronic trail and then filed away what he knew about her, thinking it might be useful at a later date.

The other guy, Robert Woods, was more problematic. He didn't have an electronic trail. There were a couple news articles about him. Gil pulled them up and printed them out. The guy was old, probably didn't know anything about computers. Gil's dad had resisted computers to his dying day.

His next foray into cyberspace was to find the victim. He never knew the full name of his victim ten years ago, and the blog only used a first name and gave no address. Gil knew it wouldn't be a problem to ferret that information out for himself. He could access so many databases that he had no business accessing.

When he found the girl, he sat back and laughed. She was right in his backyard, living in Lancaster, working for an ambulance company. And she had family living even closer, here in Tehachapi. If he could still stand, he would have been dancing. He doubted that she would be able to identify him now, but seeing her name and remembering the night she got away made him angry. He picked up the grip strengthener he kept on his desk and began to squeeze, five times with the left hand, and then transfer to the right.

The anger took him back in time to when he had two legs

and the perfect MO. Picking up stupid girls, doing what he wanted with them because he was stronger and smarter, was a blast, proving each and every time he was at the top of the food chain. He'd successfully dumped three empty-headed girls out in the desert before this one, and it irritated him to no end that she got away. That night, when he saw her running, and then the other headlights, he panicked. The first and last time he'd ever given in to that emotion.

He'd fled, knowing that he was headed out of the country the next day. It was an irony. He'd been trying to get out of the trip to Iraq, was having too much fun hunting girls, had even considered not showing up and letting the plane leave without him, no matter the consequences. As it was, he was the first guy to arrive at the staging area, congratulating himself because being in Iraq was the perfect alibi.

He remembered thinking he'd finish the job with the girl when he returned home, but the accident changed everything, changed him forever. Until this stupid pair of cold case warriors reminded him of his one great failure, Gil had actually begun to think of life after the accident as different, but better. He'd proven he was still as dangerous and capable as ever, maybe more so because of his talent with computers.

This could not stand. He had to deal with this girl, put an end to any investigation as soon as possible. He knew that he could; he had the skills. But he needed to figure out the best way, the most devastating way. And he would. Maybe he'd even take care of Faye Fallon as well.

CHAPTER

-45-

ABBY PRAYED about her meeting with Althea. She wasn't sure what the woman could want with her, but she knew it was the right thing to accept the invitation.

Grounds Bakery & Café was one of Abby's favorites, but she didn't make it to the shop on Spring Street often. Abby arrived early and ordered coffee, hoping that by having it in hand, and already sipped, her nerves would settle.

She took a seat in a corner where she could look out the window and saw Althea arrive. There was a man with her, and Abby tensed. Was this some kind of setup?

The couple stopped at the curb and seemed to be arguing. Althea was insisting he stay outside—Abby could discern that much by her gestures—while the man was trying to keep her from going inside. A lot of hand gestures and angry expressions went back and forth before Althea turned away from the man. Was he the lawyer, Freeman? Abby had never seen the man, so she didn't know. But Althea left him standing there fuming and strode into the bakery.

Abby stood and the woman saw her immediately. Althea was

a striking woman. Adonna had looked like her mother. Smooth chocolate-brown skin; tall, lean frame; she'd played professional basketball and moved purposefully, like an athlete. But her lean frame was thinner today, painfully thin.

Her features were set in pain—Abby could see that and almost feel it when the woman saw her. She pointed to the coffee counter, and Abby understood she was going to purchase a beverage. Nodding, Abby sat down in her chair again, fiddled with her coffee cup, and worked to stay relaxed. People in pain were dangerous; she knew that and fought the jolting urge to leave, to say this was a bad idea.

A few minutes later Althea arrived at the table and sat across from Abby. She was silent for a moment and sipped her coffee. She shifted in her chair and looked up. "Thank you for meeting me, Detective Hart."

"Please, it's Abby." She gestured to the man outside, who was still there, pacing and occasionally looking their way. "I take it that man didn't want you to meet me."

"No. That's my brother. He can't forgive you. He wants me to sue, to get you fired." A muscle jumped in her jaw, and she set the cup down, looking toward her brother. "Part of me can't forgive either. It hurts. I've lost my family."

Abby paid no attention to the threats of lawsuits or of a firing. Althea's pain was too obvious, her struggle too apparent. Abby felt it across the table, and a lump rose in her throat.

"If there were anything I could have done differently, I would have done it," Abby said, voice thick.

"I try to put myself in your place." Voice breaking, Althea drew in a breath. "I hate what happened, but I can't hate you." A tear rolled down her cheek; bracelets clanked on her wrist as she swiped it away. "I know you did your job. It's not just forgiving you I struggle with; it's forgiving Clayton as well. He never should have rushed out there like he did." She paused to blow her nose and looked Abby in the eye. "I've been on my knees in prayer about this. I know I will see my baby girl and my man again in heaven someday. I also know I can't honor their memory if I stay bitter and angry like my brother. I hurt worse than I ever thought I could hurt and still be standing. I needed to look you in the eye and say that I forgive you." She reached her hand across the table and gripped Abby's. "It's only by saying it that maybe, one day, I'll feel it."

Abby couldn't stop her own tears from falling as she held Althea's hand. "I'm so sorry. I thank you, Althea; I do."

"Don't thank me. Thank the Lord we both serve. The Lord can and does bring good out of the bad, the painful. And I know that you know my hurt. My prayer for you is that you keep working for those like my Adonna, to make sure we are safe, even if you run into more people like Clayton who can't wait for justice and try their own way."

"I promise you that I will." With those words, and the burning in her throat and eyes, Abby resolved never to run and hide from the work she did. Her calling was law enforcement, and she gritted her teeth and vowed to remember the most important thing: being a voice for those who couldn't speak, catching killers. Even through the tears she knew her vision was clearing.

CHAPTER

-46-

AFTER MEETING WITH FALLON, Luke and Woody returned to their hotel room and set up a mini investigation board. Luke ignored the raised eyebrows Woody tossed his way at the mention of Faye's invitation.

"Gil Barone is all we have to explore right now," Luke said.

"I agree," Woody said. "I've been racking my brains looking for another angle but . . ."

The buzz of Luke's phone stopped his response. It was Faye.

"Good news," she said. "Molly wants to talk to Abby."

"You sound surprised," Luke said.

"I guess I am. But Abby's background touched Molly. The only thing is, Molly's mom wants to meet her first."

"I'm sure that will be fine. We'll call Abby, and my bet is that she'll head up here first thing tomorrow. Why don't we plan on meeting again for lunch at the same place?"

Faye agreed, and when Luke disconnected, he asked Woody to call Abby.

Woody got her voice mail and left a message.

While they waited for her call, they returned to Barone and discussed how to handle his interview.

"I'd like to get a feel for the guy," Luke said. "I realize this is a long shot . . ."

"But right now it's our only shot. If he doesn't pan out, we're back where they were when the tips began to dry up."

"If he comes up hinky, how do you want to handle it?"

"I thought about trying to put together something of a six-pack, or just asking Molly to take a good look, but . . ."

"We're not sure how strong Molly is, what her frame of mind is like."

"Right, so maybe the best thing to do would be to try to get an opportunity DNA sample and have it tested and wait and see."

"That's an idea." Luke wrote that on the board with a question mark. He knew the term. An opportunity sample was obtained by recovering something the suspect touched, drank from, or smoked. He'd read about officers getting viable samples by swabbing the door handles of the suspect's vehicle, or from discarded cigarette butts or coffee cups. If Barone did prove to be suspicious, Luke doubted he'd voluntarily give a sample.

Woody's phone rang. From the conversation, Luke recognized it was Abby returning his call. She was excited about being able to help and would be up the next day around lunchtime to meet them. Woody looked at Luke as he relayed the news.

Luke hiked a shoulder. They were planning on a side trip to Bakersfield regarding Lucy Harper tomorrow. "We'll be back in time, I'm sure."

Woody told Abby about the deli and made the meeting firm before ending the call. Luke shot off a text to Faye that they were set for the next day.

They worked for a little while longer before calling it a day. The plan was to stop at the computer shop on the way to Bakersfield. Whatever happened with Barone, they would still continue the search for Lucy Harper. Again Luke found himself bothered that they had not mentioned the possible Triple Seven lead to Abby.

He calmed his anxiety by telling himself they really wouldn't know anything until they found Lucy, if she was even the right person, so his worry was useless.

———————◼▶

The computer store was one of three businesses in a corner center. There was a Starbucks on one end, an Italian restaurant in the middle, and then the Tehachapi Computer Depot, and it was on the way out of town. As Luke turned into the lot and parked, Woody's phone rang.

"You go ahead," he said to Luke. "I need to answer this. Be right behind you."

Luke nodded and headed into the Depot. The store was well stocked with all types of electronics, reminding Luke of a RadioShack. There was a glass case that spanned the back wall where the cash register was, and a man Luke assumed was an employee standing behind it. Because there was no way the skinny guy with a pockmarked face was Gil Barone. He was helping someone with a laptop, and he reminded Luke of one of the nerds from *Revenge of the Nerds*.

Not wanting to interrupt, Luke browsed, slowly moving

closer to the counter. The shop was neat, orderly. Barone took care of Apple computers and PCs. He sold home security systems and electronics of all kinds, even drones. It was a fascinating shop, and Luke almost wished he were here to make a purchase. He did need a new security system, and it'd be cool to be able to take home a drone and play with it.

The customer finished, thanked the salesman, calling him Bart, and then left the store. Luke approached the counter.

"Can I help you?" Bart asked.

For a second, Luke thought he saw recognition cross the man's face and he wondered why but let it pass. "I'm looking for Gil Barone."

"He hasn't come to work yet. Is there something I can help you with?"

"I need to speak with him. Will he be in later?"

"He should be."

Luke pulled out one of his cards. "Here's my card. I'll try to stop by later. He can call me if he wants."

"What is this about?" Bart frowned as he looked at the card.

"I'm investigating an old crime. Mr. Barone might have been a witness." Luke fibbed because he doubted saying that Barone was a suspect would get him anywhere. "I'd just like to speak to him." He heard the door open, and Woody walked in.

Luke turned away from Bart. "He's not in. We'll try to catch up with him another time."

Woody nodded.

Luke thanked Bart, wondering to himself what the bewildered, stressed expression on his face meant. An innocent person would likely be curious about what an investigator wanted, but a guilty person would likely be stressed. Did this employee know something about Barone that caused his stress?

Or am I just reading too much into the situation? Am I too anxious to find a suspect? Luke cautioned himself to dial it back a bit. Barone was innocent until proven guilty.

Once back in the car, Luke entered the address for Lucy Harper into his Garmin.

"You want to call first?" Woody asked.

Luke shook his head. "I've found that it's often better to just show up. Calling gives people warning; sometimes that means warning to disappear. I'm 95 percent certain this is our Lucy Harper. Let's just hope we catch her home."

As they pulled out of the lot, Luke noticed a van in the handicapped parking spot. A wheelchair ramp was being lowered, but traffic cleared, and he pulled out of the lot without seeing who got out of the van.

CHAPTER

-47-

"WHY WOULD THOSE INVESTIGATORS, the ones we're supposed to be keeping an eye on, be looking for you?" Bart asked.

Gil hated the whine that slipped into Bart's voice when he was stressed. He looked down at the card in his hand. "I have no idea."

"You don't think they're onto us?"

"What?" Then realization dawned. Bart was afraid this had something to do with their hacking. Even though the crime they were supposedly looking into happened long before he'd begun hacking and had nothing to do with computer crimes. That was what stress and panic did to a person, made them think stupid. Gil smothered a smile. *Maybe I'll just let him think that. It might ensure that he keeps his mouth shut.*

"I don't see how they could be. Even if they are, those are just two private investigators. Not real cops. Nothing to be afraid of."

"He said it was an old case and that you might be a witness. Before, when I spied on Faye, I thought he was looking into an old rape."

Gil shook his head. "Like I said, I have no idea what they want," he lied. "I guess we'll have to wait until he comes back."

"You're not going to call him?"

"Nah. If he wants to talk to me, he'll be back. I've got work to do."

He rolled into the back room to work on a computer someone had dropped off because it crashed. But he had another reason for wanting to be in the back. The card unnerved him more than he'd ever let on to Bart. Murphy had surprised him and he hated surprises. Why did the rent-a-cops want to talk to him? If they were working on that old rape case with no new evidence, what was it that brought them to him? He'd lived in Northridge when he picked up the girl, not the AV.

Working calmed his nerves and cleared his thinking. He refused to let the surprise visit diminish his spirits. He'd dug into the victim's life in his effort to think of a way to deal with her, settle the score he had with her, and he'd learned something that made him laugh. The victim had a sister, a girl Gil knew well, a girl he'd toyed with because he didn't really think her worth his time. But he'd been careful to Haskellize her just the same.

I'll just have to come up with something to deal with this problem sooner than I thought. But he already had a plan forming. He'd show those stupid cold case warriors just what they'd stepped into.

"I am the top of the food chain," he muttered under his breath. "And they'll regret the day they crossed my path."

CHAPTER

-48-

THE DRIVE TO BAKERSFIELD was about forty minutes, and it took another fifteen to find the address for Lucy Harper. The neighborhood was working class, but neat. The houses were small and close together, and the business district they passed through before they turned on Lucy's street sported Spanish language signs and storefronts. Luke knew there was a lot of farming in and around Bakersfield and a large population of migrant workers.

The address they parked in front of was a clean, bright single-story house painted a cheery yellow.

"Let's just go knock," Luke said in response to Woody's questioning gaze. The two men got out of the car and walked up a short path to the front door.

The woman who answered their knock was definitely not Lucy Harper. She was at most in her twenties, too young.

Luke introduced himself.

The woman frowned. "You the police?"

"No, I'm a private investigator. I'm looking for Lucy Harper."

"Why?"

"I just want to ask her questions about an old crime."

"She didn't do nothing." Fear spread across the young woman's face, and she started to close the door.

"I'm not accusing her of anything. She was a witness."

The girl shook her head. "My mom isn't here. You should go."

"Wait, please." Luke held his hand up, as it was clear the girl was going to shut the door. "Just give your mom my card. I only want to ask her a few questions. Please."

The door was now only open a crack, but at least it was still open. Luke quickly pulled a card from his wallet. "Here, give this to your mother. Ask her to please call me anytime." He held the card out and for a moment feared that the girl would not take it. But eventually she did take the card and then slammed the door all the way closed. Luke could hear the dead bolt being set.

"That went well," Woody said.

"Win some, you lose some," Luke said with a shrug as the pair got back in the car and returned to Tehachapi. "She was definitely afraid of something."

"Agreed."

When they were on the road again, Woody said, "I'm wondering if maybe we're going at this case wrong."

"What do you mean?"

"We're dealing with skittish women all the way around. Maybe a couple of ugly mugs like us aren't going to get what we need from them."

Luke frowned. "You suggesting we ask Abby to help us with this as well as with Molly?"

"Maybe. We'd have to let Abby in on this eventually."

Luke said nothing, hoping his face didn't betray just how he felt about the thought of Abby helping them with everything they were working on. He'd love it. This would solve the problem of keeping things like Lucy Harper from her. But he wasn't entirely sure she'd be happy that they hadn't told her about the woman. Would she want to help if she thought they were keeping secrets?

"Do you want to hit that Barone guy again?" Woody asked when Luke neared the off-ramp for Tehachapi.

"We don't really have time. Abby should be here shortly. Let's head to the deli. Why don't you try your friend again, the one looking into the reason Barone got kicked out of school?"

"Good idea. I'm sure he got my message. I'll double-check."

"We could be barking up the wrong tree, digging into someone who is perfectly innocent."

"Well—" Woody shrugged—"from what Brenda Harris said, this guy is anything but completely innocent. At the very least, he's worth talking to." He activated his phone and punched in a number.

Luke reached the deli and saw Abby was already here. It was good to see her. It seemed to make everything about the day, all the misses, easier to swallow somehow. It didn't hurt that he saw her smile at him, even before she saw Woody. He wondered how Abby and Ethan were doing. Woody had told him that the week she spent in Oregon involved working with Ethan on one of his projects.

Sighing, Luke knew the attraction to Abby was going nowhere, and since it was Ethan she was with, he should rejoice. Ethan was a solid guy. A guy who would be good to Abby, a guy she deserved.

CHAPTER

-49-

KELSEY KNEW THERE WAS GOING TO BE TROUBLE after she read the transcript of the interview. The reporter had the audacity to ask Lowell Rollins about Gavin Kent and his murder confession followed by suicide.

"Did you actually have a longtime aide who was a confessed murderer and not know anything about it?"

Lowell was a politician. He made it through the interview without losing his composure, and Kelsey knew the friendly reporter was satisfied.

But her employer was not happy and as expected went ballistic. Kelsey kept her mouth shut as her boss raged to the point of histrionics, even throwing a glass into the fireplace to shatter into a thousand pieces.

"I want her dealt with now!" Pointing at Kelsey. "Do you know where she is?"

"Of course. You wanted me to keep tabs on her."

"Well, finish her and that stupid PI. I want her and Murphy out of the way permanently."

Kelsey saw the bloodlust in her boss's eyes and cringed

inside. For the first time since she took the job Gavin's death had given her, she wondered if she really wanted it. Was this position, this shot at a life in the national spotlight, worth what this person asked of her? But where would she go if she quit? A lifetime of choices had brought her to this place, choices she couldn't take back.

When she didn't immediately respond to her boss, the rebuke came. "What? You don't have the stomach to handle this? Do I need to find someone else?"

"I'll handle it," Kelsey said. There was no point in saying that Hart's death, especially if it was violent and unexplained, might open up a whole other can of worms. Nope, she'd do what she was told and deal with the fallout when it came.

"See that you do. And just because I want to be certain, take Quinn with you."

"Quinn? He's part of the personal protection detail. Why—?"

"We have plenty of protection in place. This is important. I want that woman and everyone connected with that investigation erased permanently, now. I've already told Quinn he's with you for a couple of days. He'll do what he's told and keep his mouth shut."

Kelsey was left speechless and dismissed. Quinn, the person Kelsey hated most in the organization, was to be her partner. He was a Brit. He'd been a bobby but quit to join a global security company. That's where Gavin found him when he was looking for extra help. Gavin and Quinn connected on a macho he-man level, but Kelsey never liked him, hated the way he looked at her and the way his accent always made him sound condescending and smug. Her employer, on the other hand, loved the accent, considered it class while everyone else thought it pretentious.

She left the office and headed for her car in a daze. Though it had been threatened before, it had never occurred to her that her employer would want to be separated from Quinn during this frenzy of fund-raising. Kill two people? Quinn could do it without raising his pulse rate, of that Kelsey was certain.

Maybe she should see this as a positive, let Quinn do the dirty work. But once she stepped off the elevator and saw Quinn smirking at her in the lobby, she knew there was nothing positive about this situation. He had a travel bag slung over his shoulder. She'd been ordered to kill, to murder two people, and Quinn must detect no hesitation to her steps in that direction.

Her hands went numb as she pulled the car keys from her purse and motioned for the big oaf to follow her to the parking lot. Feeling cornered, and surprised she had any left, she fought the tears that threatened. She wished she could hold Gavin one more time and ask him how the two of them ever got to this point. Meanwhile, her grip slipped completely and she felt herself falling off the cliff, deep into a pit that had no bottom.

CHAPTER

-50-

BEFORE ABBY LEFT FOR TEHACHAPI, Ethan called with the news that he was driving back to Long Beach. He'd be getting in late but wanted to see Abby the next day.

"It's great you'll be home, but . . ."

"Are you back to work already?"

"No . . ." She explained to him where she was going and what she'd be doing.

"Are you really needed there? I think Woody would have a good grip on things."

"I want to help. I feel for the victim. I don't think I'll be there more than a night, maybe two."

"I'm leaving for Malawi soon. We really need to talk."

"Ethan, I'll do my best to hurry back."

He didn't sound happy with her answer but ended the call by asking her to be careful and telling her that he'd be praying.

That touched Abby deeply because she knew Ethan was praying for her welfare, not that she would bend to his will. "I love that, Ethan, and know that the reverse is true." For the rest of the drive she wondered if she should have cancelled her trip to Tehachapi to be there when Ethan arrived. After a struggle she decided, no, she needed to help Molly if she could.

She easily found the deli Woody had told her about on the phone. She reached it just before Luke and Woody pulled up. Luke smiled when he saw her and held up his hand, and she felt giddy. Chastising herself, she smacked the center console, wondering if the fleeting irritation she felt with Ethan was fueling this attraction to Luke. No, she decided, she liked Luke for a lot of reasons. But he was and always would be a colleague, nothing more, even with their Triple Seven connection.

It's not a social day. This is work, she thought as she got out of the car.

"How'd your interview with the suspect go?" she asked as a gust of wind pushed her toward the street. This high desert town was a windy place; no surprise it was the wind farm capital of Southern California.

"He wasn't there, so we struck out for now." Luke reached out to steady her. Abby wanted his touch, but she didn't want it and struggled not to feel awkward or react from the shot of heat that resulted from the contact. She couldn't deny it, no matter how hard she tried; his presence and his smile were warm, friendly, and something she hoped to see more of.

She saw that Woody was still in the car and felt the need to shift focus. "What's up with Woody?"

"He's talking to a friend who works for campus police at Cal State."

"Sheldon?"

"You know him?"

"Yep, he was a friend of Woody's from his academy class.

But he didn't make it through field training. Cal State police eventually hired him; he's the chief there now."

"Whoa, I'm impressed. Woody has friends in high places."

"We'll probably get some good info."

Woody climbed out of the car.

"Anything?" Luke asked.

"Sheldon researched. Your boy did get kicked out of college. He was caught peeping."

"Peeping?"

"Yes, at the dorms. Several complaints. That, and there was also a charge of sexual battery. He was cited, but the case was dropped, and then the college asked him to leave."

"The college cops cited him?"

"No, LBPD did. The east division commander stepped in and persuaded the victim to forgive and forget, from what he says. Sheldon remembers the incident. He was a sergeant then, and apparently the fact that Barone's dad was a sheriff's deputy helped. Sheldon thinks the dad might have even intervened. He might have spoken to the east commander at the time— you know, asked for a little professional courtesy. All of this is hearsay, of course, but I think it probably paints a good picture of what happened. This was in 2001."

"Yeah, I can see that picture," Abby said, thinking of how a father would intervene for his dirtbag son. She fell back as another gust of wind caught her off-balance.

Woody nodded. "Why don't we go inside before we all blow away?"

Abby appreciated getting out of the wind, but she still felt bowled over, even after they were led to a table and Luke's arm brushed hers.

The gooseflesh wasn't from the wind.

"I forgot to tell you guys what happened the day I left for Oregon. Talking about the east division made me think of Kelsey Cox."

"Did you run into her?" Woody asked.

"Sort of." She told them about the governor and Kelsey's visit.

"Both of them? Guess the governor really wants you on his protection team," Woody said.

Abby made a face.

Then a beautiful blonde woman swept into the deli. Luke saw her and stood. Woody looked toward the door and did the same.

"Hello, Faye, great to see you again," Luke said.

So this was the blogger, Faye Fallon. Abby couldn't help but notice Luke's reaction to the beautiful woman. His face brightened; he seemed transfixed. She'd seen the same kind of reaction from male officers sometimes, when contacting pretty female complaining parties. A sick knot formed in the pit of her stomach. She worked hard to keep her face from showing emotion, knowing that of all the people in her life, it was Luke who read her the best. Almost as quickly as the feeling overwhelmed her, she fought back, wondering why on earth she thought she had any claim on Luke. For as long as she'd known him, she'd been involved with Ethan. Why was this so weird?

It took great effort to keep her expression neutral as the woman extended her hand. "You must be Detective Hart."

Abby accepted the hand as Luke pulled out the chair next to her and the blogger took a seat.

"Please, it's Abby," she said, fighting the urge to look for flaws in the beautiful face—a pimple, a stray hair, anything.

"I'm so glad to finally meet you. I've read every article I

could find about you, and I know that you understand what Molly faces."

The only thing Abby could find in the woman's visage was compassion, a true concern for a victim of a horrific crime. Swallowing, she said, "I think I do."

Everyone settled around the table, and Fallon announced, "Julia Cavanaugh will be joining us here today. She also wants to meet Abby."

A young server stepped up to the table, and everyone ordered lunch.

"Hi, Callie," Faye said, turning to Luke. "This is Molly's younger sister." To the girl, "These people are the ones working on your sister's case."

Callie didn't look all that excited about the information.

As she walked away, Faye sighed. "This crime has taken a toll on the entire family."

"I understand that," Abby said before addressing Luke, still mentally beating herself up over the petty emotions that almost overwhelmed her regarding a woman who appeared to be completely genuine.

"Tell me about this guy who might be your suspect, the peeper," Abby said. She saw that Woody had brought a file in with him. "Maybe this is a good lead and not false hope."

Luke took the file from Woody. "He's really just a person of interest at this time, someone we want to talk to. He runs a computer shop, name is Gil Barone."

Callie returned with their drinks. "Oh." She'd obviously heard the last part of what Luke said. "You guys know Gil?"

Luke looked at her. "Uh, no, we'd like to meet him. Do you know him?"

Callie beamed. "Everyone knows Gil. He's a genius with computers. And his prices are reasonable, not like the big computer stores. He's a war hero too, got blown up in Iraq."

"He did?" Woody asked.

Callie's blonde head bobbed. "Yes. His tank rolled over a bomb. He's lucky to be alive. And he's humble about it. The whole town wanted to pitch in and get him a motorized wheelchair. When he got the money, he thanked everyone but said he didn't mind pushing himself around, said it kept him sharp. Instead, he used the money to buy a WWII vet the chair."

Callie was obviously impressed by that gesture, Abby thought.

"I didn't know he was in a wheelchair," Luke said.

"Paralyzed from the waist down. He can use his arms. Never bitter about it either. He's an inspiration." She moved away to another table.

"Now I know why that name was familiar," Fallon said. "I've read about the guy. He's a local hero around here."

Abby saw Luke raise an eyebrow and cock his head to look at Woody.

"What?" she asked.

"Injuries notwithstanding, Mr. Barone did not serve in any branch of the armed services," Luke said. "I checked."

Woody shook his head. "Could be he embellished the tale to impress the ladies. Wouldn't be the first time a guy did that."

"We'll have to wait and ask him."

"A peeper and a liar," Abby observed. "He's looking more and more interesting."

For the rest of lunch they talked about the case, and Abby found herself more intrigued than ever.

They lingered over lunch waiting for Mrs. Cavanaugh. She arrived a little after one thirty. Luke saw the sturdy-looking woman, dressed in pressed jeans and a yellow sweater, come into the restaurant. She walked directly to their table, where Faye Fallon stood and greeted her with a hug, then made all the necessary introductions.

"I'll confess that I've done a little research about all of you on the Internet. Mr. Murphy and Detective Hart, I feel I know you. Mr. Woods, you're a little more enigmatic."

"Yes, that's me," Woody said with a smile. "Enigmatic."

Luke pulled out a chair for Julia and she sat. Before they could get started, Callie reappeared.

"Hey, Mom," she said to Julia. "Can I get you something to drink?"

"Some tea." Julia's sad gaze followed Callie. "Poor Callie. As hard as this has been on Molly, it's been hard on her as well."

The profound sadness on Julia's face gave Luke pause. Briefly doubt crossed his mind. *Are we giving this family false hope?*

Julia sighed. "At first, Molly was so strong. We're a Christian family, and the church rallied around, and it appeared as though she would come through this trauma okay, but . . ."

"She doesn't understand why the bad guy was never caught." Abby spoke and Luke looked at her, glad she was there. Abby understood, even better than he could, what Molly was dealing with.

Julia nodded. "For a few years she was fine, standing on her own two feet. She lived in a condo in Lancaster and was working on an ambulance; she's an EMT and wants to be a paramedic.

But it seemed as if she lost ground every time an anniversary passed. The tenth anniversary was the worst. She started wondering if her own memory was faulty. Did the attack even happen? There were bad dreams, illusions that people in the community didn't believe her, but worst of all, she's begun to believe that God has failed her."

Abby said, "I think I know what she's feeling."

"Do you?" Julia asked. "Do you really? The reason I wanted to meet you here is to really make you understand that I don't want you to get my daughter's hopes up. She's been through so much. I won't let you talk to her if I think you'll make things worse."

"Julia, I know from firsthand experience that Molly has to be okay, really okay, with either eventuality, the guy being caught or not. And she has to know here—" Abby placed her hand over her heart—"that whatever happens, God is in it. He is sovereign over either eventuality."

Luke agreed and held her gaze. "And, Mrs. Cavanaugh, I can't guarantee you anything except this: We're here because we believe that your daughter's case is solvable. We will do everything in our power to catch the perpetrator. But ultimately we know, as I'm sure you do, that he will never escape God's justice."

CHAPTER
51

SHORTLY AFTER JULIA ARRIVED, Faye, Luke, and Woody excused themselves so she and Abby could talk. Luke and Woody wanted to try to connect with Barone again. As much as Abby wanted to be in on that interview, she knew the sooner she met with Molly, the better.

Watching Luke and Faye leave threatened to throw Abby off her game, force her to lose her focus, so she worked doubly hard to concentrate on Julia.

"Molly has good days and bad days," Julia explained. "She's healing from the accident she had and is just starting to feel better, to walk around. We're hoping this doesn't end her career. When she has a good day, she's like her old self. But when she has a bad day . . ." Julia shook her head. "It's like she crawls into a dark place and won't come out."

"I can relate." Abby thought about her own few days trying to hide under the covers at her aunt's. "She lived through a traumatic event, so it's understandable. Even though she survived, the trauma can resurface and create problems."

"Yes, that's what happened. She was having flashbacks, but lately that's been better. She's perked up in some ways and her therapist is very optimistic that she's responding well to treatment. In my opinion the biggest issue right now is her faith. It's fractured. It's almost as if after waiting ten years with no resolution, she's decided that God has failed her. She's stopped going to church. She's actually more open to talking about the old case than about her faith crisis."

"I've been there as well." Abby shared with Julia her own faith journey. "My aunt helped me immensely by pointing out that I was hiding. When I came out of hiding, I realized that my foundation had slipped. I had to get back to the basics. Maybe that's where Molly is now."

Julia put a hand on Abby's. "I think you do understand. The hard thing will be getting Molly to listen."

"I wish I could hang around in case you need my help, but I have quite a few commitments in Palmdale that I need to take care of," Faye told Luke as they stepped outside the deli.

"It'd be nice to have your help," Luke said, losing himself in her deep-blue eyes. "But we understand, and we have it covered." He extended his hand.

She took it in both of hers. "Call me as soon as you have any information, if you are able."

"Will do."

He realized she let him hold her hand probably longer than he should have when he heard Woody clearing his throat.

Letting go, Luke stepped back so Woody could say his good-bye to Faye. They watched her get into her car and drive away before heading for their rental.

"Uh-huh," Woody said as he unlocked the car doors.

"What?"

"Pretty woman. She sure does like you." He arched an eyebrow Luke's way.

Luke gave a dismissive wave and climbed into the car, pulling at his collar as the heat rose in his face.

As they returned to the computer store, Luke couldn't help but think about the last ten years of scrupulously avoiding any kind of entanglements with women as he worked hard on being Maddie's dad and getting his business going. To suddenly be so attracted to two women staggered him a bit. He prayed for focus as he drove.

"Looks like he's here," Luke said as they pulled into the parking lot. The same van was in the handicapped spot in front of the store. Since he now knew that Barone was in a wheelchair, he figured this was his transport.

"Let's go check him out."

When they entered the store, the same guy they'd spoken to earlier saw them immediately.

"Gil, they're back," he called out.

As they reached the counter, a man in a wheelchair, presumably Barone, rolled out of the back room toward them. Luke studied the bearded face. The eyes could be the eyes from Molly's composite. The bone structure, what he could see of it, looked right. But how long had this guy been wheelchair bound? His arms and shoulders were ripped, powerful, not something Molly ever mentioned about her attacker. Luke could see that this guy spent a lot of time with weights. Was that to compensate for the loss of his legs?

"The private eyes," Barone said, a sneer in his voice. "What is it you want?"

His antagonistic attitude immediately made Luke's dirtbag detector buzz. He introduced himself and Woody.

"We just had a couple questions about an old crime, a rape that happened in Lancaster a while ago."

"How long ago?" The way Barone asked the question, the tone of his voice, gave Luke the feeling that the guy was toying with them.

"Ten years. May of 2005 to be precise."

"I was in Iraq then." He held his hands out. "Came back with this wonderful chair."

"Did you serve?"

Barone shook his head. "I was a truck driver for ACME. They were civilian trucking contractors. They had me moving supplies, ran over an IED. So there—I can't have any information about what happened in the AV if I wasn't here, can I?"

He was mocking them. Luke felt his temper simmer. But there was nowhere to go. He cast a glance at Woody, who had his cop face on, unreadable. They had no leverage, no choice but to leave and check out his story.

"Can I get back to work now?"

Woody put a hand on his shoulder, kept Luke from saying something he shouldn't.

"Thanks for your time, Mr. Barone," Woody said. He turned to leave, tapping Luke's arm, but Luke was locked into a stare with Barone. There was no way to dial back the vibe he was getting. He knew the man was lying, knew the man was evil.

He finally broke away to leave with Woody. As soon as they were out of the store, he said, "That guy is dirty."

"I agree," Woody said, "but we have to prove it."

"What a couple of dorks," Bart giggled. "Guess you showed them."

"Top of the food chain," Gil said. He wheeled himself into the back room, leaving Bart to help some customers who just entered. As soon as he was out of Bart's view, his grin faded.

Despite all of his bravado for Bart's benefit, Gil feared now that his luck had run out. He'd lied about the date he was in Iraq, and the two detectives would figure that out eventually. They'd be back. He'd considered trying to Haskellize them, but the younger one—there was something about his eyes. When he looked into them, Gil knew at a gut level that there would be no snowing that guy.

He'd researched the crime. They had his DNA because his victim had lived to be examined. They would put two and two together soon enough. And while he could hack into a lot of things, because of the way DNA samples were entered, hacking CODIS was out of his realm of expertise, even if he had the time.

He grabbed his grip strengthener and tried to think. If he was going to go down, he would go in a big way. No way was he going to prison, not in a wheelchair. No way.

CHAPTER

52

ABBY WAS ON HER WAY to talk to Molly. Luke read her text when he and Woody returned to their car. He thought about having her ask Molly if she'd seen Gil. They already knew that her sister had. But not knowing how Molly was doing made him hesitate. He'd wait until he talked to Abby. Right now he needed to ferret out the truth about Barone's story.

He sat down with his laptop as soon as he and Woody returned to the hotel. Looking up ACME Transport was easy enough, but when he narrowed it down to a company that would have been operating in Northridge or the Antelope Valley, the areas they were most certain Barone had been in, he came up with a company that had gone bankrupt in 2008.

Sitting back in his chair, Luke ran a hand over his head. "Argh. No one to talk to at ACME. It's a bust."

"He knew that. That's why he threw us that bone," Woody said, but Luke noticed that he was looking down at his phone while he talked, working on a text.

"You got a new girlfriend?" Luke asked. He grinned when Woody looked up at him.

"I guess in a way you could say that. I've been in contact with that rescue agency lady, Carol. She's trying to find me a dog. Ed's been mopey since Ralph left us. The neighbor boy taking care of him while I'm here called me to say he was worried. So I want to find him a friend." He put the phone down. "I'm not that handy with the computer, but I can put a hold on this until after we're finished if you have something for me."

Luke waved him off. "There's not a lot for us to do right now. We're kind of at a dead end. I've got to find someone to talk to me about ACME and then, depending on what I learn, get ahold of Jones and give him what we have so far. You're fine. I hope you find a dog."

"Thanks." His attention went back to the phone.

"But you never cease to amaze me." Luke shook his head in wonder. He picked up his own phone and called Orson, leaving a message, asking if there was any way he could find a contact person for ACME, a bankrupt civilian contractor for the Army.

He'd no sooner set the phone down than it rang.

"That was fast. Are you screening?"

There was silence for a moment and then a female voice said, "Excuse me?"

Luke double-checked the number and saw that it wasn't Orson on the other end.

"I'm sorry. This is Luke Murphy. Can I help you?"

"You left a card at my house. You were looking for Lucy Harper."

"Yes, I did. I am." He sat up straight and tapped Woody on the shoulder, mouthing, *"Lucy."* "I'm looking for Lucy Harper, a woman who used to live in Long Beach, California. Is that you?"

"How did you find us?"

"I'm a cold case investigator, a private investigator."

There was a long pause and Luke held his breath.

"Why do you want her?"

"I think she may have information about a crime that happened a long time ago. I would just like to talk to her, ask her a couple of questions. She's not in any trouble."

"Mr. Murphy, my mother had a stroke. She doesn't speak anymore."

"Oh." Luke closed his eyes, then looked at Woody, who understood that this was another dead end. "I'm so sorry to hear that. Does she communicate at all?"

"No. But there is something." The woman paused. "I have something of hers I would like to give you. Maybe it's what you want."

"What is that?"

"Some papers. My mother had them in a safe-deposit box. She's had them since she lived in Long Beach. I almost threw them away. If you want them, I'll meet you somewhere and give them to you."

Luke crossed his fingers, wondering if this was a bone, something helpful, or simply another waste of time. What would it hurt to take a look?

"Sure, I'll meet you. Name the place. Right now I'm in Tehachapi."

They made arrangements to meet the next morning at a gas station off the highway between Tehachapi and Bakersfield.

Luke disconnected, praying that this was the smoking gun, something both he and Abby could rejoice over.

CHAPTER

-53-

"THAT'S YOUR PLAN? Go after the guy first?" Quinn sneered at Kelsey.

"I'm saying it will be easier to get to him out there. And we'll have time to decide the best course of attack. I have an eye on him there."

"Meaning you don't have an eye on the woman."

"She's either in Long Beach or out in the desert with the guy."

"You can't be sure one way or the other?"

"My contact told me she planned to go out there. I'm just not certain she's there yet."

"It would be to our advantage to take care of both of them at the same time."

"I agree. That's why I think the best place to start is out there."

Quinn started to say something, then stopped. *At least the sneer is gone,* Kelsey thought. *He sees my logic.*

"The eye you have on the guy out in the desert, he trust-worthy?"

"He owes me, so yeah, I think he is."

"Call him. Make sure our guy is where you think he is and then let me talk to him."

Kelsey bit her tongue, hating having to take orders from Quinn. She called Jerry while Quinn drove. They'd picked up a nondescript rental car, and the only thing she didn't mind about this arrangement was him driving.

She asked Jerry to confirm where Murphy was. He told her the PI was staying in Tehachapi, at the La Quinta hotel.

"You've seen him?" Quinn asked. The call was on speaker.

Jerry hesitated.

"It's okay, Jerry. He works with me," Kelsey said, hoping to allay Jerry's fear.

"I have a guy I trust in town watching him—"

Quinn shot Kelsey a dirty look. "Who?" he demanded. She knew he was mad that another person was involved. She was upset as well; she hadn't known that Jerry would involve someone else, but she wasn't going to let her irritation show.

"Guy who runs the local computer shop. His dad was a deputy. I trust him. He does a lot of stuff besides computers." The implication in Jerry's voice was that this man did illegal things. "He sent me the guy's license plate and confirmed the guy is there, investigating an old crime."

"I want his information," Quinn demanded. "Can you text it to us?"

"Kelsey, what is this?"

"Trust me. Just send me what you know about this guy. It's no big deal; we're just checking up. Your work is finished. You'll be paid. The money will be in your account tomorrow."

That seemed to placate Jerry. Kelsey disconnected.

"Money he'll never spend," Quinn said.

"What do you mean?" she asked, unease spreading through her gut.

"You don't think we can leave any loose ends, do you? You've made more work for us. There are two more names to add to the list."

She shivered. A few seconds later the text from Jerry came through.

Rubbing her forehead, she realized she was in far deeper than she'd ever wanted to be. Stuck in a car with a dangerous moron like Quinn, heading out to kill two people—now four—she was trapped. Her employer had gone around the bend letting this guy off his leash. His presence and his accent were already grating on her nerves; now they made her afraid.

She'd also lost her grip on the ledge and was in free fall, without the energy to fight with him. He'd probably dictate the plan, and once they set it in motion, they'd have to strike quickly or she'd lose her nerve. As it was, when they hit the 14 freeway and traffic jammed to a stop, she knew it would be dark before they arrived in Tehachapi. Part of her wondered if she should just give in, point a gun at Quinn, and make him turn around. Then she'd march into the homicide office and tell the truth about those murders so many years ago.

She heard Gavin's voice in her head saying that that would be quitting.

But you quit on me! her mind screamed. She barely kept the tears at bay, knowing that to show such weakness in Quinn's presence would be her death.

I'm crazy, she thought, *certifiable, talking to a dead man. But once this is over, my place on Rollins's team will be solidified, set in concrete. All I need to do is be thorough, careful, and this ugly chapter in my life will be over for good.*

Fists formed so tight her knuckles turned white and her fingernails cut into her palms as traffic inched forward.

CHAPTER

-54-

THE MORE ABBY AND JULIA TALKED, the more the woman reminded her of Dede. While in Faye Fallon Abby had seen the compassion she always saw in her aunt, in Julia she saw the patience and kindness that radiated from Dede. She was on the phone now, checking to see if it was okay if Abby came over.

She disconnected and smiled. "Molly's home and she'd like to talk to you. Why don't you follow me over, and I'll introduce you."

"I'd love to."

All the way over, Abby prayed for the right words, for the wisdom to know what to say to this girl, this survivor.

The Cavanaughs lived in a subdivision not far from a park. After parking at the curb, Abby followed Julia into the house.

"Molly?" she called out.

"In here, Mom."

Abby and Julia walked into what looked to Abby like a family room. Her eye was immediately drawn to a bookcase on the wall to her right. There were awards and trophies lined up. Molly's name was on several swimming awards. She knew the girl worked on an ambulance and was an EMT. There was a plaque citing her for bravery, for pulling a motorist out of a burning car.

"Molly, this is Detective Hart, the police officer I told you about."

"Hello, Molly." Abby stepped toward the girl, who set down the controls to a video game but didn't stand. She wore a brace on one wrist and a knee-high walking cast on one leg. That foot sat up on an ottoman. The girl's expression was bland, uninterested.

As Abby looked at Molly, her chest tightened. She smiled and stepped forward to extend her hand.

It was a few seconds before Molly reciprocated and they shook. Molly's eyes were haunted and Abby recognized them; they were victim eyes. This girl had endured brutality, lived through it, and discovered it was often harder to survive than it was to escape.

Abby had struggled with the loss of her parents in much the same way. But when she heard the message of Christ, the burden lifted. *But Molly knows the message, yet she is in despair.*

Please, Lord, help me to help this girl, Abby prayed as she saw the scars on Molly's uncovered wrist. Abby knew they were there because she'd been cutting herself—not to commit suicide, but to replicate the cuts the rapist's ropes left all those years ago. Like her mother had said, because he'd never been caught, the girl doubted her own memory of the attack.

Suddenly Abby's world, her focus, shifted into clarity.

The years of her own obsession.

The pain and disappointment of coming so close to a solution only to have it snatched away.

The shooting.

And everything that pressed on her own soul and sent her running away to her aunt.

But Dede had helped her to realize there's really no place to hide if you live life with a purpose. And her purpose for five years had been acting as a voice for those who had theirs brutally silenced. Abby knew that well now, as well as she knew that God was sovereign in all things, good and bad. Althea had even said it: *The Lord can and does bring good out of the bad, the painful.*

Helping people like Molly to see that she couldn't let that one evil act define her—drain the life from her, keep her from her purpose—was Abby's calling.

How can I help her to see all of this? How can I help her to stand whether or not her bad guy is ever caught?

"You think you can help me, huh?"

Taken aback by the semi-hostile tone, Abby ignored the challenge. "I'm Abby." She pointed at the plaque. "You pulled someone from a burning car? Impressive."

Molly hiked one shoulder, but something flickered in her eyes. Pride maybe? "My partner and I rolled up on a crash that just happened. We had to help; there was no way we could drive past. That was a few years ago."

"Still, it takes courage to face fire like that. I hate fire."

"Can I get you something to drink, Abby?" Julia asked. "Tea? Soda? Molly, do you want anything?"

"I'm fine." Abby moved to take a seat.

But Molly stopped her and pushed herself up. "I feel like a walk, like being outside. Do you want to take a walk, Detec— uh, Abby?"

"That would be great. But your cast?"

"I've got a kneeling walker." She pointed and Abby noticed the walker by the side of the couch. "It finally doesn't hurt so much. I just need to go slow."

Julia wrung her hands. "I think that means she'd like to just talk to you and not have Mom hovering. It's a nice day. Go; have a good talk." She smiled nervously and motioned for Abby and Molly to leave.

Abby was unsure for a minute, but when Molly moved past her, grabbed the walker, set her knee on it, and pushed toward the front door, she followed, deciding to let the young woman set the tone of the meeting and the speed of the walk. She agreed with Julia; it was a nice day. But the wind was annoying.

"It's always windy here," Molly said as if reading Abby's mind.

"I guess I'll have to get used to eggbeater hair." Her comment got no reaction, and Abby wondered if she could reach this girl, if Molly would open up.

They were almost to the park when Abby saw Molly's frown, the anger in the close-knit brows.

"What is it, Molly? Are you in pain?"

"Pain?" She huffed derisively. "Lately, I don't know what it's like *not* to be in pain."

Struggling to find words, the right response, Abby was surprised when Molly turned and opened up, venting with both barrels.

"My mom thinks you can help me. Well, everything in my life sucks." She hopped on one leg and turned the walker to better face Abby. "You can help with that? Good luck. My mom keeps praying for me, keeps calling on the prayer chain to lift me up." She raised one hand in a mocking gesture and rolled her eyes. "I just don't believe all that anymore. God is not good. He's supposed to be all-powerful. Then why did he let what happened to me happen? I was a good kid; I believed in all the God malarkey then; I even wore a purity ring. Then out of the blue I'm kidnapped and raped. And on top of all that, a car hits me. Talk about piling on! If you believe all the stuff my mom does, then tell me: Why has he deserted me? Why doesn't he care?"

Taken aback by the vehemence but not the questions, Abby motioned to a bench. "Why don't we have a seat?"

She'd asked the same questions herself but made peace with not knowing all the answers. She tried to think of what to say to this angry victim. What would Dede say?

She realized in an instant that for her answer to matter, to mean anything at all, it had to be hers. It had to come from Abby and from her own struggle and solution or it would mean squat to Molly.

"Molly, I asked those same questions when I lost my parents. I barely understood the concept of God then, but I thought he was someone who helped good people, and as far as I was concerned, my parents were good."

"I made one mistake, accepting that ride. And I paid. God punished me."

"Sweetie, God doesn't work that way. I was only six when my parents died. Do you think he was punishing me?"

Molly looked at her, sniffling, but not crying.

"What horrible sin could a six-year-old commit that would make God punish her with the loss of her parents?" Abby asked.

Voice dripping with bitterness, Molly asked, "But what

happened to me feels like punishment, like God was mad. If he wasn't mad, why did that guy get away? And since God was so quick to punish me, why has he taken so long to punish the bad guy?"

Abby pushed her hair back from her face, working to keep her tone calm, her posture relaxed. Molly was spoiling for a fight, but that wasn't why Abby was here. "What happened to you was evil, period. The man who kidnapped you deserves to be in jail. Why is he still free?" She threw her hands up. "I can't answer the why questions for you any more than I can answer the why questions for me. But I've learned so much in the last twenty-five years about God. He is good; he loves us; he sent his Son to die for us before we were even ready to repent from our own evil."

Molly raised the front wheel of the walker and slammed it down. "I've heard that so often that it makes me want to puke. After I was rescued and home safe, I prayed for justice, for that man to be caught so I could see him get what he deserved and feel better. God failed me. He didn't listen then, and he's not listening now."

Abby shifted gears. "I read the report. You told the officers when you were rescued that you prayed for God to save you and then the trunk popped open. At the time you said you thought it was an answered prayer, a miracle."

"I remember." She made a face as if smelling something bad. "But over the years I've decided that there's no such thing as miracles. I was just lucky he had a newer car with a latch inside to pop the trunk, and I was fortunate enough to hit the latch."

The wind whipped and Abby paused, unsure how to reach this girl who seemed content in her self-pity, her anger at God.

Althea came to mind. Althea, who had lost so much yet stepped out of her pain to forgive Abby. What was it she'd said? She couldn't honor her loved ones' memories by staying bitter. Molly had lost her innocence, any illusion that the world was a safe place, and her faith in God. Staying bitter would only make it worse for her. But how to get through to her?

Dede didn't pull any punches to get to me. Maybe that's the tack I need to take. Praying she was right, Abby stared at Molly, who was looking away.

"Why do you want the bad guy to win?"

Molly jerked around, her face scrunched in disbelief. "What? I don't want him to win. I want him in jail, punished for what he did to me."

"Every day you're stuck in the past, whining about how God failed you by letting that man get away, you're letting him win."

"He's already won because he got away scot-free. That's not fair."

"I agree it's not fair. I agree it sucks. It makes me angry. When I was a kid, I used to scream and yell at God all the time, demand to know why he let my parents be taken."

"And you got your answers? Is that why you're fine now?" Her tone was brittle, dripping with sarcasm.

"No. I didn't get any answers, at least not the ones I wanted."

"Now you're going to tell me I just have to learn to deal with it? I don't want to!"

Abby shook her head. "What's the alternative? Are you going to stay a prisoner in the trunk of the car? Are you going to let him keep you tied up and cowering for the rest of your life? If so, then he's won the Publishers Clearing House of life."

"What do you mean? I'm nobody's prisoner."

Abby stood and grabbed her wrist. "Look at this. Look at you. Staying here in your parents' house, hiding from the world. I know what happened to you is awful. I understand it's easy for your parents to protect you, to allow this to go on because they love you and want to keep you safe. News flash: the world is out there. It's not pretty at times and it's not safe. But you have a life to live, and every day you waste by hiding, you're letting that man take away from you."

Molly yanked her hand out of Abby's grasp and said nothing.

Abby tried again. "Molly, people who say they believe in God need to know the God they believe in. He never promised life in this world would be easy or pain free. What he did promise was that he would be with us, no matter what. He was with you in that car ten years ago and he's with you now. He may tell you why it all happened. He may not. He will judge the man who hurt you whether we catch him or not."

"I'm tired of hearing what *will* happen. I want it to happen *now*. I'm tired of hearing everything works together for good sometime in the *future*. I don't deserve to be forgotten." Molly stood scowling, arms folded.

Abby saw herself in Molly but knew she was losing the battle with this girl.

"Every step you take away from God is letting the bad guy win. Throwing a temper tantrum and stomping your feet is letting the evil win. We may catch this bad guy; we may not. You have no control over that. You do have control over how you live the life you have in front of you."

"I was wrong," Molly said. "I thought you would be different. I thought you would understand, but you're just like everyone else. God failed me; that's it." She wrenched the walker around so she could stand and rest her knee on it and leave.

Abby grabbed one side of the handlebar to stop her. "God doesn't fail. I'm sorry I can't answer the why questions you have. But I do know that God is still God. No one escapes his justice. There is nowhere to run, nowhere for anyone to hide. You need to stand up straight, beat the man that hurt you by living your life, stepping forward with your head up no matter what you face."

Molly looked away, but Abby didn't let go. "You proved that you could do that when you ran into the flames to pull that person out of the car. Stuff like that beats the man who hurt you. Stuff like that honors all you lost and smashes all the evil done to you."

Still no response.

Abby let go. "I'm staying at the La Quinta. I'll be there at least until tomorrow. Call me if you want to talk any more."

Molly hopped away with a determined push of the walker.

Abby watched her go, and her heart broke with the failure she felt.

CHAPTER

-55-

GIL WAS CLOSING UP SHOP. Bart had already left with the day's earnings to make a deposit at the bank. A couple minutes before he could get to the front door to lock it, a big man in a suit walked in. He looked to Gil like a cop. Gil moved to the counter, where he had a gun within reach. He didn't want to go out that way, but if this guy—he might even be a fed—forced his hand, so be it.

"We're just closing," Gil told the man.

"I won't be a minute. Are you Gil?"

The British accent threw Gil. This guy wasn't a fed; was he?

"Who's asking?"

"My name's not important. Your friend Jerry sent me." He pulled an envelope out of his pocket and from that counted out some bills, five hundred-dollar bills. "I need something."

"You look like a cop."

"I'm no cop. I'm looking for some things. Jerry says you can help." He put a handwritten list on top of the bills.

Gil read the list. It was all stuff he had, but he didn't trust this guy at all. And he didn't have time to play games with anyone, much less someone who was probably a bad undercover cop. He needed to stall, give himself time to think.

"When do you need it by?"

"ASAP, Ace. ASAP."

"Soonest I can do it would be tomorrow morning."

"First thing?"

"Around ten."

"Nine?"

"Fine, nine."

"This money is a down payment." The Brit slid the money to Gil. "There'll be five more when you deliver."

"See you tomorrow."

The guy nodded and left Gil alone in the shop. Gil crumpled up the list and tossed it in the trash. The money he shoved into a drawer before he rolled himself to the door to lock up and head home.

CHAPTER

-56-

ORSON RETURNED LUKE'S CALL about ACME a short time after Lucy's daughter called.

"I do have the name of someone from ACME. The CEO is retired now, but I met him once. He did some logistics consulting after the company failed. I'm not sure if he'll be able to help you with simple personnel matters, but he might be able to put you in touch with someone who can."

Luke thanked Orson and then spent the better part of an hour on the phone before he hit pay dirt. After three referrals, he reached a man who had been Gil Barone's immediate supervisor.

"Barone, yeah. I remember that jerk."

"Great. I'm trying to figure out the exact dates he was in Iraq and exactly how he was injured."

"You're lucky. I kept a file on the guy. I expected a big lawsuit from him, so I documented everything. He was gearing up to sue, but I remember that his dad died and left him some cash. I kept the file because guys like him never go away completely."

"Why would he sue you? Rolling over an IED is hardly your fault."

"IED? Is that what he told you? Ha!" The guy laughed for a moment; then he continued. "That's rich. That coward didn't get anywhere near any IEDs. The first week we were in Qatar, he got liquored up and crashed a company truck. Karma bit his butt. He ended up paralyzed. He was mad at me because there was a clause in his contract that said if he did get hurt in a combat-related situation, like an IED, he'd get a cash settlement. He wanted me to lie and not write the real reason for his crash on the paperwork that went home with him. Fat chance. I wasn't putting my job in jeopardy lying for the likes of him."

"I see." Luke knew they were on the right track looking into Barone. Just one thing needed to be nailed down. "What day, exactly, did you leave for Qatar?"

"May 17, 2005. It's funny, but back then Barone was a pain in my backside. He was only given the job because his dad knew the owner. Anyway, I'd have bet money he wasn't going to show up. The closer our departure date got, the more squirrelly he was. But when it was time to stage for the flight, he was the first one at the warehouse all shiny and eager to go."

Luke gave the man his e-mail and asked that he send him what he could about Barone. He'd forward everything to Jones at the Los Angeles County sheriff's office. He thanked the man and disconnected. He grinned at Woody. "He left the day *after* Molly's rape."

"So he is a good suspect, looking better and better now. Are we going to give all that to Jones?"

"Yeah, he'll have the power to pull Barone into an interrogation and pin him down about his whereabouts that day."

Luke checked the clock. "Why don't you call him first thing in the morning and tell him what we've found. My meeting with Lucy's daughter is early."

"Will do. Not sure he'll have enough to order a DNA swab, though."

"Even with all the lies the guy has told?"

"I'm no lawyer. We could still try to pick up an opportunity sample."

"Maybe." Luke drummed his fingers on the desk. "It bothers me that he's so close to Molly. Remember that her sister, Callie, seemed to think a lot of the guy."

"Well, he's not the same guy he was ten years ago, and he has a lot to lose now. He's a businessman, ties to the community and all that. Going after Callie would be stupid. My guess is he'll lawyer up and stonewall us and the sheriff."

"Maybe you're right, but what if we just spook him and he runs?"

Woody shrugged. "Not a whole lot we can do. We found a viable lead to give to the locals. We can warn Molly and her family."

"Which reminds me—have you heard from Abby?"

"Yeah, while you were on the phone, she texted she was tired and turning in early."

"Did she say how it went with Molly?"

"Nope, sorry. I did make plans to meet her for breakfast around eight or eight thirty. We'll eat next door." There was a restaurant adjacent to the hotel.

"Good idea. I might be back in time to grab a cup of coffee."

When he went to sleep, Luke thought about Abby and Molly and winced inside for Abby as much as for Molly at the thought that the meeting might not have gone well. They all wanted to

help the girl, especially Abby, but maybe it was all too much
for Molly to recover from. Like that soldier he and Woody had
found living under a bridge. At the time he'd wondered if the
man would ever recover. The soldier's mom didn't think so, but
she was committed to caring for him.

Maybe with Molly it was the same. She was lost and would
need to be cared for by her parents. Luke fell asleep praying that
whatever Lucy's daughter had to give him would be helpful, at
least to Abby.

"I'm not certain I helped her at all," Abby said when she and
Woody met for breakfast. She played with her eggs, sipped
her coffee, and felt utterly defeated. "I tried a little tough love,
but . . ." She threw her hands up. "So where's Luke?"

She wouldn't admit to Woody how disappointed she was
to not see Luke with him. She wanted to talk to Luke, go over
the discussion with Molly. For some reason she was sure Luke
would understand more than Woody did. Maybe that wasn't it.
Maybe in reality she just wanted to see Luke.

What about Faye?

"He had an appointment to keep. Let me tell you about this
guy Barone. He's as dirty as they come." Woody told her what
they had found out, but Abby wondered why he dodged the
question about Luke. Woody's description of Barone sidetracked
her for a minute.

"That sounds great, gold. If it were my case, I'd be all over
him."

"I called and left a message for the sheriff about all that we
found." His phone buzzed with a text.

"Is that Luke?"

"No, it's that dog rescue lady, Carol. She's found me a dog to look at. I figured since I was up here, if I had time, I'd look into adopting a rescued dog. Never thought she'd find one so quickly."

"Woody, that's great. What kind of dog?"

"Lab mix. If you guys don't think you'll need me, I'm going to head out there and take a look."

"I think that would be fine. You've done all you can do by forwarding what you found to the Los Angeles County Sheriff's Department. Go get a dog. I'm happy for you."

Woody smiled. He bent to text. "There, we're set. As soon as Luke is back, I'm going to see a woman about a dog."

His grin brightened Abby's day, but it still bugged her. Where was Luke?

CHAPTER

-57-

KELSEY BARELY SLEPT. When they'd arrived in Tehachapi, they'd found the hotel easily enough. They even located Murphy's car. Kudos to Jerry for giving them the license plate. That was when the fight started with Quinn.

"I have enough C-4 to blast his car to the moon."

"Nothing subtle about you, is there?"

He'd cursed. "I know how to get the job done. Why do you think I'm here?" He'd stormed away from her to his room, but later Kelsey heard him go out again. She could only guess where. And that was when it dawned on her the answer to his rhetorical question. She knew why he was there. He was going to kill her as well. It was foolish to think that her employer sent him along for any other reason. Like Jerry and the computer guy, she was a loose end. The only question was, when would he strike and would she be ready?

Quinn had asked her exactly what Murphy was doing here, and she'd played stupid, wondering if having that information gave her any advantage at all. Kelsey already knew what Murphy was doing, of course, but it behooved her to make Quinn believe she was as incompetent and blind as he thought she was. He'd make his move when he didn't need her anymore. Maybe he'd even kill Murphy and then make certain she was blamed for it. Thinking out possible scenarios had kept her up all night.

She swallowed an energy drink and changed her clothes, struggling to make herself presentable. There was no way to get rid of the bloodshot eyes.

It was dawn and the sun was brightening everything now. They'd stayed at a different hotel. Kelsey wondered if Quinn would want to do a drive-by of the La Quinta to be certain Murphy was still there. She double-checked her weapon, a habit from work she'd never tried to break. A knock on the door made her jump.

"Yes?"

"Just me." Quinn. "You ready to go?"

"Be right with you."

When she stepped out of her room, Quinn was leaning against the wall across the way like a male model. He looked like a *GQ* secret service agent, and the smirk on his face troubled her.

"Let's saddle up." He headed for the door, Kelsey on his heels. "I spoke to the chief," he said as he walked, without turning toward her. "There's been a change in plans."

Kelsey's hand was on her gun. Quinn called their boss *chief* simply to grate on her nerves. Kelsey herself had retired as a deputy chief, and for some reason Quinn thought that was a failed career. Their boss had never been chief of anything. And that their plans would change without Kelsey's input was troublesome.

"What do you mean?" she asked as they stepped out into the parking lot.

"The chief likes my solution for Murphy. So I'm taking the lead here." He stopped at the car and turned to face her. "You got a problem with that?"

Would it matter if I did? Kelsey thought. What she said was, "No, just as long as you get the job done and don't screw it up."

"Ha-ha. Like that would happen. I'm not you." He opened the car door, laughing at his dig while all Kelsey could do was hurry around to the passenger side.

CHAPTER

-58-

GIL DIDN'T KNOW what time it was when he killed Bart. After they'd been home for a bit last night, Gil tried to explain to his friend who he was and told him the big secret of his life: that he used to rape and murder stupid girls and dump their bodies in the desert. He thought Bart would understand, that he'd want to join him in designing a big exit strategy. He did need Bart's help with some things. But after hearing everything, Bart freaked out, practically wet his pants, and couldn't accept what Gil was saying. There was nothing Gil could do but shoot the moron and shut him up.

There was no turning back now. He'd wanted more time to plan, more time to make his departure spectacular. He admired those guys who could hijack a plane and then fly it into a building. That was showmanship, making a statement. But nothing like that was available to him. Still, he'd do his best to cook up something. He needed a few things from his shop. And he kept thinking about the one that got away, Molly.

He thought about her as he trussed up Bart. It was an effort to drag him behind the chair and get him outside, but it was worth it. The guy was stinking up the man cave. Once that task was over, he showered, trimmed his beard, and dressed. He put on a new company polo shirt and made sure every hair was in place. He wanted to look good when his picture was plastered all over the news.

He drove to the shop as the sun began spreading a ripple of bright across the sky. There were just a few things he needed, and then he had to get into position for the most important part of his plan. He filled a bag with his needs, then wheeled back, turning his clock sign around. It read *Be back at* and pointed to the time on a clock. Gil set the hands to read twelve, then remembered the cocky British guy. He reset the hands to say eight, grinning at the thought of the stupid Brit stopping by and being frustrated by his absence. He took one last look around the shop and briefly wondered if maybe there was another way. Remembering Bart in his backyard put his mind right, so he locked the door and got back into his van.

He parked at the corner, pleased that morning traffic wasn't heavy yet. He knew she'd have to ride her bike by here on the way to the deli. He'd just opened the side door and made the transfer from the driver's seat to the wheelchair when he saw her, pedaling down the street on her way to work.

When she got within earshot, he called out. "Callie?"

She stood up on the pedals and looked his way. He smiled and waved. Her frown disappeared and she smiled back, directing her bike to come to a stop next to his van.

"Hi, Mr. Barone! What brings you here?"

"I'm having a little problem. Bart is sick today and I dropped the keys to the shop in the van. I think they rolled to the back and I can't get them. It's a good thing I saw you. Do you think you can get them for me?"

"Oh, you bet. No problem." She climbed off her bike, took her backpack from her shoulder, and hung it on the handlebars. "Can I lean the bike against the van?"

"Sure, sure."

Once the bike was stable, Callie stepped up into the van and turned her back to Barone. "Where do you think—?"

The words died in her throat as Barone grabbed her from behind, encircling her neck with his powerful arm, putting her in a choke hold, something he'd learned from his father years ago. Stupid girl didn't even ask what he was doing there. Flexing the muscles in his biceps and forearm, he cut off the blood flow in her carotid arteries, keeping the grip tight until she went limp in his grasp. He then released her to fall to the floor of the van and made sure she was still breathing. He didn't want her dead . . . yet.

He peeked out the door and saw no one around. As quick as he could, he duct-taped her mouth and hands. Her bike was a problem. Glancing down at her, hoping she didn't wake up, he rolled to the van's chair platform and lowered it so he could grab the bike. When he did, the backpack fell off and slid under the van, out of his reach. Cursing because there was no time to get it, he raised the platform and laid the bike on top of Callie, who was just starting to stir.

He pushed the button to close the side door and transferred back to the driver's seat. He planned to be home before the girl was fully awake and felt the tires of the van roll over the backpack as he accelerated away from the curb. That couldn't be helped, and in the big scheme of things he didn't think it mattered much anyway.

CHAPTER -59-

LUKE SAW ABBY WITH WOODY in front of the restaurant and his heart raced. His arrival at the hotel following his meeting with Lucy Harper's daughter must have coincided with their finishing breakfast. They stood at the edge of the parking lot between the restaurant and the hotel. Though he had not read what Harper had given him, he felt in his soul that it would be important to Abby, that it would help her, help both of them clarify the horrific losses in their past. He hurried toward them. When Woody faced him, the expression on his face made Luke slow. When his gaze came to Abby and he saw the frown, the body language tight and angry, he almost stopped.

"I just told Abby where you were—all of it," Woody said as Luke reached them, and the air bled out of Luke's sails.

"How could you?" Abby asked.

"I—" He looked from Abby to Woody, suddenly at a loss.

Abby turned to Woody, her tone softer as she said, "It's okay. I know that you want to go see about the dog."

Woody looked unsure and, for the first time since Luke had known him, old and tired. Luke tossed him the car keys, and

Woody took off for the car, leaving Luke to face Abby. Luke squared up, struggling for the right words.

"What do you mean this person Lucy Harper might have seen my dad after the fire?" She stared at Luke, and he ached at the pain he saw in her eyes. Abby's anger seemed to burn through him. "How could you keep this from me?" she asked. "The two of you just said in plain English that you don't trust me." Her hurt, smoldering green eyes held him in place.

"That's not it at all—"

"So what's your excuse?"

"Her name was in the papers we got from Asa's safe—"

"You've known about her for weeks and you never told me?"

Luke felt the wind pushing him, and Abby kept moving hair out of her face.

"We didn't know if it was a legitimate lead. We—I wanted to be sure we had something solid before I told you."

He could see the pain of perceived betrayal all over her face, and it pierced him to the center of his soul.

"You didn't consider that I should know this bit of information pertaining to the murders of my parents?"

"It's not like that. It's just that you were having a tough time with the shooting. Lucy Harper may have been a wild-goose chase. We didn't want to get your hopes up."

"You didn't want me to lose my mind. You didn't want me to wind up the crazy person."

"Abby, that wasn't it at all. I'm sorry you see it that way."

"Yeah, I'm sorry too." She turned to leave.

"Here, please take this." He pulled what Lucy had given him out of his pocket. "I haven't read it. But she thought it was something your father wrote."

Abby looked at him. For the first time since he'd met her, Luke didn't like what he saw in her beautiful eyes. Mistrust, anger, and hurt. Luke felt his heart break apart in his chest.

She took the envelope from him.

"I'm really sorry. I—"

Just then a car squealed into the lot. By reflex Luke put a hand on Abby's elbow to move her out of the way.

Then Luke recognized Molly Cavanaugh behind the wheel.

"Detective Hart! Detective Hart!" The distraught girl leaned out the driver's window.

"What is it?" Abby started toward her and Luke stepped up as well.

"It's Callie; she's been kidnapped. My sister—she's gone."

The stricken look on the girl's face hit Luke like a sledgehammer.

"It's Barone," he said, and both women turned toward him.

"The computer guy?" Molly asked, going stone still.

"Yes. I was going to tell you, warn you. We sent the information to the county sheriff. I think he's the rapist. Do you know where he lives?"

A look of horror crossed Molly's face. "You mean . . ." Her voice trailed off, and Luke feared he'd hit her too hard, that she'd retreat back into her PTSD.

They had to find Barone.

CHAPTER

-60-

"WHERE IS THIS GUY?" Quinn looked at his watch. "Sign says eight, and he told me nine. He was supposed to be here half an hour ago." He turned to Kelsey. "Where does he live? Did Jerry send you that information?"

They'd been sitting in front of the computer shop since quarter to nine. Smug and pleased with himself, Quinn had been talkative this morning and told her over breakfast that he needed some electronics. He had the C-4 to make the bomb, but he needed something to set it off and explained that he'd talked to the guy the night before and been promised the supplies.

Kelsey knew enough about bombs to know he could probably find something at the Home Depot, but for some reason he didn't want to go there. A sickening feeling in the pit of her stomach told her why. He planned to kill the computer guy and eliminate any possible connection being made to him. Now he wanted to go to the guy's house, which she was fairly certain would be ugly, but she'd roll with it.

"I've got it on my phone," Kelsey said as she found the text message. She was happy to give him the address. She wanted to move this thing forward and wondered if she'd be able to save herself when Quinn made his move on her. She plugged the address into the GPS.

"I'll get this dude out of bed and into the shop, where he belongs," Quinn muttered as he left the lot and followed the directions on the screen.

Kelsey kept her hand on her gun, feeling surprisingly calm. Her only hope was that she wouldn't make anything easy for the big oaf, Quinn.

The drive to the computer guy's house didn't take very long. He lived at the top of a hill. The street ended with a jog to the left but nothing off to the right and nothing behind. The house had an unobstructed view of the whole valley, but the dead-end, private nature of the location probably appealed to Quinn.

"I'll be right back," he said as he pulled into the driveway. He left the car running and strode to the front door.

Still not certain what he was up to, Kelsey kept an eye on him but took her hand off her gun. The hand was cramping because of the tight grip she had on the butt of her weapon. She was looking down at her hand when a huge explosion rent the air, and debris rained down on the car.

Kelsey was thrown back against the passenger seat, and the passenger window spiderwebbed as it shattered, but the safety glass stayed in place. A loud thud sounded, and the car shook when something large hit the front fender and then slid off.

Ears ringing, in shock and not really processing what had just happened, Kelsey tried to open her car door, but it wouldn't open. She shoved hard and the obstruction moved. She slipped out of the car.

In horror she looked down and realized the obstruction—the object that had hit the car—was Quinn's bloody body.

CHAPTER

-61-

"KIDNAPPED?" Abby forgot her anger with Luke and Woody and
stared at Molly.

"Yes, she didn't show up for work." The girl's wide, frightened eyes went back and forth from Luke to Abby. "They found
her backpack in the street. You really think he's got her?"

"I do," Luke said.

Abby saw the certainty in his face and remembered all the
circumstantial evidence Woody had shared with her. Yeah, he
was probably right, and she hated to think of what that might
mean for Callie.

"We need to go by his shop. Do you know where he lives if
he's not there?"

Molly nodded. "Everybody does. It's not far from the shop.
I'll show you." She opened the car door and slid out, standing
on her good leg. Luke moved close to steady her.

"No, you need to call the police."

"They won't believe me. Everybody loves the computer guy.
Please, if he has her, every minute counts."

Abby looked from Luke to the girl.

"She's right," Luke said. "We're wasting time. Woody has the car."

"Then let's go in mine." Abby gripped Molly by the shoulders. "Just tell us where he lives. I'm not putting you in danger."

"I'll get back in my car and follow you if you don't let me come. I can show you where he lives. I'm not staying out of this to sit and wait." There was a stubborn set to her jaw.

Shaking her head in frustration, Abby hit her key fob to unlock the car doors, not wanting to take Molly but realizing what a waste of time it was to argue.

"We need to hurry. Direct me to the shop, and if he's not there, his house." Luke helped Molly into the backseat. Abby noted she put some weight on her casted leg.

"I'll call the locals and tell them why I'm so sure he's the bad guy," Luke said as they climbed into Abby's car. "I'll persuade them to meet us there."

"I pray that you can make them understand," Abby said as she started the car and burned rubber out of the lot.

Kelsey shifted into survival mode immediately. Not bothering to waste time going around the car, she slid back into the passenger seat, continuing over to the driver's seat. Throwing the car in gear, she pressed the gas and reversed out of the driveway, then shoved the lever into drive and lurched away, not truly comprehending what just happened but knowing she should not be here when the local authorities arrived.

She took the left road jog and drove, not even sure of where she was going. After descending and making several turns, feeling safe in a residential area, she stopped and pulled to the curb, heart pounding.

What did she and Quinn step into?

There was no way to know. As Kelsey inventoried her situation, she realized Quinn's body might present quite a problem for the boss, the "chief." He'd be identified quickly, and there would be questions—lots of them, no doubt. The boss's wrath would rain down for certain. She realized at that moment that she no longer cared.

She typed the freeway into the GPS, and directions popped up. The sooner she got out of Tehachapi, the better. As she followed the line on the screen, she heard sirens in the distance, behind her, no doubt headed to the computer guy's house.

Accelerating, she let her mind drift to what story she would tell the rental car company about the broken window and the dent and the blood from Quinn.

CHAPTER

-62-

BARONE JUMPED when he heard the front door booby trap go off, then cursed.

They're early.

He wasn't ready yet.

In his mind's eye he saw an army of SWAT team officers scratching their heads, trying to figure out how to get to the smartest guy they'd ever encountered. He'd wanted to wire the entire house to blow and kill the whole stupid macho team. He was only halfway done.

But he'd killed Bart too soon. Gil could do a lot of things and do them well, but he was slowed by the inability to use his legs. He'd failed to realize just how much he'd come to count on the guy. Now someone was here; someone had tripped that first explosive setup. The only thing that calmed him was knowing they couldn't get to him in the man cave from the house. He was still in control. He'd confront them the way he wanted to confront them.

He stopped what he was doing and tried to think. There was no way he'd have the house wired in time. He had no idea how many people were at his front door, and in any event, the blast was sure to bring the troops, the negotiators. Barone had no intention of negotiating. He put down the tools he was working with and rolled to where he could see his outside monitor feed. All he saw was snow and he figured they'd cut the feed. Either that or the blast had disabled it.

No matter, he thought. *I'll just go with plan B.* He slid into a thick bulletproof vest and grabbed his assault rifle. The heavy bag of ammo clips he placed on his lap, not certain he'd be able to use them all but planning to give it a try. He rolled into the garage, toward the door control. He could hear the girl whimpering and struggling in the van; he hadn't had time to pull her out yet.

For a second he paused at the van, wondering if he should just put a bullet in her head.

Nah, he didn't want to take the time. He was about to go out in a big way, and it was imperative that he prove to everyone that he was at the top of the food chain.

Stopping at the door button, he slapped a clip into the rifle and then chambered a round. He was ready to rock and roll and take as many with him as possible. He punched the button and prepared to fire as soon as the door was up high enough.

CHAPTER

63

MOLLY WAS RIGHT. As Abby listened to Luke try to explain to the local police why he was certain Gil Barone had Callie, she could tell they were skeptical.

"Turn here." Molly pointed. "He lives at the very top of this street."

Though she knew there was no guarantee Barone was headed home—after all, he'd tried to dump Molly in the desert—Abby followed her instructions because there was no other option at the moment.

Luke disconnected from the police, letting out an exasperated breath. "They're sending someone to the shop, even though I told them that we just drove by and he's not there."

She glanced at Luke and saw the frustration on his features. "He does all their computer work; we must be wrong," he said, throwing up his hands.

"They eat lunch with the guy. Callie has seen every cop in town with him." Molly's voice was tight, grim.

As they climbed the hill, Abby prayed Callie was okay, that

they weren't too late. Just then she heard a loud boom and saw a puff of smoke in the distance. She slammed on the brakes.

"What was that?"

"Gunshots?" Molly asked.

"Sounded like a bomb, an explosion," Luke said.

More smoke billowed ahead. Abby turned to Molly. "That's his house there?"

"At the very top. It's the last house on the street. What if it's on fire and Callie's in there?"

Abby stepped on it and continued up the hill. From the corner of her eye she saw a car, or the tail end of a car, disappear to the left, but she wasted no time looking after it. Her attention was on the house at the end of the street.

"That's it," Molly said as a large single-story ranch came into view.

The driveway split; to the left was the garage and to the right the front entryway, which appeared to be smoldering. There was also a brick retaining wall about four feet high off to the left, winding around the front of the house, that Abby noted would provide decent cover. That thought made her question the wisdom of bringing Molly along. But that wasn't what made Abby stop the car. What made her stop was the body she saw in the driveway.

"Luke . . ."

"I see it." He turned to Molly. "Get down in the backseat, call 911, and tell them what you've seen and heard."

She nodded. "Callie?"

"We'll check," Abby said. "I promise. But call; we need the troops here. Something bad is going down."

Molly slid down on the floor and pulled out her phone.

Abby nodded to Luke and they both got out of the car.

She'd brought her .45 on this trip and removed it from the door panel. Luke was unarmed, and Abby prayed that whatever had happened here was already over.

She'd stopped the car back about thirty feet from the body. She and Luke approached it cautiously.

"Is this Barone?" she asked Luke.

He shook his head. "Never seen him before."

The man was obviously dead. His face was a bloody mess, and the waxy color of his skin told Abby that the heart was no longer pumping. Abby was tempted to check for ID when she heard a rumble that indicated the garage door was opening.

"Cover," she said to Luke and they trotted toward the retaining wall. Before they reached a safe place, she saw a man in a wheelchair appear in the opening and raise an assault rifle. He started shooting.

At first the shots went wild until he found his target. As Abby dove for cover, she saw the man look their way. At the same moment they reached the safety of cover, bullets began pinging the wall, kicking up dirt, shredding the plants, pulverizing the brick wall. They didn't have much time. He was screaming as he fired, but Abby couldn't make out what he was saying.

"Do you hear sirens?" Abby yelled to Luke.

"All I hear are bullets." He glanced back toward the car. "If he decides to shoot up the car, Molly doesn't have a prayer."

He voiced Abby's greatest fear. The troops were coming, but did they have the luxury of time?

"I agree. I'm open to suggestions."

"He'll be reloading soon." He pointed across the driveway. "I'll draw his fire and you take a shot."

She stared at him.

He smiled. Those sharp, clear eyes held no hint of fear or doubt. He put a hand on her shoulder as the shooting paused. The sound of an empty clip bouncing on the ground was followed by the clang of a fresh clip being jammed into place.

"He has to be stopped," Luke said. "I trust you."

He was up and running before Abby could argue.

She stood, training her weapon on the man in the wheelchair as he raised his rifle to aim at Luke.

He was wearing a ballistic vest.

"O Lord, protect Luke," she prayed as she shifted her aim and fired.

CHAPTER

-64-

THE RIFLE CLATTERED TO THE GROUND and Barone tilted forward, screaming. He fell out of the chair. Abby kept her gun trained on him, ready to shoot again if he tried to reclaim the rifle. But he didn't. He simply writhed and bled a lot. Luke was there in a flash, kicking the rifle away. Sirens were closer, but Abby could tell by the bright-red blood she'd hit an artery. She'd aimed for his shoulder, a part exposed and free of the vest, and had hit where she wanted. Obviously the bullet had done a lot of damage.

"He's a mess." Luke knelt next to him.

Abby approached them, gun pointed away. "We have to find Callie."

"He'll bleed to death."

"I won't let him die."

They both turned as Molly limped toward them, grimacing in pain, sweatshirt off. She got on her good knee, casted leg out to the side next to Gil, and made a pressure bandage with her sweatshirt. He writhed around but was obviously growing weaker.

"I've got this," Molly said, face confidently set. "Find Callie."

Abby looked at Luke and he stood. Together they jogged into

the garage. Behind them the first emergency vehicles pulled up. They heard Molly yelling to them that Barone needed immediate attention.

With the sounds of emergency vehicle traffic behind them, Abby called for Callie and strained to hear if there was any response. In spite of the noise of diesel engines as fire trucks pulled up, Abby heard banging.

"Over here." She pointed to the van and Luke tried to open the side door.

"It's locked. I need to find the key to get it open." He glanced at the scene around Barone and knew asking him for the keys was not an option. He moved around to the front of the van and peered in the window. "I can't see anything." He tried the front door, and it too was locked.

He looked around and grabbed a bat leaning against the wall. Abby stepped back as he smashed the window. In another second he had the side door sliding open.

Abby was aware that several officers had joined them in the garage as Luke jumped inside, moved the bike, and tenderly picked up the bound girl. Abby watched as his large, strong hands gently removed the duct tape from the weeping girl, telling her it was all going to be okay now.

"Callie!" Molly called out. Abby saw that the paramedics had taken over with Barone, and Molly came toward them, supported by a firefighter.

Luke lifted Callie out of the van and set her on shaky legs, and the girls embraced. The officers turned questioning looks their way, and Abby explained what had happened as the firefighter stepped forward to check Callie's injuries.

Molly wiped her eyes and looked at Abby. "You were right

yesterday. I know that now." She hugged Abby. "Thank you for not letting the bad guy win."

"Thank God, Molly. Thank God. He is our help in every situation." Abby wiped the girl's tears.

Molly nodded. Callie called for Molly and she went to her sister.

"Amen to that," Luke said as Abby stepped back to where he stood. His warm gaze soothed her and he held out his hand. "Great shot. I knew you'd have my back. Faye will be thrilled by our success today."

His brilliant smile cut Abby two ways. She wanted his excitement and happiness directed her way but realized she was too late; he was already captivated by someone else.

Abby was still processing the events of the morning when her phone rang.

"Abby, where are you?" It was Bill, and his voice sounded uncharacteristically tense.

"I'm in Tehachapi with Luke and Woody. Why? What's the matter?"

She and Luke were sitting in an office at the police station, eating sandwiches. They'd spent hours at the scene as the local cops went through Barone's residence. Besides the body in the driveway, there was a second body in the backyard, identified as Barone's partner, Bart Meechum. But the man in the driveway had no ID. His face had taken the brunt of a blast that had been tentatively identified as a bomb, a booby trap rigged to explode at the front door. Who he was, why he was there, and why Barone killed him were mysteries.

Luke and Abby had been excused to get something to eat and were waiting for a debriefing by the detectives in charge.

"Something has come up," Bill said. "A family doing an excavation in their backyard—they were going to put in a pool. They dug up a skeleton."

"Yeah?" Wary now, Abby frowned. "What does that have to do with me?"

Luke reached over and placed his hand over hers, apparently reading her angst.

"Body had been wrapped in plastic and the clothing was still intact, and in the back pocket was a wallet with ID and credit cards. The ID . . . Well, Abby, the ID belongs to your father, Buck Morgan."

"What?" Abby's body went numb. She felt a roaring in her ears as her pulse raced.

Luke tightened his grip on her hand, but she barely noticed. She saw him staring, concern in his eyes. He mouthed something—it might have been "What's wrong?"—but she couldn't hear the words.

"We'll need DNA to be certain," Bill was saying, "but this might be your dad."

CHAPTER

-65-

WHEN ABBY DISCONNECTED the phone call with Bill, she turned to Luke and told him what her partner had said. Luke couldn't find his voice for a minute.

"I think it would be important to find out who owned that house twenty-seven years ago," he said finally, worried about Abby and what this could mean to the investigation that affected them both. The information had rocked her world; he could tell that by the expression on her face.

"Bill said they were looking into it," Abby said, her voice not even sounding like Abby.

"It's okay if you want to leave, to go home and be briefed on what's up with this news," Woody said. He'd arrived just after lunch, having missed all the action at Barone's house because he was out with the dog rescue agency. "Maybe I should even drive you."

Abby looked away and said nothing for a moment.

Luke knew this information was a 9.9 on the Richter scale, but he had no idea how to help Abby deal with it.

"I can fill the local cops in on anything they might be missing," he said.

After a minute she sighed and turned back to them. She was herself again. The news had unsteadied her but not knocked her down.

"I'll wait. I want to speak to Molly once more before I head home. That's the most important thing right now, not me. Bill will call when he has more information."

Luke relaxed. She was fine. This wasn't affecting her like an earthquake. He'd been so wrong about reading her lately. Was that a good thing or a bad thing?

"I need to apologize again for keeping the information about Lucy Harper from you. It's obvious to me that you have peace where that investigation is concerned. Knowing about her would never have thrown you for a loop. I'm embarrassed I ever thought it would."

"I'm not fragile. Part of me understands a little bit why Woody would have tried to protect me, but not you. I thought you knew me better than that. You should have trusted me with the information when you first got it."

Swimming in guilt, Luke started to say something but she stopped him.

"You just reminded me—I never read what you gave me. I never had a chance to look at what was in the envelope."

"That's right." Luke looked around. "Where is it?"

"Still in the car." She stood and left Woody and Luke in the office.

"You didn't read it?" Woody asked.

Luke shook his head. "It's for her, not for me."

"Sorry about reading that situation wrong; we should have told her."

"Don't blame yourself. I could have just as easily argued harder. Water under the bridge now." He tried to swallow the regret he felt but knew it would be a long while before he forgave himself. He prayed that whatever was inside would be good news for Abby.

Abby returned to the room. She sat down and tore the envelope open. Luke held his breath.

"It's a letter from my dad." She frowned. "'To whom it may concern.'" After a second she looked up, amazement on her face.

Kelsey was almost home when her phone buzzed, startling her. When she saw that it wasn't the *chief*, she relaxed. She was in the back of a cab, having dumped the rental car in a rough section of LA and hailed a taxi to take her home. Quinn had rented the car; there was nothing in it to connect to her, and she had no interest in explaining the broken window. She'd taken his bag of C-4 with her but wasn't certain what she'd do with it. The phone call was from an old PD friend, and she answered it.

"There's something up at Gavin's old house."

"What?"

"You know, the place he had on Granada. The people who live there now dug up the patio to put in a pool—"

Kelsey went numb and barely heard the rest of the sentence.

"Anyway—" he was still talking—"turn on the TV. You'll see the pictures from the helicopter circling above."

She thanked him for the information and disconnected as the taxi pulled up in front of her town house.

Her friend had been wrong on one count. The house on Granada had not been Gavin's; it had been hers. He'd lived there with her when they were engaged. But what had just been dug up in the backyard was the reason she had him move out, the reason they'd eventually cancelled the wedding. She'd lived there only another year before selling. She'd lost track of how many times it had changed hands since then.

It was only a matter of time before a connection to her was made.

She opened the front door, stepped inside, and closed it, leaning back against the solid wood as fatigue crushed her like a hammer. Kelsey couldn't think; she couldn't plan. It was the proverbial rock and hard place. Her life was over if she turned on her employer, but would her employer help her if suspicion crouched on Kelsey's doorstep?

After what seemed an eternity, Kelsey mustered the strength to take the bag of C-4 to the garage. There she unlocked the large gun safe. There was only one gun in the safe; the rest of the shelves were home to a paper trail. Some of what she had here might save her from some trouble, but a lot of it would damn her in more ways than one.

A question plagued her, something she couldn't answer at the moment: what was she going to do with all of it?

CHAPTER
-66-

IN SPITE OF KNOWING that there was a big mystery waiting for her in Long Beach, and that Ethan was back and wanted to talk, Abby spent another night in Tehachapi. Things at Barone's house hadn't been completely wrapped up the day before, and she, Luke, and Woody weren't released to go back to their hotel until after midnight anyway. Abby wanted to speak with Molly. So after breakfast and one more meeting with the local cops, their part was finished for the time being and Abby got her chance to reconnect with the girl.

"I'm okay," Molly said. She was back on her rolling walker and upbeat in spite of the dark circles under her eyes. Abby guessed she hadn't gotten much sleep after the disturbing day they'd spent sorting out Barone and all that he'd done. "I hated you for a while. I told my mom you were nothing but a big bully."

Abby couldn't suppress a chuckle. "I imagine that's exactly what I was the day we met."

"I needed it. Everyone but you treated me like I was breakable. It took almost losing my sister to realize that the last thing

I wanted to be was fragile. And I also saw that by staying stuck where I was, I was letting him win. He still had me in the trunk of his car."

Abby could tell by her face that she was being honest, that she'd finally won a resounding victory over what had happened all those years ago. Abby knew what a good feeling it was to be in that place.

"I'm so glad to hear it. And how is Callie?"

"She's okay. He didn't do anything to her—I mean, he choked her and tied her up, and that was bad, but he didn't do anything else. I'll make sure she stays okay. And she can't believe how that guy totally fooled everyone in town. How is he doing?"

"Last I heard—thanks to you—he'll live to stand trial. He lost a lot of blood, but he'll live."

"I heard him, you know, heard him yelling. Even with the gun firing, I understood what he was saying. I heard him screaming that he was the top of the food chain."

"You did? I couldn't understand a word. So you knew then that he was your bad guy."

Molly nodded. "Yeah, and I'll confess that while I was holding my sweatshirt against his wounds, pressing to stop the bleeding, I wanted him to live so that he would know what it's like in a trunk. I think being locked in a jail cell will be just like that."

"He'll receive justice for what he did, even more than for what he did to you. He killed at least two people, maybe more." Abby paused, wondering if Molly was ready for the rest of the news that the police search of Barone's house had brought. She decided that the girl was okay all the way around. "By the way, the police found a lot of interesting things in Barone's house.

One item was a shoe box that contained three IDs and some jewelry. This is preliminary, but it appears as if the stuff belongs to three girls who went missing around the same time you were attacked." Abby watched Molly process this new information.

"You mean there were girls who didn't get away?"

"It looks that way, though it will be difficult to prove in court. Officers are working hard to prove what they can."

Molly bit her bottom lip and looked down for a minute. When she looked up again, she said, "So the families of the missing girls will have a little bit of closure?"

Abby nodded. "As much as is possible if Barone doesn't want to talk."

"I hope I have the chance to help some of them, if I can."

"That's a wonderful thought. You might be a big help."

Molly smiled. "Thank you for everything, especially Callie." She wrapped Abby in a hug.

"Seeing you on a firm foundation is thanks enough."

Abby left Tehachapi with a light heart. Helping Molly was satisfying on many levels, and she hoped to be able to help others like her. Molly's smile and new, confident demeanor resonated with her for a long time. While Abby loved catching killers, putting people in jail so they couldn't victimize anyone else, she realized that seeing life pour back into a tortured soul was as, if not more, satisfying. *After all,* she thought, *I know what it's like to emerge from a tunnel of darkness to find my footing on the other side. Helping people like me, like Molly, feels like a journey worth taking, a vision worth having.*

We're survivors.

Luke and Woody had left town already, about half an hour before she did. The dog rescue people had found Woody a female Lab, half-starved, wandering in the desert, probably dumped by some idiot, Woody said. He had to wait for her to pass a medical exam and then be spayed, but he was looking forward to driving back out in a couple of weeks or so to pick her up.

Abby's phone rang, and she saw it was Ethan, again. He'd called yesterday, but she'd not been able to answer or return the call. She picked the phone up but realized that she didn't want to talk to Ethan at the moment. Feeling guilty, she nonetheless put the phone down and let the call go to voice mail.

I'll call him after I get to Long Beach, when I know more about the buried body they discovered. I'd rather have the whole story to tell him. . . . Yes, that's best, she told herself as she let her thoughts return to the find in Long Beach.

Abby planned to meet Luke and Woody at the house on Granada where the remains with her father's ID had been unearthed. Because of the contents of the letter Luke had gotten from Lucy Harper's daughter, Abby was 99.9 percent certain they were her father's remains.

"What does it say?" Luke had asked.

"It's from my dad." Abby took a deep breath; the letter had shaken her but had not knocked her off-balance. *"He gave it to Lucy with instructions that she take it to the police if anything happened to him. It's dated two days after the fire."*

"She didn't do as he asked."

Abby shook her head. *"I guess not. She was probably frightened. She had kids and no particular loyalty to my father."* She looked into Luke's eyes, then to Woody. Both of her friends were obviously concerned. *"I'm okay. He confirms a bit of what*

Sanders said. Gavin was the shooter. He killed my mom and my
dad killed Piper Shea. My dad agonized over running off and leav-
ing your uncle and me. What he hoped to do was prove he'd acted in
self-defense and be reunited with me. And he says he was certain she
would have ordered Gavin to kill me on the spot if he hadn't fled."

"She?"

"Yep. Alyssa Rollins was there giving all the orders."

Abby had considered that Alyssa was involved, but assumed
her involvement included her husband, Lowell Rollins. But her
father made it clear that he didn't believe Lowell was involved
at all, that it was only Alyssa who was behind the threats that
eventually led to the shooting. The day after the fire Buck had
tried to reach Lowell but failed. His next thought was to appeal
to Kelsey Cox. He was going to turn himself in, but he didn't
know where Abby was and he wanted to be certain what he did
would not jeopardize her.

That's why, after he left the letter with Lucy Harper, he went
to the house on Granada—Kelsey Cox's house, the place that
ended up being his tomb.

Abby was on her way there. She wanted to see her father's
temporary grave and pray about what move to make next.

The letter would never be considered proof enough to even
approach Alyssa Rollins, much less formally accuse her, but
maybe it would be good enough to pressure Kelsey into reveal-
ing what she knew.

At least that was what Abby hoped.

CHAPTER

-67-

LUKE CALLED FAYE as he and Woody were leaving Tehachapi. He'd been so busy the day before, he'd not been able to call but knew that Molly's mother had already relayed the good news.

"Oh, Luke! I've been on cloud nine since I heard from Julia. You and Woody are knights in shining armor."

"We just followed the lead." He smiled, glad she couldn't see him blush and happy at the joy in her voice.

"No, you did so much more. I confess, even though I knew you both were competent, I had my doubts. I really thought this case was too cold and too tough. Thank God you proved me wrong. I'm on my way to Tehachapi as soon as I post my blog update. Can I buy you lunch?"

"Uh, that would have been nice, but we're heading back to Long Beach today. Something has come up there about another cold case."

"Does it have anything to do with the body they found in that backyard?"

"Yeah, as a matter of fact it does. Are you clairvoyant?"

"I saw that on the news."

Luke explained to her what had been found.

"Oh, my goodness! Poor Detective Hart. This must be hard for her."

"Hard?" Luke frowned. "I think this will answer a lot of questions."

"Maybe it will, but coming face-to-face with your father's murder would not be easy. I still would like to take you to dinner—you and Woody. Please, let me do that. Okay?"

Luke cleared his throat. "I'll talk to Woody and get back to you. Fair?"

"Fair. Thank you both, again."

Luke disconnected and realized he liked the idea of seeing Faye again, even as he worried about how hard reliving her father's murder would be for Abby.

⎯⎯▶

Bill was waiting in front of the house on Granada with Luke and Woody when Abby arrived.

"Luke filled me in on the letter," her partner said. "I sure wish it was a smoking gun."

"Me too," Abby said. "Can I go back and take a look?"

"Sure. Even though evidence collection is finished, the homeowners agreed to let us keep everything secure until after you came by." Bill led them to the backyard, through a gate, and under police tape.

It was a big yard for Belmont Shore. Abby could see why the owners wanted to put in a pool. Most of the yard had been pressed concrete. A beautiful design had once been there from what Abby could see of what was left. A huge part had been broken up and removed, and in the center was a large hole where the dirt had been scooped out, uncovering her father's remains.

Abby's chest felt tight. She'd thought she was ready for this, ready to stay cop blank and strong. But it was emotional as the full import hit her hard. Her father died here. She wiped her eyes and felt Luke at her shoulder.

"You okay?"

She nodded, unable to speak at the moment. The words from Dad's letter replayed in her mind. Three times her dad had expressed concern for his daughter. All he wanted was to be certain that his daughter was safe. How was it he ended up wrapped in plastic and buried under inches of concrete?

The guys let her have a minute of quiet before Bill spoke. "Twenty-seven years ago this house belonged to—"

"Kelsey Cox," Abby finished for him.

"I remember her talking about putting a pool in."

Everyone looked at Woody.

"She was going to put a pool in?" Luke asked.

"It's a vague memory. She and Gavin were engaged. They lived together—I guess here; I was never close with them. We were at a graduation party and she was crowing about having a pool and spa to spend her honeymoon in."

"So it was before the Triple Seven burned?" Bill asked.

Woody grimaced. "Must have been, but my memory is foggy. She obviously changed her mind about it."

"Probably because she needed a place to hide my father's body," Abby said and the guys all looked at her. Her legs were back; she was solid again and working on figuring out how to confront Kelsey Cox.

"I'm done here, Bill." She turned to leave.

"What are you planning?" Luke asked as he and Woody fell into step with her.

"Not sure. Maybe the direct approach: just walking up and asking the woman."

They walked out to the front of the house, and Abby noted an SUV driving by. It was familiar but didn't register right away. Then she locked eyes with the driver. Time slowed and the realization hit like a kick to the gut. The vehicle accelerated away.

That was Kelsey's SUV, and she was the woman behind the wheel with a deer-in-the-headlights expression on her face.

"That's her!" Abby sprinted around to the driver's side.

"Who?" Luke asked.

"Cox. I'm going to confront her right now." Abby was in the car starting the engine before anyone could stop her. She didn't even hear what they were yelling as she peeled away from the curb.

CHAPTER

68

ABBY POUNDED ON THE ACCELERATOR as soon as the engine caught. She saw Kelsey's taillights three blocks away as they disappeared to the right at the corner. She was heading north. Abby bet she was going home. The woman had a town house in North Long Beach. Abby knew that because from time to time she had read in the LBPD daily log of officers being dispatched there to pick up paperwork when Cox was a deputy chief.

Squealing tires and narrowly avoiding a collision with an unsuspecting motorist, Abby made the same right the fleeing woman had and saw nothing. She was forced to cool her heels at a red light. Tapping the steering wheel while she tried to calm down and think clearly, Abby prayed she was right and it was the townhome Cox was headed to.

She floored it when the light changed and drove for the Bixby Knolls area of North Long Beach. When she turned onto the main street that ran along the town house complex, she slowed until she saw Cox's car parked illegally at a fire hydrant red curb.

Abby yanked the wheel and parked in front of Kelsey's

vehicle, half on the sidewalk. As she lurched from her car, her phone began to ring. Guessing that it was Luke or Woody probably trying to calm her, she ignored it and, taking only her gun, sprinted for Kelsey's home.

In the middle of the complex, all the units looked alike. Abby paused to get her bearings, trying to remember the number. She wandered, the minutes ticking, frustration growing. Then she recognized the address and charged toward it.

The door was unlocked, and she shoved it open. Stopping at the threshold, she tried to calm her breathing and racing heart.

"Kelsey?" she called out and listened. She heard a rustling of papers and smelled smoke. Had she set her own place on fire?

Gun up in a two-handed grip, Abby peered inside. "There's no way out. Just come clean. I know you weren't the ringleader in all of this."

Tiptoeing forward, Abby entered a small, tiled entryway. Straight ahead was the living room; to the left a kitchen and to the right a staircase. The smell of smoke was in the air, and Abby felt a nudge of urgency, but which way?

The floor creaked upstairs, and Abby made her decision and quickened her gait, gun extended in front of her as she climbed the stairway. The smell of smoke was stronger here, and she heard the whirr of a bathroom fan. The sound of rustling paper was louder.

At the top of the stairs to the right was the master bedroom, and Abby slowly moved that way. A tendril of smoke curled from the top of a doorway inside the bedroom and ran along the ceiling.

Abby inched into the bathroom and brought her gun on target. Kelsey Cox was feeding pieces of paper into the bathtub, where a fire greedily devoured them. The bathroom fan was on, but it was not successfully removing all of the smoke.

"Stop!"

"Or what? You'll shoot?" Cox pointed a gun of her own but kept dropping paper in the fire. "I don't think so. I should have started this so much sooner. I just don't trust a shredder to do the job."

Rage welled up in Abby as she realized she was once again going to be denied proof of the truth. Her finger tightened on the trigger, knowing the shot would be justified.

But killing Cox would solve nothing. Her anger cooled.

Gritting her teeth, she lifted her finger from the trigger and placed it along the frame but kept the gun on target. "You killed my father?"

Cox laughed and sounded a little hysterical. "Yeah, I did. He threatened to expose Gavin as the Triple Seven killer. Wouldn't you kill to protect the man you loved?" More papers fell onto the fire.

"Why not just take him to jail? He killed Shea. He wouldn't have been a credible witness against Gavin."

"I did what was necessary at the time. I made the hard choice. I'm good at that, always have been."

For a second her attention was distracted as the fire flared, and Abby stepped toward her.

"Not so fast!" The gun swung around. Kelsey dumped the rest of the papers from the counter into the tub.

The fire sputtered and then flared again, and the flames shot up. Cox coughed, and Abby herself felt the sting in her eyes and the burn in her throat. Then the plastic shower curtain caught, and pungent black smoke filled the air.

The fire kindled the beginning of fear inside Abby, and the sudden screech of the smoke alarm in the bedroom almost made her squeeze the trigger.

She backed out of the bathroom, coughing, a headache starting because of the smoke.

Kelsey followed, wiping one eye and keeping her gun trained on Abby.

What was her endgame? Abby wondered and almost asked.

But Kelsey started talking. "I had no problem with your parents; neither did Gavin. We were planning on having our wedding reception at the Triple Seven."

She swung her gun up and smashed the smoke alarm, mercifully ending the screech while the smoke got blacker and thicker. Abby had no chance to react. Cox quickly had the gun pointed at her again.

It doesn't matter, Abby thought. She could already hear sirens in the distance. She retreated from the bedroom, wanting relief from the smoke. "Gavin killed my mom. I know Alyssa ordered it."

That surprised Cox, knocked her back a step.

"How'd you know it was Alyssa? She drove Gavin and Piper to the restaurant that day, and she was the reason it all went bad. They were just supposed to scare your folks into quitting the buyout talk. But your mom was intractable. She threatened Alyssa with throwing a wrench into Lowell's career. Gavin told me that she claimed to know something that would end any political dream Alyssa and Lowell had. And that was what got her killed. You don't threaten Alyssa."

More smoke, and another alarm went off in a different part of the condo.

"My dad left a letter. He said it was all Alyssa. He could have stopped her then. Why did you kill him?" Abby repeated the question; suddenly the answer was so important. She was at the top of the stairs now, wanting to take Kelsey into custody, get the gun out of her hand, but how?

"Your dad showed up at my house on Granada a couple days after the fire. He'd been told to disappear permanently, but as usual, he didn't listen. Gavin was still limping around with his leg injury. Buck wanted to take him to the station and get the whole story out, tell the investigators what really happened. He hoped that he could prove self-defense in the killing of Piper Shea, and get you back. But he knew Gavin would have to be arrested for your mother's death. That was the only way all the truth would come out." Harsh coughing interrupted Cox briefly. "What a sap your dad was. He truly believed that if Gavin went to jail, Lowell would finally see what a manipulator his wife was."

The smoke thickened and the harsh hacking worsened, but Cox kept her gun up. "They were arguing. He didn't see me come in behind him. I hit him with a shovel."

Abby felt numb and she tightened her grip on her gun. The dense smoke made it difficult to see, to breathe, to think.

"Just so happens we were putting in a pool. There was a grave ready and waiting for your father. Imagine the pool company's surprise the next day when we told them we'd changed our mind and now we wanted a concrete patio instead of a pool. I never imagined anyone would dig that backyard up ever again."

Cox collapsed in a coughing fit as the pop of breaking glass sounded from the bedroom.

Abby flinched and fought the urge to turn and run down the stairs and out of the burning town house.

"You better let me go," Cox said, voice harsh and raspy, "or we'll both die here."

"You're not going anywhere but prison." Except Abby was already weakening, the smoke close to incapacitating her. She knew she had to do something.

Before she could move, the carpet caught fire behind Kelsey, and she screamed. She dropped her gun and dove forward, tackling Abby and knocking the gun from her hand. Chest burning, Abby tried to stay on her feet but couldn't. She and Kelsey fell in a tangle down the stairway.

They stopped when Abby's head hit the tile floor at the bottom, hard. The last thing she thought before losing consciousness was that she was going to burn to death with the woman who killed her father.

CHAPTER

-69-

LUKE DROVE AS FAST as he could to North Long Beach. Woody was certain that Kelsey was heading home with Abby on her tail. Luke prayed he was right because they had no plan B. Woody knew Kelsey's address, and Luke worked hard to stay calm as he drove, praying they would arrive in time to keep Abby safe.

"There, there!" Woody pointed, and Luke saw Abby's car.

He stomped the brakes, and his car squealed to a stop next to Abby's. He was out of the car in a rush. Woody had told him the number to look for, and he took only a second to get his bearings and was off in the direction indicated on a directory sign.

He could hear sirens, and as he neared the unit, he saw why. Smoke was pouring out an upstairs window. Neighbors were gathered on the ground nearby, several on cell phones.

Luke didn't waste time asking them anything. He burst into the townhome. "Abby!"

The smoke and the heat stung his eyes. Luke saw the two women in a tangled heap at the bottom of the stairs, neither one moving. His heart stopped when he saw the blood. Fire greedily descended the carpeted staircase toward the women. Dropping to his knees, he gently moved Kelsey off Abby.

"Abby!"

She moaned and coughed. She was alive. He scooped her up, intending to come back for Kelsey, but as he stood, two firefighters appeared at his shoulder. He thanked God as one of them helped him and the other tended to Kelsey.

All Luke could do was nod as the firefighter led him out of the smoky entryway with Abby limp in his arms.

Abby came to, coughing and sputtering in the oxygen mask paramedics had affixed to her face. She recognized that she was on an ambulance gurney.

"Cox . . . she started the fire . . . burned her papers." She tried to say more but collapsed in coughing. Strong hands gripped her shoulders, holding her until the fit passed. When it did, she looked up into Luke's worried eyes.

"She's being tended; medics are working on her. She cut her head, but it looks like she'll be okay. Relax." Luke pointed.

Abby followed his gaze and saw that paramedics were treating Kelsey and getting ready to transport. Her head was wrapped, and when Abby looked down and saw blood on her own shirt, she realized it was Kelsey's.

"She's not going anywhere but to the hospital, and Bill is on his way. I'll tell him what you said. It all will be sorted out, I promise." His hand brushed her face as he replaced the mask that had moved with her coughing fit. "You took in a lot of smoke."

Abby nodded and thought better than to try to speak again.

She took deep breaths from the mask, hoping to clear her lungs and ease the burning in her throat. She was conscious of Luke's hand holding hers, and she squeezed it, loving the rough, warm strength there. His very presence made her feel safe and secure.

But the back of her mind niggled with the thought of Ethan and the fact that she'd never returned his calls.

"We're ready to go." A paramedic stepped around to her even as Kelsey's ambulance pulled away.

Abby started to protest that she didn't need to go to the hospital when another coughing fit struck.

"Calm down, kid." Woody stepped up. "Let them look you over. You were out cold when Luke picked you up. We'll be right behind to take you home when it's time."

"Listen to your training officer," Luke said, letting go of her hand.

Abby relaxed, hoping by the time she got to the hospital, she'd be able to speak without coughing.

Besides the smoke inhalation, Abby had a slight concussion. She was cleared to go home after a couple of hours in the emergency room. By that time, aside from a raw throat and a slight headache, she felt okay. Luke, Bill, and Woody joined her in the emergency room, and she learned a little about Kelsey as they chatted and waited for the doctor to sign her release. In a hoarse voice Abby told Bill what happened in the town house and what Kelsey had said.

"She said she killed my father; she hit him with a shovel." She felt better now, stronger.

Bill nodded. "I just got a preliminary report from the coroner on the body we dug up. That would fit with the probable cause of death. The skull was fractured. In any event, Cox has a lot to explain. The bomb squad was called out. After the fire was knocked down, firefighters checking for hot spots found a bag of C-4 explosive in her garage, along with a wallet and ID card. I ran a check on the ID; it belongs to a man who works for Lowell Rollins, part of his protection team."

"Well, Kelsey works for him as well," Abby said. "That doesn't surprise me, but explosives?" Unease nagged at her about the situation, but her thinking was still foggy, smoky. One glance at Luke and Woody, and the concern she saw in their faces made her decide to shelve questions and worries for the time being.

"Like I said, she has a lot to explain, but she's not talking," Bill continued. "Her injuries are minor, but she'll be in the hospital at least overnight. I'm working on getting a warrant issued for when she's released medically. I'll charge her with starting the fire and possession of explosives." Bill checked his phone and said, "I'm glad to see that you're okay, but I've got a lot of work to do." He left them just before the doctor came in and signed her out.

"I'll go get the car," Woody said, leaving Luke to help Abby out.

Abby looked at Luke. His hazel-brown eyes warmed her, but at the same time she saw a distraction there, like his mind was elsewhere, and she remembered Faye. She realized her mind should be elsewhere as well, with Ethan, not Luke.

"We have all the answers now," he said, "don't we?"

She thought before responding. Yes, they did have answers, answers she'd spent most of her life trying to find.

Turning her attention back to him, she said, "Answers but no solutions."

"By 'no solutions,' you mean because the responsible parties have not all been held accountable."

She nodded, and he cocked his head knowingly, holding out his hand to steady her as she slid off the exam table.

"They will be eventually, I know," Abby said. "But part of me wants it now."

"Well, let's see how all this shakes out. After you feel better, maybe we'll find an opening, a way to have justice now. What say we hold off closing any doors until we hear definitively what kind of story Kelsey will tell?"

Peering into Luke's sharp, clear eyes, she held his gaze. "Might be a long wait."

He shrugged. "Used to that. Anyway, I'll keep busy. It's time to concentrate on other people's cold cases."

They walked out to the curb to wait for Woody, and Abby let her mind wander. She doubted Kelsey would say a word. The woman had been caught burning evidence; she wasn't ready to step up and do the right thing.

On the other hand Abby thanked God that she had her father's letter. But she was disappointed that she would never know why Lucy hadn't gone to the police with it right after her father disappeared. Still even there Abby could see God's hand in things. It was possible Lucy might have trusted the wrong cop back then, someone like Kelsey Cox, and the letter would have been destroyed. Perhaps Lucy might have been collateral damage. As it was, Abby now had the letter and would keep it safe, if for no other reason than because it was like hearing her father speak, and that was special to Abby.

And Luke was right about waiting right now for things to shake out. Maybe Kelsey would decide to come forward with everything she knew.

Abby could be patient; at least at the moment she was too tired to think about anything else.

CHAPTER

-70-

"A DATE?" Maddie looked up at Luke, hands on hips.

"Yep, a real date." Luke smiled at his daughter. "And I didn't even have to join a computer dating service."

"That's probably best. I don't know that I would like a girl the computer spit out." She gave him a hug and settled back into finishing her schoolwork before dinner.

Luke chuckled in agreement and once again checked his image in the mirror, working to calm his nerves. He'd not been on a date since he courted his wife, and he felt rusty to say the least. He stopped on his way to the car when something on the television news his mother was watching caught his attention. It was about Lowell Rollins.

In the week since the incident at the retired deputy chief's town house, a firestorm had erupted around Cox and her connection to Lowell Rollins. Added to the mix was the unknown dead man at Barone's house in Tehachapi. He'd eventually been identified as the man whose ID Cox had in her garage. He was also on the governor's payroll. As a result the would-be senator's campaign had been hit with a barrage of questions and intense scrutiny. What was the man doing there? Why did he have C-4 as Cox claimed?

The only information Kelsey Cox volunteered was that the C-4 belonged to the man named Quinn. Beyond that she would not talk. She was in jail for arson. Though she had confessed to killing Abby's father all those years ago, Luke knew from Bill that they needed to build a case before they could charge her with murder. And her lips were sealed when it came to answering questions about Alyssa Rollins's involvement in anything.

Abby had called him after the revelation that the dead man in Barone's driveway had been positively identified as Quinn Rodgers, Alyssa Rollins's bodyguard.

"Does the fact that Cox had explosives she claimed belonged to a man employed by Alyssa Rollins—a man who was found dead in Tehachapi, where we were both working—bother you as much as it does me?"

"Yes, it does," he said, but maybe more, he thought, when he considered the danger Alonzo Ruiz had brought to his doorstep. *"I believe his being there had something to do with us. The locals certainly found no connection between him and Barone. Cox was probably there as well. My speculation is that Alyssa sent them there to deal with us. Though why she would consider us a threat is beyond me."*

"As long as Alyssa Rollins is free and clear, we have no assurance the danger is past, no assurance everyone involved has been stopped. I believe Alyssa was trying to get rid of us. I don't want to live looking over my shoulder, wondering if she'll try again."

"Do you have an idea about how we can be certain she won't?"

"No. That's why I called. I can only guess what she planned in Tehachapi. At least right now she has her hands full; the press is all

over this story. I've even gotten calls. Gunther is practically camped on my doorstep. Everyone who was in the Triple Seven that day, except for me, is dead."

"Did you tell Gunther about the letter?"

"No. I, uh . . . The letter is mine. It's personal. It would never hold up in court without corroborating evidence. I don't want to go through an authentication fight or have to answer questions about chain of custody."

"You don't have to justify that decision to me. I understand. But you do know that even if you lay off of Alyssa and keep quiet, that doesn't mean she'll stop. The Triple Seven invest is closed tight, and still, for some reason, she sent Kelsey Cox and Quinn Rodgers after us."

"But it's not closed anymore."

"What?"

"My father's body has reopened the case. Since it wasn't him next to my mom, homicide has to find out who it was."

"Piper Shea?"

"It has to be proven."

Luke considered this for a moment. *"You're right, and while the governor is caught in this firestorm about Kelsey and Quinn, I doubt Alyssa can do anything."*

They had agreed to wait and watch. But as Luke listened to the news report, he wondered if waiting would be possible. His jaw dropped as the newscaster read a statement issued by Governor Rollins. It said that Quinn had been in Tehachapi investigating a possible hacker. One of the governor's campaign offices had been hacked, and Quinn had been unofficially following up a lead. The governor was not at liberty to discuss specifics because of an ongoing federal investigation.

Luke knew that the officers who searched Barone's house had found a setup they thought was related to hacking. As the press's questioning got lighter and lighter, Luke felt a sinking in his chest and knew that Rollins would weather the media volcano. The major news outlets were buying the explanation and the governor would likely emerge from this unscathed.

Luke no longer wondered if it would be the end of his campaign. The man would never give up the quest to be a senator. Alyssa was winning.

Abby put the letters away when she saw the clock. Ethan would be there any minute and she wasn't ready. She just couldn't put the letters down. Uncle Simon had mailed her all of her father's letters. The visiting approval had not yet come through, and he didn't want to keep her in suspense.

Her father had written messages to his brother overflowing with love for his wife and his daughter. She'd never known how much her father loved her; she'd only been able to guess. But now she knew. In his own words Buck Morgan laid open his heart. All her life she'd heard how important the restaurant was to her father, but in the letters he barely mentioned the place. It was all about his daughter.

Little Abby is the best thing to ever happen to us, Simon. I wish you could see her, watch her play, see her smile. She makes the dreariest day bright. When she was a baby, if I came home from having a bad day, all I had to do was stand at her crib and watch her sleep and the badness went

away. Pat thinks she's a daddy's girl, and I have to agree.
I love it. If you could see the grin on my face right now,
you'd laugh. When I pick her up and see her smile . . .
Bro, my heart is full; my life is perfect.

There were four letters in all, written in the two years before her father's death. In them he also talked about his faith, telling Simon about Jesus, about salvation, and how he wanted his brother to see a chaplain and give his life to God. Simon said that he had followed his brother's advice and that had turned his life around. This information took Abby's breath away. All her life she'd heard that her father was a wild child, pugnacious, ready to start trouble. To learn that he was a Christian had knocked her back a step.

And there was something else in the letters, words that had taken Abby completely by surprise—her father's affection for Lowell Rollins. They were truly good friends. Abby wanted to ask Simon about that when they finally got to visit. Before he went to prison, Simon would have known Lowell.

A picture of Lowell formed now in her mind that rocked her world. And she began to believe that only Alyssa was the evil one. Lowell was complicit in one respect: according to her father, Lowell never wanted to see the petty, mean streak in his wife, so he turned a blind eye. True, the man could have changed in thirty years, but Abby had a feeling that wasn't the case, and now she had to figure out how to put together all the pieces she had in a way to stop Alyssa cold.

But at this moment her heart and her mind had to be with Ethan. They had only talked on the phone for the past week, even though he was back in Long Beach. He'd spent several days in LA working on passports and visas for a couple of his team members.

She hated to think that she dreaded this visit from him, but she did. She knew he was not happy with what had happened with Cox, with the danger she'd put herself in. The tone of his voice and his choice of words told her that he was ready to call it quits where their romantic relationship was concerned.

Sad thing was, she agreed. Her heart would never be in overseas mission work, and that was where Ethan's heart would always stay.

Then she heard his knock at the door. Taking a deep breath, and praying that God would help her with this difficult meeting, she went to the door.

She gave him a hug, even as she noticed his disapproving glance at the fading bruises on her arms from the tumble down the stairs.

"How've you been?" she asked, suddenly feeling the nervous drive to speak.

"Good. Packed and ready for Malawi." He walked to the dining table and sat. "I'm so ready to head out again. I had a great Skype chat last night with the team members who are already there." He rubbed his face with both hands and then looked up at her. "We need to talk."

Sighing, Abby sat across from him. "I know."

"You feel it too?"

"I think so."

He took her hand. "I've been praying the Lord would change your heart, or change mine, but that doesn't seem to be happening."

"Ethan, I—"

He waved her quiet and spoke softly, sadly. "The week I was with you after the shooting, while you were healing, I prayed that you would see the incident and aftermath as a sign—a door closing and a new opportunity arising for you to make a life change." He paused and swallowed. "I even hoped when you saw how much good the church build did for people . . ." His voice trailed off and almost broke.

She squeezed his hand.

He cleared his throat. "But you love your work as much as I love the mission field—I see that now. If you didn't, you wouldn't have been hurt so bad by the shooting. So I understand we've come to a crossroads. I know that we will always be friends. I just don't see us being married. We want very different lives."

Abby swallowed a lump, amazed at the conflicting emotions that swirled within: pain, sadness, and realization of truth. And even a sense of relief.

"I agree." She gripped his hand in both of hers. "I do value your friendship. We've known each other so long. I don't want to lose that." She reached out to hug him and he returned the gesture.

"You won't," he whispered. "I'll be in touch, and pray for you often," he said, and a few minutes later he walked out of her house.

⊱━━⊰

Abby sat on the couch with Bandit, trying to reconcile her feelings. She knew the breakup was right, and she knew they'd always be friends, but there was still a sense of loss and a very sharp pain as she contemplated the future without Ethan's steady presence.

She turned on the TV and flipped through the channels before she caught an announcer saying that up next was an important statement from Governor Rollins. Putting the remote down, she waited through the commercials for the statement.

"He's gonna quit the race, Bandit. I know it," she said to the little dog. She'd seen the chaos swirling around the campaign. His opponent was hitting him hard with everything that happened in Tehachapi, with Kelsey, Quinn, and Gavin. In an odd way she felt sorry for Rollins even as she struggled to think of a way to get to Alyssa.

When the commercials ended and the press conference began, Abby's expectation changed to anger. She put Bandit down and stood, staring at the TV screen in disbelief.

"No, no. He's getting away with it. He's turning the negative to a positive."

There was even an FBI agent confirming the ongoing investigation regarding Gilbert Barone and the hacking of a large financial institution.

She'd heard enough. Slapping a hand to her forehead, she switched the TV off. She fell to the couch and stayed there for a long time, numb, wondering how a man whose career never should have gotten going in the first place now seemed completely bulletproof.

CHAPTER

-71-

LUKE HAD A FEW MINUTES to help Maddie with her geography lesson before his date. She was studying the African continent and along with boundaries and capitals, she was learning about Christian persecution. He normally liked helping Maddie when he could, but this subject made him think of Ethan and all the work he did in dangerous countries, places where he could literally lose his life for his faith.

He shook his head; he had feelings for Abby, but he knew he had no right to those feelings. She would marry Ethan.

And I have to get over it.

That's what tonight was all about. Meeting Faye Fallon had been the high point in the midst of this turmoil. Woody had coyly declined her dinner invitation, so it was going to be just Luke and Faye. He'd rather think about her than Ethan Carver. Or Lowell Rollins.

There was still a lot of uncertainty about life with another woman swirling around in his heart. But if things went well with Faye, Luke was willing to think about the future with a new woman in his life permanently.

"Dad, hello." Maddie tapped the top of his head.

"What? Oh, sorry, Mads." He returned his attention to her lesson.

"Did I get the spelling right?"

Luke bent to the task of checking the paper. "Let me see." He looked over the paper and silently thanked God that his daughter was smart and she studied hard.

"Yep, 100 percent." He put his knuckles up for a fist bump.

"Cool. Can I go play basketball now?"

"Double-check with Grandma—"

Just then Grace stepped into the room.

"Luke, you have a visitor." Grace moved aside and into the room stepped Abby Hart.

"Oh." He stood, heart thumping. "Abby."

"I didn't mean to interrupt," she said, looking more than a little ill at ease.

"You didn't," Maddie said brightly. "I'm done. Aced it." She waved the paper at Grace. "Basketball now?"

Grace smiled. "Sure. Just change your clothes first." With that, Grace and Maddie left the room, leaving Luke and Abby alone.

"Is something wrong?" he asked.

Abby shook her head. "No. But I have something to ask you. Sorry to just stop by unannounced. It looks like you were on your way out. A date?"

"Yeah, actually. With Faye Fallon."

A flicker of something Luke couldn't quite define crossed Abby's face. "I'll make this quick then," she said. "We know most of what happened at the Triple Seven all those years ago, and it points squarely to one person. I'm going to use that information to find some way to take down Alyssa Rollins. Are you in?"

EPILOGUE

"WELCOME TO THE COLD CASE SQUAD."

Glad for the welcome, Luke was distracted; something that had been happening to him all too frequently lately, he thought. But could he help it if events in his life seemed to collide and explode, showering contingencies in all directions?

He and Woody took a seat in a conference room in the federal building on Ocean Boulevard in Long Beach. A few other members of the new cold case task force were also there.

FBI Agent Todd Orson went over the squad's mission statement. It was to review cold cases and close them, preferably with prosecution, but if prosecution was not possible, closure for families was the next-most-desirable outcome. A secondary objective was to help smaller jurisdictions with limited resources clear cold case backlogs.

Orson had said that there would be a change in the makeup of the squad. Just before he played a brief video welcome from Senator Harriet Shore, the woman behind the formation of the cold case task force, the door to the room opened and in walked Abby. Orson nodded to her as she took a seat, and then started the video. Luke was the only one besides Orson who knew why she was there.

On-screen, the petite redheaded senator began by saying, *"I want to thank you all for stepping up to join this endeavor. I know firsthand how difficult it is to lose a loved one to violent crime. About the only thing worse than bearing up under that loss is knowing that the perpetrator of the crime still walks this world free."*

Luke agreed wholeheartedly and turned to see Abby nodding. He tuned out the rest of the introduction as Shore outlined the process by which money was appropriated for the squad.

When the video ended, Orson passed out some literature about information and records sources.

"Okay, people, right now we have the money and the mission. The best way to keep the money coming is to solve cases and put bad guys in jail." He pointed to the whiteboard behind him, where he'd written, *Success opens the money stream.*

"You'll find in the packet I gave you a little more information about how cases are chosen for investigation. Take a minute and look everything over."

Luke noted Abby got the same packet and suppressed a smile as he skimmed over the paperwork. Law enforcement agencies were asked to submit digital summaries of cases to an office in DC, where a team of retired FBI agents would review them and send the ones deemed workable to Orson, who would in turn parcel them out to the appropriate investigative team.

"What's the new dimension to this gig?" Luke asked, pretending ignorance and looking at Abby, who grinned. He felt an earthquake in his soul and chastised himself. He was dating Faye, and his relationship with Abby needed to stay where it was: professional.

"Figured you'd ask that, Bullet." Orson smiled and jabbed a thumb in Abby's direction. "The new dimension is this: the cold case squad is now a joint task force. This means we are forming each cold case task force with an agent, which would be me, and a sworn law enforcement officer. Detective Abby Hart will be working with the cold case task force. She's been loaned to us from LBPD for a year. You guys know Abby," he said to Luke and Woody. He then introduced her to rest of the team.

"Think you mugs can take orders from such an accomplished detective?"

"You bet," Luke said, keeping his expression neutral. He knew that this job, with the reopening of the Triple Seven case, would allow Abby more freedom to peel away the layers protecting Alyssa Rollins. And Luke was the optimist, confident that they would ferret out something new and substantial.

But a question haunted him. If they did find everything they were looking for, and Alyssa was finally behind bars, would Abby walk out of his life forever?

TURN THE PAGE

for a sneak peek at the next book in the

COLD CASE JUSTICE SERIES.

"PLEASE STATE YOUR NAME FOR THE COURT."

Abby Hart had to admit to feeling a bit sorry for the woman sitting before the judge today. Less than a year ago, Kelsey Cox had retired as a deputy chief after a thirty-year trailblazing law enforcement career. And here she was in a prison jumpsuit, no makeup, bad hairstyle, and looking so painfully thin, Abby winced.

Cox cleared her throat. "Kelsey June Cox." She stared at the microphone she spoke into, seemingly oblivious to anyone else in the judge's private chamber. This had been one of Kelsey's demands—along with the plea to speed up the process and have her hearing as soon as possible—that she be able to give her statement in private, with only a few people present. All in exchange for a mere fifteen-year sentence.

Yeah, I'm getting a confession, Abby thought, *but why do I feel as though in our effort to close this, we've dealt away justice, real justice?*

Abby was glad police reporter Walter Gunther had crashed the party and was here with her, but she really wished it were Luke Murphy. He had more skin in the game and would be a tower of support.

"Please proceed with your statement, Ms. Cox, about what occurred on the night of June 16, 1988."

After a sip of water, Cox began. "On that night, I left work late, after 10 p.m., and returned to my home on Granada, in Long Beach, to hear arguing." Her voice was thin and reedy, not the same one Abby remembered barking orders when Kelsey Cox was a supervisor in patrol.

"At the time I shared the home with Gavin Kent. He was a fellow officer and my fiancé. I recognized his voice, but it was only when I stepped out onto the patio that I saw who the other person was. It was Buck Morgan." She paused to take a drink of water. Her gaze flickered briefly to Abby, then back down on the mic.

"Was Buck Morgan an acquaintance?" the judge asked.

"Buck Morgan was known to me as one of the owners of a restaurant that had burned down, the Triple Seven. The fire had occurred two nights previous and it was assumed by everyone that Morgan had died in it."

"When you stepped out onto the patio, did the two men see you?"

"No, uh . . . I mean, I think Gavin saw me, but I was behind Buck."

"Could you hear what the argument was about?"

"Bits of it—it really didn't make sense, and like I said, I thought Buck was dead, and that concerned me. What if he had faked his death? It occurred to me that he might be a killer; he might have killed his wife and set the fire . . ."

Abby was almost up out of her seat. Beside her, DA Drew gripped her hand, and Gunther shook his head. Face hot, heart pumping, Abby slowly settled back into her chair. For the first time Cox steadily looked her way, expression blank.

The judge cast a frown Abby's direction and then nodded for Cox to continue.

"I didn't really know what to think, or what was happening, but I could see that Buck was trying to get Gavin to go somewhere with him. Fearing for Gavin, I moved in behind Morgan."

"Did you have a weapon?"

"I'd left my duty weapon in the house, and I didn't want to waste time by going back to get it. I grabbed a shovel—we were having work done in our backyard and there was one handy. I moved in behind Morgan as he was getting more agitated. I was afraid for Gavin; he'd hurt himself and was not 100 percent."

"How had he hurt himself?"

"Helping with the yard remodel."

Abby could not hold back a snort. Gavin Kent had killed her mother, that much she knew, and been wounded by a shotgun, fired by her father, before Kent ran out of ammo and had to flee for his life. Another angry glance from the judge, and she forced herself to nod an apology.

"What happened then?"

"I just reacted. I saw Morgan move toward Gavin, and I swung the shovel and hit him in the head as hard as I could."

* * *

Abby left the courthouse angry and frustrated. She remembered a time when she was a kid in foster care, filled with anger. She used to pound big rocks into smaller rocks and pretend she was pounding the people who had murdered her parents. It had been a long time since so much anger boiled inside—rage, really. Rage that made her want to pound something—or someone.

"Hey, Abby, hold up."

She stopped and turned. She'd tried to ignore Gunther but wasn't angry enough to make the old guy chase after her. Besides, he wasn't the one who infuriated her.

"Trying to give me a heart attack?" He caught up to her, breathing hard, bending over, and putting his hands on his thighs to catch his breath. "You stormed out of there and made the judge mad. Hope you don't have to try any cases in front of him right away," he said after he straightened up.

"I don't know what I expected in there. I didn't want a trial any more than Drew did—too risky with the shaky evidence we have—but somehow what Kelsey had to say just didn't sit right with me. She wanted my dad to be the bad guy, threatening Gavin Kent. And Kent is the man who killed my mother!"

Gunther raised both hands. "Calm down. I'm on your side here."

Abby took a deep breath, glancing around the street in front of the courthouse at the people coming and going. This was the place where people came for justice, she thought bitterly. On one level she knew she had no right to be so angry. She had more answers now about the murders of her parents than she'd had a year ago. After Gavin Kent killed her mother, her father tried to take Kent to the police, but Cox killed Buck Morgan. Then she buried him under tons of concrete in her backyard, where he'd lain hidden for all these years.

Now, at least there would be one person in jail, sentenced for part of the crime. The only person not already dead or in custody was the one person responsible for ordering all of the carnage, and Abby's angst was in no small part aroused because of this fact.

A part of Abby had hoped Kelsey would finally point the finger at that person: California's first lady, Alyssa Rollins. But after hearing Cox's self-serving confession, it stung like a thousand beestings to Abby's heart that Alyssa seemed to slip through every crack and stay free.

She looked at Gunther. "I know you are. This is just aggravating."

"Well, step into my office." He pointed to a street hot dog vendor. "Let me buy you lunch and we'll talk about it."

In spite of everything Abby laughed. "Yeah, that used to be Asa's favorite place to take me for lunch too." Her old partner Asa Foster had been the one to introduce her to the crusty reporter Gunther. "But he did it because he was cheap."

"I resemble that remark," Gunther said with mock offense.

"Thanks for the offer, but I've got some training to get back to for the cold case squad. Rain check?"

"Sure." He stepped close. "I'd still like to pick your brain about the Triple Seven someday. It's not settled in my mind, and I don't think it's settled in yours either."

Abby cocked her head and shrugged, then continued toward the parking structure.

It's not settled, she thought, *and I doubt that it will ever be. At least not to my satisfaction.*

ABOUT THE AUTHOR

A FORMER LONG BEACH, CALIFORNIA, police officer of twenty-two years, Janice Cantore worked a variety of assignments, including patrol, administration, juvenile investigations, and training. She's always enjoyed writing and published two short articles on faith at work for *Cop and Christ* and *Today's Christian Woman* before tackling novels. She now lives in a small town in southern Oregon, where she enjoys exploring the forests, rivers, and lakes with her two Labrador retrievers—Maggie and Abbie.

Janice writes suspense novels designed to keep readers engrossed and leave them inspired. *Burning Proof,* the second title in her new Cold Case Justice series, is the sequel to *Drawing Fire.* Janice also authored *Critical Pursuit, Visible Threat,* and the Pacific Coast Justice series, which includes *Accused, Abducted,* and *Avenged.*

Visit Janice's website at www.janicecantore.com and connect with her on Facebook at www.facebook.com/JaniceCantore.

DISCUSSION QUESTIONS

1. At the beginning of *Burning Proof*, Detective Abby Hart walks into a horrible life-and-death scenario. Does she make the right choice, or is there another option? As she and others rehash the situation, are her actions sufficiently justified? How does this fictional account change how you might view similar events in real life?

2. Abby and her fiancé, Ethan, face some tough choices about their relationship. How important is it for spouses' career and ministry goals to be compatible? What advice would you give them?

3. Luke Murphy is trying to put the mistakes from his marriage behind him and consider a future with a new woman. Do you think he will be successful? Should he put aside his feelings for Abby too and pursue someone else? What do you think the author has in mind for the final book in this series?

4. In some ways Kelsey Cox is a victim of her own past choices. How do you feel about her character? What options does she have now? What do you think she will

do? Is there a situation in your life where you feel stuck because of choices you've made in the past? How might you begin to change your course?

5. Why does Woody insist on keeping Abby in the dark after he and Luke uncover a clue that could give her some answers about her parents' deaths? Should Luke have pressed the issue and told Abby earlier? Why or why not?

6. During a time when she doesn't feel like she can pray, Abby is touched to know that her aunt Dede is praying for her. Think of a time in your life when the prayers of others ministered to you in this way. How is it different from being able to pray on your own behalf? Is there someone in your circle of influence who's facing a situation that you might pray for?

7. Dede suggests that Abby's foundation was weak—that she got into police work for the wrong reasons. How does Abby's calling become clearer to her? In what ways have you discovered your calling in life—or if you're still searching for it, what are some possible ways God might be directing you?

8. Althea Joiner asks to meet with Abby after the shooting death of her husband. She tells Abby, "I needed to look you in the eye and say that I forgive you. It's only by saying it that maybe, one day, I'll feel it." Has there ever been a situation in your life when you found it difficult, if not impossible, to forgive someone who had hurt you—whether or not the hurt was intentional? Do you agree that by saying we forgive someone, it can become easier to feel it? What are some other ways to move

toward forgiveness in a difficult situation? Why is it important to take steps in that direction?

9. Molly Cavanaugh is understandably haunted by her kidnapping and rape as a young teen. What did you think of Abby's confrontational style, telling the girl to let go of the past? Are Molly's parents right to shelter her and try to protect her from further pain? How can we help those we love to live healthy lives while still protecting them in appropriate ways?

10. Gil Barone seems like an incorrigibly evil person. Do you believe some people are like that, totally beyond redemption? Why or why not? What do Molly's actions toward him at the end of the story show?

11. What does Abby learn about her family in talking with her uncle Simon? Were you surprised at the depiction of Buck Morgan that was painted in the letters he and his brother exchanged?

12. Where do Abby and Luke land on Lowell Rollins's culpability in the Triple Seven fire and murders? Do you agree with their conclusion? Why or why not? How would you rate Lowell's chances of winning the senate race?

PACIFIC
COAST
JUSTICE
SERIES

ABDUCTED

ACCUSED

AVENGED

TYNDALE
FICTION

www.tyndalefiction.com

Available now at bookstores and online.
www.janicecantore.com

CP0564